William Tooke, Charles Churchill

The Poetical Works of Charles Churchill

Vol. II

William Tooke, Charles Churchill

The Poetical Works of Charles Churchill
Vol. II

ISBN/EAN: 9783337003173

Printed in Europe, USA, Canada, Australia, Japan

Cover: Foto ©Andreas Hilbeck / pixelio.de

More available books at **www.hansebooks.com**

THE POETICAL WORKS OF
CHARLES CHURCHILL

WITH A MEMOIR BY JAMES HANNAY
AND COPIOUS NOTES BY
W. TOOKE, F.R.S.

REVISED EDITION IN TWO VOLUMES

VOL. II

LONDON:

GEORGE BELL & SONS, YORK ST., COVENT GARDEN

AND NEW YORK

1892

CONTENTS OF VOL. II.

THE AUTHOR.

THIS Poem was published in December 1763, and for it and the Duellist, Churchill obtained from Mr. Flexney and Mr. Kearsley the sum of £450. The sale was very extensive, and the price of half a crown required for so short a poem rendered it a profitable concern to the booksellers. The Rosciad, of nearly four times the length, had been first published by Churchill at the moderate price of one shilling.

By contemporary critics "The Author" was highly praised, and was considered the most agreeable and unexceptionable of Churchill's poems. Nor is this popularity surprising; the first part of the poem is devoted to a vindication of the "censorial power of the press," and could not fail to please the literary profession. The age in which Churchill lived was remarkable for the swarms of lampoons, satires, and political pamphlets which issued from the press. The time was one of great excitement, and the public eagerly devoured the trash that came out—tasteless enough in itself, but strongly flavoured with insinuation and libel. The writers generally indicated the objects of their abuse by dashes, or by initials only; which served the double purpose of screening themselves and stimulating the curiosity of their readers. "Strange," says Cowper—

> "Strange! how the frequent interjected dash
> Quickens a market, and helps off the trash;
> The important letters that include the rest,
> Serve as a key to those that are suppressed;
> Conjecture gripes the victims in his paw,
> The world is charmed, and Scrib escapes the law."

Nearly all these writings are now forgotten. The authors
of them had all Churchill's virulence, without his force: but
no doubt they thought themselves poets, and the natural
guardians of public morality. "The Author" defends the
satirist; and they thought it was a defence of them.

ACCURSED the man, whom fate ordains,
            in spite,
        And cruel parents teach, to read and
            write !
What need of letters ? wherefore should we spell ?
Why write our names ? a mark will do as well.
    Much are the precious hours of youth misspent
In climbing learning's rugged, steep ascent ;
When to the top the bold adventurer's got,
He reigns, vain monarch o'er a barren spot,
Whilst in the vale of ignorance below
Folly and vice to rank luxuriance grow ;   10
Honours and wealth pour in on every side,
And proud preferment rolls her golden tide.
    O'er crabbed authors life's gay prime to waste,
To cramp wild genius in the chains of taste,
To bear the slavish drudgery of schools,
And tamely stoop to every pedant's rules ;
For seven long years debarr'd of liberal ease,
To plod in college trammels to degrees ;
Beneath the weight of solemn toys to groan,
Sleep over books, and leave mankind unknown ;   20
To praise each senior blockhead's threadbare tale,
And laugh till reason blush, and spirits fail ;
Manhood with vile submission to disgrace,
And cap the fool, whose merit is his place,

Vice-Chancellors, whose knowledge is but small,
And Chancellors who nothing know at all,
Ill-brook'd the generous spirit in those days
When learning was the certain road to praise,
When nobles, with a love of science bless'd,
Approved in others what themselves possess'd. 30
    But now, when Dulness rears aloft her throne,
When lordly vassals her wide empire own;
When Wit, seduced by Envy, starts aside,
And basely leagues with Ignorance and Pride;
What, now, should tempt us, by false hopes misled,
Learning's unfashionable paths to tread,
To bear those labours which our fathers bore,
That crown withheld, which they in triumph wore? .
    When with much pains this boasted learning's
        got,
'Tis an affront to those who have it not: 40
In some it causes hate, in others fear,
Instructs our foes to rail, our friends to sneer.
With prudent haste the worldly minded fool
Forgets the little which he learnt at school:
The elder brother to vast fortunes born.
Looks on all science with an eye of scorn;
Dependent brethren the same features wear.
And younger sons are stupid as the heir.
In senates, at the bar, in church and state,
Genius is vile, and learning out of date.   50
    Is this—O death to think! is this the land
Where merit and reward went hand in hand?
Where heroes, parent-like, the poet view'd,
By whom they saw their glorious deeds renew'd?
Where poets, true to honour, tuned their lays,
And by their patrons sanctified their praise?

Is this the land, where, on our Spenser's tongue,
Enamour'd of his voice, Description hung?
Where Jonson rigid Gravity beguiled,   59
Whilst Reason through her critic fences smiled?
Where Nature listening stood whilst Shakespeare
    play'd,
And wonder'd at the work herself had made?
Is this the land, where, mindful of her charge
And office high, fair Freedom walk'd at large?
Where, finding in our laws a sure defence,
She mock'd at all restraints, but those of sense?
Where, Health and Honour trooping by her side,
She spread her sacred empire far and wide;
Pointed the way, Affliction to beguile,
And bade the face of Sorrow wear a smile,   70
Bade those who dare obey the generous call,
Enjoy her blessings, which God meant for all?
Is this the land, where, in some tyrant's reign
When a weak, wicked, ministerial train,
The tools of power, the slaves of interest,
    plann'd
Their country's ruin, and with bribes unmann'd
Those wretches, who, ordain'd in Freedom's cause,
Gave up our liberties, and sold our laws;
When Power was taught by Meanness where to go,
Nor dared to love the virtue of a foe;   80
When, like a leperous plague, from the foul head
To the foul heart her sores Corruption spread;
Her iron arm when stern Oppression rear'd,
And Virtue, from her broad base shaken, fear'd
The scourge of Vice; when, impotent and vain,
Poor Freedom bow'd the neck to Slavery's chain;
Is this the land, where, in those worst of times,

The hardy poet raised his honest rhymes
To dread rebuke, and bade Controlment speak
In guilty blushes on the villain's cheek;   90
Bade Power turn pale, kept mighty rogues in awe,
And made them fear the Muse, who fear'd not law?

How do I laugh, when men of narrow souls,
Whom folly guides, and prejudice controls;
Who, one dull, drowsy track of business trod,
Worship their Mammon, and neglect their God;
Who, breathing by one musty set of rules,
Dote from their birth, and are by system fools;
Who, form'd to dulness from their very youth,
Lies of the day prefer to Gospel-truth;   100
Pick up their little knowledge from Reviews,
And lay out all their stock of faith in news;
How do I laugh, when creatures, form'd like
        these,
Whom Reason scorns, and I should blush to please,
Rail at all liberal arts, deem verse a crime,
And hold not truth, as truth, if told in rhyme?

How do I laugh, when Publius, hoary grown
In zeal for Scotland's welfare, and his own,
By slow degrees, and course of office, drawn
In mood and figure at the helm to yawn,   110
Too mean (the worst of curses Heaven can send)

---

[88] Andrew Marvell. He was member for Hull during
several Parliaments, from the Restoration till his death.
Being a man of no property, his constituents gave him an
income sufficient for his maintenance, during the whole time
he represented them. Marvell made himself so obnoxious
to the Court by his public spirit and integrity, that towards
the close of his career his life was considered in danger. He
died in 1678, in the fifty-eighth year of his age, not without some suspicion of his having been poisoned.

[97] Smollett, then editor of the Critical Review

To have a foe; too proud to have a friend;
Erring by form, which blockheads sacred hold,
Ne'er making new faults, and ne'er mending old,
Rebukes my spirit, bids the daring Muse
Subjects more equal to her weakness choose;
Bids her frequent the haunts of humble swains,
Nor dare to traffic in ambitious strains;
Bids her, indulging the poetic whim
In quaint-wrought ode, or sonnet pertly trim, 120
Along the church-way path complain with Gray,
Or dance with Mason on the first of May!
" All sacred is the name and power of kings;
All states and statesmen are those mighty things
Which, howsoe'er they out of course may roll,
Were never made for poets to control."
    Peace, peace, thou Dotard, nor thus vilely deem
Of sacred numbers, and their power blaspheme.
I tell thee, Wretch, search all creation round,
In earth, in heaven, no subject can be found   130
(Our God alone except) above whose weight
The poet cannot rise, and hold his state.
The blessed saints above in numbers speak
The praise of God, though there all praise is weak:
In numbers here below the bard shall teach
Virtue to soar beyond the villain's reach;
Shall tear his labouring lungs, strain his hoarse
        throat,
And raise his voice beyond the trumpet's note,
Should an afflicted country, awed by men
Of slavish principles, demand his pen.   140
This is a great, a glorious point of view,
Fit for an English poet to pursue,
Undaunted to pursue, though, in return,

His writings by the common hangman burn.

How do I laugh, when men, by fortune placed
Above their betters, and by rank disgraced,
Who found their pride on titles which they stain,
And, mean themselves, are of their fathers vain;
Who would a bill of privilege prefer,
And treat a poet like a creditor,   150
The generous ardour of the Muse condemn,
And curse the storm they know must break on them!
" What, shall a reptile bard, a wretch unknown,
Without one badge of merit but his own,
Great nobles lash, and lords, like common men,
Smart from the vengeance of a scribbler's pen?"

What's in this name of Lord, that I should fear
To bring their vices to the public ear?
Flows not the honest blood of humble swains   159
Quick as the tide which swells a monarch's veins?
Monarchs, who wealth and titles can bestow,
Cannot make virtues in succession flow.
Wouldst thou, proud man, be safely placed above
The censure of the Muse—deserve her love:
Act as thy birth demands, as nobles ought;
Look back, and, by thy worthy father taught,
Who earn'd those honours, thou wert born to wear;
Follow his steps, and be his virtue's heir:
But if, regardless of the road to fame,
You start aside, and tread the paths of shame;
If such thy life, that should thy sire arise,   171
The sight of such a son would blast his eyes,
Would make him curse the hour which gave thee
            birth,
Would drive him, shuddering, from the face of earth,
Once more, with shame and sorrow, 'mongst the dead

In endless night to hide his reverend head ;
If such thy life, though kings had made thee more
Than ever king a scoundrel made before ;
Nay, to allow thy pride a deeper spring,
Though God in vengeance had made thee a king,
Taking on Virtue's wing her daring flight,   181
The Muse should drag thee trembling to the light,
Probe thy foul wounds, and lay thy bosom bare
To the keen question of the searching air.

Gods ! with what pride I see the titled slave,
Who smarts beneath the stroke which Satire gave,
Aiming at ease, and with dishonest art
Striving to hide the feelings of his heart !
How do I laugh, when, with affected air,
(Scarce able through despite to keep his chair, 190
Whilst on his trembling lip pale anger speaks,
And the chafed blood flies mounting to his cheeks,)
He talks of Conscience, which good men secures
From all those evil moments guilt endures,
And seems to laugh at those who pay regard
To the wild ravings of a frantic bard.
"Satire, whilst envy and ill-humour sway
The mind of man, must always make her way ;
Nor to a bosom, with discretion fraught,
Is all her malice worth a single thought.   200
The wise have not the will, nor fools the power,
To stop her headstrong course ; within the hour,
Left to herself, she dies ; opposing strife
Gives her fresh vigour, and prolongs her life.
All things her prey, and every man her aim,
I can no patent for exemption claim,
Nor would I wish to stop that harmless dart
Which plays around, but cannot wound my heart

Though pointed at myself, be Satire free;
To her 'tis pleasure, and no pain to me." 210
    Dissembling Wretch! hence to the Stoic school,
And there amongst thy brethren play the fool;
There, unrebuked, these wild, vain, doctrines preach:
Lives there a man whom Satire cannot reach?
Lives there a man who calmly can stand by,
And see his conscience ripp'd with steady eye?
When Satire flies abroad on Falsehood's wing,
Short is her life, and impotent her sting;
But when to truth allied, the wound she gives
Sinks deep, and to remotest ages lives. 220
When in the tomb thy pamper'd flesh shall rot,
And e'en by friends thy mem'ry be forgot,
Still shalt thou live, recorded for thy crimes,
Live in her page, and stink to after-times.
    Hast thou no feeling yet? Come, throw off pride,
And own those passions which thou shalt not hide.
Sandwich, who from the moment of his birth
Made human nature a reproach on earth,
Who never dared, nor wish'd behind to stay,
When Folly, Vice, and Meanness led the way, 230
Would blush, should he be told, by Truth and Wit
Those actions, which he blush'd not to commit.
Men the most infamous are fond of fame,
And those who fear not guilt, yet start at shame.
    But whither runs my zeal, whose rapid force,
Turning the brain, bears Reason from her course;
Carries me back to times, when poets, bless'd
With courage, graced the science they profess'd;
When they, in honour rooted, firmly stood

---

[218] The 1st edition has,—
     "Short is her life indeed, and dull her sting;"

The bad to punish and reward the good ;   24ᵗ
When, to a flame by public virtue wrought,
The foes of freedom they to justice brought,
And dared expose those slaves who dared support
A tyrant plan, and call'd themselves a Court?
Ah! what are poets now? as slavish those
Who deal in verse, as those who deal in prose.
Is there an Author, search the kingdom round,
In whom true worth and real spirit's found?
The slaves of booksellers, or (doom'd by Fate
To baser chains) vile pensioners of state,   250
Some, dead to shame, and of those shackles proud
Which Honour scorns, for slavery roar aloud ;
Others, half-palsied only, mutes become,
And what makes Smollett write makes Johnson
          dumb.
    Why turns yon villain pale? why bends his eye
Inward, abash'd, when Murphy passes by?
Dost thou sage Murphy for a blockhead take,
Who wages war with vice for virtue's sake ?
No, no, like other worldlings, you will find
He shifts his sails, and catches every wind :   260
His soul the shock of interest can't endure :
Give him a pension then, and sin secure.
    With laurell'd wreaths the flatterer's brows adorn,
Bid Virtue crouch, bid Vice exalt her horn ;

---

²⁵⁰ Dr. Johnson in his Dictionary defined a pensioner as " a dependent, a slave of state." He afterwards accepted a pension ; but it was unaccompanied with any political stipu lation.

²⁵⁴ It is said the government paid Smollett for his defence of them in the " Briton ;" but no stated pension was ever conferred on him.

²⁵⁶ See Rosciad, l. 67, note.

Bid cowards thrive, put Honesty to flight,
Murphy shall prove, or try to prove it right.
Try, thou state-juggler, every paltry art;
Ransack the inmost closet of my heart,
Swear thou'rt my friend; by that base oath make way
Into my breast, and flatter to betray;   270
Or, if those tricks are vain, if wholesome doubt
Detects the fraud, and points the villain out,
Bribe those who daily at my board are fed,
And make them take my life who eat my bread;
On Authors for defence, for praise depend,
Pay him but well, and Murphy is thy friend:
He, he shall ready stand with venal rhymes,
To varnish guilt, and consecrate thy crimes,
To make corruption in false colours shine,   279
And damn his own good name, to rescue thine.

  But, if thy niggard hands their gifts withhold,
And Vice no longer rains down showers of gold,
Expect no mercy; facts, well grounded, teach,
Murphy, if not rewarded, will impeach.
What though each man of nice and juster thought,
Shunning his steps, decrees, by honour taught,
He ne'er can be a friend, who stoops so low
To be the base betrayer of a foe?
What though, with thine together link'd, his name
Must be with thine transmitted down to shame?
To every manly feeling callous grown,   291
Rather than not blast thine, he'll blast his own.

  To ope the fountain whence sedition springs,
To slander government, and libel kings;
With Freedom's name to serve a present hour,
Though born and bred to arbitrary power;
To talk of William with insidious art,

Whilst a vile Stuart's lurking in his heart,
And, whilst mean Envy rears her loathsome head,
Flattering the living, to abuse the dead,   300
Where is Shebbeare?   Oh let not foul reproach,
Travelling thither in a City-coach,
The pillory dare to name : the whole intent
Of that parade was fame, not punishment ;
And that old, staunch Whig, Beardmore, standing by,
Can in full court give that report the lie.

With rude unnatural jargon to support,
Half Scotch, half English, a declining court ;
To make most glaring contraries unite,
And prove beyond dispute that black is white ; 310
To make firm Honour tamely league with Shame,
Make Vice and Virtue differ but in name ;
To prove that chains and freedom are but one,
That to be saved must mean to be undone,

---

[301] Dr. John Shebbeare, a physician and notorious Jaco-
bitical writer, was, in 1759, prosecuted for writing a seventh
letter to the people of England, and sentenced to the pillory,
and to two years' imprisonment. In the execution of the
former sentence, Shebbeare went to the pillory in one of the
city coaches, with Beardmore the under-sheriff, and stood
upon the platform of the pillory, instead of being confined
in it, whilst a servant in livery held an umbrella over his
head. Beardmore was prosecuted for allowing this, fined
£30, and committed into custody for two months.

Shebbeare, on the accession of George the Third, had a
pension of £200 per annum conferred upon him, and thence-
forth wielded his pen in defence of government. He died
in 1788.

[307] William Guthrie compiled a peerage on the plan of
Sir William Dugdale and Collins, each article being sub-
mitted to the representative of the noble family treated of.
Notwithstanding this care, it was found when published to
contain an unpardonable number of errors, many of them as
gross as those mentioned by the poet.

Is there not Guthrie? Who, like him, can call
All opposites to proof, and conquer all?
He calls forth living waters from the rock;
He calls forth children from the barren stock:
He, far beyond the springs of Nature led,
Makes women bring forth after they are dead: 320
He, on a curious, new, and happy plan,
In wedlock's sacred bands joins man to man;
And, to complete the whole, most strange, but true,
By some rare magic, makes them fruitful too,
Whilst from their loins, in the due course of years,
Flows the rich blood of Guthrie's English Peers.

Dost thou contrive some blacker deed of shame,
Something which Nature shudders but to name,
Something which makes the soul of man retreat,
And the life-blood run backward to her seat? 330
Dost thou contrive, for some base private end,
Some selfish view, to hang a trusting friend,
To lure him on, e'en to his parting breath,
And promise life to work him surer death?
Grown old in villany, and dead to grace,
Hell in his heart, and Tyburn in his face,
Behold, a parson at thy elbow stands,
Lowering damnation, and with open hands
Ripe to betray his Saviour for reward,
The Atheist chaplain of an Atheist lord. 340

Bred to the church, and for the gown decreed,
Ere it was known that I should learn to read—
Though that was nothing, for my friends, who knew
What mighty Dulness of itself could do,

327-340 These lines were originally written for the threatened "Elegy, or Ayliffe's Ghost." See *Epistle to Hogarth*, l. 140, note.

Never design'd me for a working priest,
But hoped I should have been a Dean at least—
Condemn'd (like many more and worthier men
To whom I pledge the service of my pen)
Condemn'd (whilst proud and pamper'd sons of lawn,
Cramm'd to the throat, in lazy plenty yawn)   350
In pomp of reverend beggary to appear,
To pray, and starve, on forty pounds a-year.
My friends, who never felt the galling load,
Lament that I forsook the packhorse road,
Whilst Virtue to my conduct witness bears,
In throwing off that gown which Francis wears.
   What creature's that, so very pert and prim,

---

[348] Our author had composed about fifty lines of a poem intitled " The Curate," and, as was his custom, repeated them to his family. In all probability he never committed them to writing, as they were not found among his papers. Indeed his memory being remarkably tenacious, he rarely wrote his poems until they were required by the printer. He had two other poems in contemplation, Woman, a Satire on Man, and a Poem founded on the battle of Culloden.

[356] The Rev. Philip Francis, the translator of Horace, chaplain to Lord Holland, at whose recommendation he was promoted to the Rectory of Barrow in Suffolk, and to the chaplainship of Chelsea Hospital. He died in 1773.

[357] The Rev. Mr. Kidgell, Rector of Horne, in Surrey, and Chaplain to the Earl of March, by the aid of Faden, the Publisher of the Public Ledger, got possession of a copy of Wilkes' Essay on Woman, which he placed in the hands of Lord March, who immediately transmitted it to the secretaries of state. A succinct narrative of the transaction was published by Kidgell in vindication of his conduct, in which he seemed to delight in quoting and dwelling upon the worst passages in the book. Kidgell, who was one of the trustees for repairing and amending the turnpike roads in the counties of Surrey and Sussex, absconded about £100 in debt to the Trust, and emigrated to Flanders, where he died, as it is said, a Roman Catholic.

So very full of foppery, and whim,
So gentle, yet so brisk ; so wondrous sweet,
So fit to prattle at a lady's feet ;   360
Who looks as he the Lord's rich vineyard trod,
And by his garb appears a man of God ?
Trust not to looks, nor credit outward show ;
The villain lurks beneath the cassock'd beau ;
That's an informer ; what avails the name ?
Suffice it that the wretch from Sodom came.
His tongue is deadly—from his presence run,
Unless thy rage would wish to be undone.
No ties can hold him, no affection bind,
And fear alone restrains his coward mind ;   370
Free him from that, no monster is so fell,
Nor is so sure a blood-hound found in hell.
His silken smiles, his hypocritic air,
His meek demeanour, plausible and fair,
Are only worn to pave Fraud's easier way,
And make gull'd Virtue fall a surer prey.
Attend his church—his plan of doctrine view—
The preacher is a Christian, dull, but true ;
But when the hallow'd hour of preaching's o'er,
That plan of doctrine's never thought of more ;
Christ is laid by neglected on the shelf,   381
And the vile priest is Gospel to himself.
   By Cleland tutor'd, and with Blacow bred,

383 John Cleland, the son of Colonel Cleland, who was a
friend of Pope's, and the Will Honeycomb of the Spectator,
was the author of an infamously licentious publication, rendered the more dangerous and seductive by its elegance of
language and assumed decency of expression, and which he
sold for 20 guineas to a bookseller, who cleared above £10,000
by the sale of it. Mr. Cleland having been summoned
before the privy council for this work, pleaded poverty as his

(Blacow, whom, by a brave resentment led,
Oxford, if Oxford had not sunk in fame,
Ere this, had damn'd to everlasting shame,
Their steps he follows, and their crimes partakes :
To virtue lost, to vice alone he wakes,
Most lusciously declaims 'gainst luscious themes,
And whilst he rails at blasphemy, blasphemes. 390
    Are these the arts which policy supplies?
Are these the steps by which grave churchmen rise?
Forbid it, Heaven ; or, should it turn out so,
Let me and mine continue mean and low.
Such be their arts whom interest controls ;
Kidgell and I have free and modest souls :
We scorn preferment which is gain'd by sin,
And will, though poor without, have peace within.

excuse, upon which Lord Granville very nobly settled an
annuity of £100 per annum upon him, on condition of his
refraining from so immoral a style of writing. This annuity
he enjoyed until his death in 1789, at the age of 82. He
had been educated at Westminster school, where he was
contemporary with Lord Mansfield, and was for a short time
consul at Smyrna.

383 In the year 1747, a riot happened at Oxford, during
which some of the students cried out repeatedly in the
streets, King James for ever! Prince Charles! God bless
the great King James the Third! Mr. Blacow complained
to the Vice-Chancellor of this, and made the most strenuous
exertions against the offenders. The Vice-Chancellor, im-
puting their misbehaviour to intoxication, endeavoured to
waive the inquiry, but at length inflicted some trifling
punishment on the delinquents. At last the Duke of Newcastle took cognizance of the offence; a prosecution was
commenced in the Court of King's Bench, against Mr. Dawes
and Mr. Whitmore, two of the students, who being found
guilty, were sentenced to walk through Westminster-hall
with a paper on their foreheads stating their crime, to pay
a fine of five nobles each, be imprisoned for two years, and
to find security for their good behaviour for seven years more.

THE CONFERENCE.

THIS Poem was published by our Author in November 1763, soon after his elopement with Miss Carr had become a general topic of remark. In it he endeavours to separate his private from his public conduct, and in the bitterness of his soul contrasts the deviousness of the one with the rectitude of the other. Churchill and Wilkes were now at the height of their popularity. They were the "observed of all observers;" all their actions were keenly watched by enemies as well as friends; and their irregularities, exaggerated by report, were the common talk of the town. Their immorality and reckless disregard of public opinion were as universally condemned as they were notorious. In The Conference, Churchill anticipated the displeasure of the public, and by confessing the pain his errors had caused him, softened the indignation which was felt at his dissipated and vicious course of life. But though Churchill acknowledged his own faults he could not see those of his friend. There is something very touching in his friendship for Wilkes. Passages in Churchill's letters to Wilkes show that the rough and surly poet loved him almost with the tenderness of a woman. Such an affection is an honour to its object. There must have been something noble in Wilkes to inspire so pure a friendship.

THE CONFERENCE.

GRACE said in form, which sceptics must
  agree,
  When they are told that grace was said
  by me;
The servants gone, to break the scurvy jest
On the proud landlord, and his threadbare guest;
The King gone round, my Lady too withdrawn,
My Lord, in usual taste, began to yawn,
And, lolling backward in his elbow-chair,
With an insipid kind of stupid stare,
Picking his teeth, twirling his seals about—
" Churchill, you have a poem coming out: 10
You've my best wishes; but I really fear
Your Muse, in general, is too severe;
Her spirit seems her interest to oppose,
And where she makes one friend makes twenty foes."
  C. Your Lordship's fears are just; I feel their force,
But only feel it as a thing of course.
The man whose hardy spirit shall engage
To lash the vices of a guilty age,
At his first setting forward ought to know
That every rogue he meets must be his foe; 20
That the rude breath of satire will provoke
Many who feel, and more who fear the stroke;
But shall the partial rage of selfish men

From stubborn justice wrench the righteous pen?
Or shall I not my settled course pursue,
Because my foes are foes to virtue too?
 L. What is this boasted Virtue, taught in schools,
And idly drawn from antiquated rules?
What is her use? point out one wholesome end:
Will she hurt foes, or can she make a friend?   30
When from long fasts fierce appetites arise,
Can this same Virtue stifle Nature's cries?
Can she the pittance of a meal afford,
Or bid thee welcome to one great man's board?
When northern winds the rough December arm
With frost and snow, can Virtue keep thee warm?
Canst thou dismiss the hard unfeeling dun
Barely by saying thou art Virtue's son?
Or by base blundering statesmen sent to jail,
Will Mansfield take this Virtue for thy bail?   40
Believe it not, the name is in disgrace;
Virtue and Temple now are out of place.
 Quit then this meteor, whose delusive ray
From wealth and honour leads thee far astray.
True virtue means, let Reason use her eyes,
Nothing with fools, and interest with the wise.
Wouldst thou be great, her patronage disclaim,
Nor madly triumph in so mean a name:
Let nobler wreaths thy happy brows adorn,
And leave to Virtue poverty and scorn.   50
Let Prudence be thy guide; who doth not know
How seldom Prudence can with Virtue go?
To be successful try thy utmost force,
And virtue follows as a thing of course.
 Hirco, who knows not Hirco? stains the bed
Of that kind master who first gave him bread;

Scatters the seeds of discord through the land,
Breaks every public, every private band;
Beholds with joy a trusting friend undone;
Betrays a brother, and would cheat a son: 60
What mortal in his senses can endure
The name of Hirco? for the wretch is poor!
" Let him hang, drown, starve, on a dunghill rot,
By all detested live, and die forgot;
Let him, a poor return, in every breath
Feel all death's pains, yet be whole years in death,"
Is now the general cry we all pursue;
Let fortune change, and Prudence changes too,
Supple and pliant, a new system feels,
Throws up her cap, and spaniels at his heels,   70
" Long live great Hirco," cries, by interest taught,
" And let his foes, though I prove one, be nought."
     C. Peace to such men, if such men can have
          peace;
Let their possessions, let their state, increase;
Let their base services in courts strike root,
And in the season bring forth golden fruit;
I envy not: let those who have the will,
And, with so little spirit, so much skill,
With such vile instruments their fortunes carve;
Rogues may grow fat; an honest man dares starve. 80
     L. These stale conceits thrown off, let us advance
For once to real life, and quit romance.
Starve! pretty talking! but I fain would view
That man, that honest man, would do it too.
Hence to yon mountain which outbraves the sky,
And dart from pole to pole thy strengthen'd eye,
Through all that space you shall not view one man,
Not one, who dares to act on such a plan.

Cowards in calms will say what in a storm
The brave will tremble at, and not perform.　9c
Thine be the proof, and, spite of all you've said
You'd give your honour for a crust of bread.

　　C. What proof might do, what hunger might
　　　　effect,
What famish'd Nature, looking with neglect
On all she once held dear, what fear, at strife
With fainting virtue for the means of life,
Might make this coward flesh, in love with breath,
Shuddering at pain, and shrinking back from death,
In treason to my soul, descend to bear,
Trusting to fate, I neither know nor care.　100

　　Once, at this hour those wounds afresh I feel,
Which nor prosperity nor time can heal,
Those wounds which fate severely hath decreed,
Mention'd or thought of, must for ever bleed;
Those wounds, which humbled all that pride of man,
Which brings such mighty aid to virtue's plan;
Once, awed by Fortune's most oppressive frown,
By legal rapine to the earth bow'd down,
My credit at last gasp, my state undone,
Trembling to meet the shock I could not shun,　110
Virtue gave ground, and blank despair prevail'd;
Sinking beneath the storm, my spirits fail'd,
Like Peter's faith, till one, a friend indeed,—
May all distress find such in time of need,—
One kind, good man, in act, in word, in thought,
By virtue guided, and by wisdom taught,

---

[113] Churchill, previous to the publication of the Rosciad,
being deeply in debt, was threatened with the horrors of a
jail; he was relieved by the interposition of Dr. Peirson
Lloyd, second master of Westminster school, who effected a
compromise with the creditors, and advanced part of the
sum required for carrying it into effect.

Image of Him whom christians should adore,
Stretch'd forth his hand, and brought me safe to shore.
  Since, by good fortune into notice raised,
And for some little merit largely praised,   120
Indulged in swerving from prudential rules,
Hated by rogues, and not beloved by fools;
Placed above want, shall abject thirst of wealth,
So fiercely war 'gainst my soul's dearest health,
That, as a boon, I should base shackles crave,
And, born to freedom, make myself a slave?
That I should in the train of those appear
Whom honour cannot love, nor manhood fear?
  That I no longer skulk from street to street,
Afraid lest duns assail, and bailiffs meet;   130
That I from place to place this carcase bear;
Walk forth at large, and wander free as air;
That I no longer dread the awkward friend,
Whose very obligations must offend;
Nor, all too froward, with impatience burn
At suffering favours which I can't return;
That, from dependence and from pride secure,
I am not placed so high to scorn the poor,
Nor yet so low, that I ' my lord' should fear,
Or hesitate to give him sneer for sneer;   140
That, whilst sage Prudence my pursuits confirms,
I can enjoy the world on equal terms;
That, kind to others, to myself most true,
Feeling no want, I comfort those who do,
And with the will have power to aid distress,

[145] Churchill's first earnings were appropriated to the full
discharge of every demand upon him (for which, by the
terms of the compromise with his creditors, he was not
legally liable,) and to the relief of his friend Robert Lloyd,
the son of his benefactor.

These, and what other blessings I possess,
From the indulgence of the public rise;
All private patronage my soul defies.
By candour more inclined to save, than damn,
A generous public made me what I am.   150
All that I have, they gave; just memory bears
The grateful stamp, and what I am, is theirs.

    L. To feign a red-hot zeal for freedom's cause,
To mouth aloud for liberties and laws,
For public good to bellow all abroad,
Serves well the purposes of private fraud.
Prudence by public good intends her own;
If you mean otherwise, you stand alone.
What do we mean by country and by court?
What is it to oppose? what to support?   160
Mere words of course; and what is more absurd
Than to pay homage to an empty word!
Majors and minors differ but in name;
Patriots and ministers are much the same;
The only difference, after all their rout,
Is, that the one is in, the other out.

    Explore the dark recesses of the mind,
In the soul's honest volume read mankind,
And own, in wise and simple, great and small,
The same grand leading principle in all.   170
Whate'er we talk of wisdom to the wise,
Of goodness to the good, of public ties
Which to our country link, of private bands
Which claim most dear attention at our hands,
For parent and for child, for wife and friend,
Our first great mover, and our last great end
Is one, and, by whatever name we call
The ruling tyrant, self is all in all.

This, which unwilling faction shall admit,
Guided in different ways a Bute and Pitt,   180
Made tyrants break, made kings observe the law,
And gave the world a Stuart and Nassau.
    Hath Nature (strange and wild conceit of pride!)
Distinguish'd thee from all her sons beside ?
Doth virtue in thy bosom brighter glow,
Or from a spring more pure doth action flow ?
Is not thy soul bound with those very chains
Which shackle us ? or is that self, which reigns
O'er kings and beggars, which in all we see
Most strong and sovereign, only weak in thee ? 190
Fond man, believe it not ; experience tells
'Tis not thy virtue, but thy pride rebels.
Think, (and for once lay by thy lawless pen)
Think, and confess thyself like other men ;
Think but one hour, and, to thy conscience led
By Reason's hand, bow down and hang thy head :
Think on thy private life, recal thy youth,
View thyself now, and own, with strictest truth,
That self hath drawn thee from fair virtue's way
Farther than folly would have dared to stray,   200
And that the talents liberal Nature gave
To make thee free, have made thee more a slave.
    Quit then, in prudence quit that idle train
Of toys, which have so long abused thy brain,
And captive led thy powers ; with boundless will
Let self maintain her state and empire still ;
But let her, with more worthy objects caught,
Strain all the faculties and force of thought
To things of higher daring ; let her range   209
Through better pastures, and learn how to change ;
Let her, no longer to weak faction tied,

Wisely revolt, and join our stronger side.
   C. Ah! what, my Lord, hath private life to do
With things of public nature? why to view
Would you thus cruelly those scenes unfold
Which, without pain and horror to behold,
Must speak me something more, or less than man;
Which friends may pardon, but I never can?
Look back! a thought which borders on despair,
Which human nature must, yet cannot bear.   220
'Tis not the babbling of a busy world,
Where praise and censure are at random hurl'd,
Which can the meanest of my thoughts control,
Or shake one settled purpose of my soul;
Free and at large might their wild curses roam,
If all, if all, alas! were well at home.
No—'tis the tale which angry conscience tells,
When she with more than tragic horror swells
Each circumstance of guilt; when stern, but true,
She brings bad actions forth into review,   230
And like the dread hand-writing on the wall,
Bids late remorse awake at reason's call;
Arm'd at all points, bids scorpion vengeance pass,
And to the mind holds up reflection's glass,
The mind which, starting, heaves the heart-felt
      groan,
And hates that form she knows to be her own.
   Enough of this,—let private sorrows rest,—
As to the public, I dare stand the test;
Dare proudly boast, I feel no wish above
The good of England, and my country's love.   240
Stranger to party-rage, by reason's voice,
Unerring guide, directed in my choice,
Not all the tyrant powers of earth combined,

No, nor of hell, shall make me change my mind.
What! herd with men my honest soul disdains,
Men who, with servile zeal are forging chains
For Freedom's neck, and lend a helping hand
To spread destruction o'er my native land.
What! shall I not, e'en to my latest breath,
In the full face of danger and of death   250
Exert that little strength which nature gave,
And boldly stem, or perish in the wave?

    L. When I look backward for some fifty years,
And see protesting patriots turn'd to peers;
Hear men most loose for decency declaim,
And talk of character without a name;
See infidels assert the cause of God,
And meek divines wield persecution's rod;
See men transform'd to brutes, and brutes to men,
See Whitehead take a place, Ralph change his pen,
I mock the zeal, and deem the men in sport,   261
Who rail at ministers and curse a court.
Thee, haughty as thou art, and proud in rhyme,

    253 This recapitulation of inconsistencies will apply unfortunately to every period of British history. The peerages conferred on Wentworth, Pulteney, Granville, and Pitt, the speech of the Earl of Sandwich in the House of Lords, against the Essay on Woman, the religious zeal of Wharton, and the intolerance of Warburton, are probably referred to in this passage. Walpole, in a letter to George Montagu, writes, "You know I have long had a partiality for your cousin Sandwich, who has out-Sandwiched himself. He has impeached Wilkes for a blasphemous poem, and has been expelled for blasphemy himself by the Beef-steak Club in Covent Garden."

    260 See *The Ghost*, Book iii. l. 95, note.

    260 Mr. James Ralph, a political writer satirized in the Dunciad. At the death of George II. he obtained, through the interest of Lord Bute, a pension of £600 per annum. He died in 1762, at the age of 54.

Shall some preferment, offered at a time
When virtue sleeps, some sacrifice to pride,
Or some fair victim, move to change thy side.
Thee shall these eyes behold, to health restored,
Using, as Prudence bids, bold Satire's sword,
Galling thy present friends, and praising those
Whom now thy frenzy holds thy greatest foes. 270
   C. May I (can worse disgrace on manhood fall?)
Be born a Whitehead, and baptized a Paul;
May I (though to his service deeply tied
By sacred oaths, and now by will allied)
With false, feign'd zeal an injured God defend,
And use his name for some base private end;
May I (that thought bids double horrors roll
O'er my sick spirits, and unmans my soul)
Ruin the virtue which I held most dear,   279
And still must hold; may I, through abject fear,
Betray my friend; may to succeeding times,
Engraved on plates of adamant, my crimes
Stand blazing forth, whilst mark'd with envious blot,
Each little act of virtue is forgot;
Of all those evils which, to stamp men curst,
Hell keeps in store for vengeance, may the worst
Light on my head; and in my day of woe,
To make the cup of bitterness o'erflow,
May I be scorn'd by every man of worth,
Wander, like Cain, a vagabond on earth,   290
Bearing about a hell in my own mind,
Or be to Scotland for my life confined,
If I am one among the many known
Whom Shelburne fled, and Calcraft blush'd to own.

   [294] William Petty, Earl of Shelburne, first Marquess of
Lansdowne. He died in 1805.

L. Do you reflect what men you make your foes?
C. I do, and that's the reason I oppose.
Friends I have made, whom Envy must commend,
But not one foe whom I would wish a friend.
What if ten thousand Butes and Hollands bawl?
One Wilkes hath made a large amends for all.   300
    'Tis not the title, whether handed down
From age to age, or flowing from the crown
In copious streams on recent men, who came
From stems unknown, and sires without a name:
'Tis not the star which our great Edward gave
To mark the virtuous, and reward the brave,
Blazing without, whilst a base heart within
Is rotten to the core with filth and sin;
'Tis not the tinsel grandeur, taught to wait,
At custom's call, to mark a fool of state   310
From fools of lesser note, that soul can awe,
Whose pride is reason, whose defence is law.
    L. Suppose, (a thing scarce possible in art,
Were it thy cue to play a common part)
Suppose thy writings so well fenced in law,
That Norton cannot find nor make a flaw—
Hast thou not heard, that 'mongst our ancient
          tribes,
By party warpt, or lull'd asleep by bribes,
Or trembling at the ruffian hand of Force,
Law hath suspended stood, or changed its course?
Art thou assured, that, for destruction ripe,   321
Thou may'st not smart beneath the self-same gripe?

----

[294] John Calcraft, Esq. M.P. the Army Agent and Con-
tractor.
[299] The First Edition has 'Foxes' for 'Hollands.' Fox
being the surname of Lord Holland.

What sanction hast thou, frantic in thy rhymes,
Thy life, thy freedom to secure?

   C.   The times.
'Tis not on law, a system great and good,
By wisdom penn'd, and bought by noblest blood,
My faith relies: by wicked men and vain
Law, once abused, may be abused again.——
No; on our great law-giver I depend,
Who knows and guides her to her proper end; 330
Whose royalty of nature blazes out
So fierce, 'twere sin to entertain a doubt—
Did tyrant Stuarts now the laws dispense,
(Bless'd be the hour and hand which sent them
      hence!)
For something, or for nothing, for a word
Or thought, I might be doom'd to death, unheard.
Life we might all resign to lawless power,
Nor think it worth the purchase of an hour;
But envy ne'er shall fix so foul a stain
On the fair annals of a Brunswick's reign.   340

   If, slave to party, to revenge, or pride;
If, by frail human error drawn aside,
I break the law, strict rigour let her wear;
'Tis hers to punish, and 'tis mine to bear;
Nor, by the voice of Justice doom'd to death,
Would I ask mercy with my latest breath:
But, anxious only for my country's good,
In which my king's, of course, is understood;
Form'd on a plan with some few patriot friends,
Whilst by just means I aim at noblest ends,   350
My spirits cannot sink: though from the tomb
Stern Jeffries should be placed in Mansfield's room;
Though he should bring, his base designs to aid,

Some black attorney, for his purpose made,
And shove, whilst Decency and Law retreat,
The modest Norton from his maiden seat;
Though both, in ill confederates, should agree,
In damnèd league, to torture law and me;
Whilst George is king, I cannot fear endure;
Not to be guilty, is to be secure.   360

But when, in after-times, (be far removed
That day!) our monarch, glorious and beloved,
Sleeps with his fathers, should imperious fate,
In vengeance, with fresh Stuarts curse our state;
Should they, o'erleaping every fence of law,
Butcher the brave to keep tame fools in awe;
Should they, by brutal and oppressive force,
Divert sweet Justice from her even course;
Should they, of every other means bereft,
Make my right hand a witness 'gainst my left; 370
Should they, abroad by inquisitions taught,
Search out my soul, and damn me for a thought;
Still would I keep my course, still speak, still write,
Till death had plunged me in the shades of night.

Thou God of Truth, thou great, all-searching eye,
To whom our thoughts, our spirits, open lie,
Grant me thy strength, and in that needful hour,
(Should it e'er come) when Law submits to Power,
With firm resolve my steady bosom steel,
Bravely to suffer, though I deeply feel.   380

Let me, as hitherto, still draw my breath
In love with life, but not in fear of death;
And if Oppression brings me to the grave,
And marks me dead, she ne'er shall mark a slave.
Let no unworthy marks of grief be heard,
No wild laments, not one unseemly word;

Let sober triumphs wait upon my bier;
I won't forgive that friend who drops one tear.
Whether he's ravish'd in life's early morn,
Or in old age drops like an ear of corn, 390
Full ripe he falls, on nature's noblest plan,
Who lives to reason, and who dies a man.

THE GHOST.

IN FOUR BOOKS.

MR. WILLIAM KENT, the postmaster of a town in Norfolk, having lost his wife in childbed, determined to quit the place, but his engagement with the post-office compelled him to stay there some months. During this interval Miss Fanny L. (the Ghost), who was sister to his late wife, resided with him as his housekeeper. The constant communication attending such a situation soon produced a mutual attachment. Mr. Kent, however, finding that he was debarred from legally uniting himself to the sister of his deceased wife, resolved to try and forget her; and came up to London with the intention of applying for a situation in one of the public offices. The girl having followed him, he at last determined to live with her as her husband.

Mr. Kent, in October, 1759, took her to his lodging in Cock Lane, Smithfield, at the house of Mr. Parsons, the clerk of the parish. Shortly after, he went into the country on business, and Parsons's daughter, a child of eleven years of age, slept in the meantime with Miss Fanny, who complained one morning to the family of both having been greatly disturbed by violent noises during the night. Mrs. Parsons, pretending to be at a loss to account for this, bethought herself of a neighbouring industrious shoemaker, whom they concluded to be the cause of this disturbance. Soon after, on a Sunday night, Miss Fanny, getting out of bed, called out to Mrs. Parsons, " Pray does your shoemaker work so hard on Sunday nights too ?" and, being answered in the negative, she desired Mrs. Parsons to come into the chamber, and hear the noises, which still continued, herself.

Mr. Kent, on his return, being obliged to arrest Parsons for £20 he had lent to him, and which he showed no disposition to repay, left his house at an hour's warning, and took another lodging in the same street; upon which the noises ceased at Parsons's house. Mr. Kent had not remained at his new lodging above a week before Miss Fanny was taken ill. A physician was sent for who had attended her before, and an apothecary was employed; in short, every precaution was taken that tenderness could suggest, as was certified by a report drawn up, and signed by her medical attendants, men of considerable professional respectability. The disorder, however, turned out to be smallpox, and Miss Fanny died of it on the 2nd of February, 1762.

The funeral was as decent as Mr. Kent's circumstances would admit; the corpse was attended by him and a female relation to the vault under St. John's Church, Clerkenwell, where it was deposited; there was no name upon the coffin, but the registry of her burial was entered in the name of Kent.

Parsons, who had been irritated by Mr. Kent's conduct, contrived a most singular species of revenge; he circulated a report that the spirit which had formerly disturbed the repose of his daughter and Miss Fanny was succeeded by the spirit of the latter herself, who harassed his house and family with her visits, which took place as soon as the child was put to bed. Upon certain knockings, flutterings, or scratchings, which seemed to proceed from under the bedstead, the child appeared to be thrown into violent fits and agitations. While in this state, the father or female attendant put questions to the ghost, and dictated how many knocks should serve for a negative or an affirmative. In this manner long conversations were carried on in public, in the course of which she charged Mr. Kent with having poisoned her by putting arsenic in purl, and administering it to her in her illness. Numbers of persons of rank and character were induced to pay their visits to Cock Lane; and though the floor and wainscotting were ripped up, the fraud remained undetected. The ghost having engaged to follow the girl wherever she might be carried, a plan was devised for removing the child to the house of the Rev. Stephen Aldrich, rector of St. John's, Clerkenwell, in order that the phenomena might be investigated by him, and other persons of known respectability.

In pursuance of this plan many gentlemen of eminent

position assembled at Mr. Aldrich's house on the 31st of January, and about ten at night met in the chamber in which the girl had, with proper caution, been put to bed by several ladies. They sat rather more than an hour, and, hearing nothing, went down stairs, where they interrogated the father of the girl, who denied, in the strongest terms, any knowledge of fraud.

As the spirit had before publicly promised, by an affirmative knock,* that she would attend one of the gentlemen into the vault under the church of St. John, Clerkenwell, where the body was deposited, and give a token of her presence there by a knock upon her coffin, it was proposed to test the veracity of the spirit.

While deliberating on this suggestion they were summoned into the girl's chamber by some ladies who were near her bed, and who had heard knocks and scratches. When the gentlemen entered, the girl declared that she felt the spirit like a mouse upon her back; but being required to hold her hands out of bed, from that time, though the spirit was solemnly adjured to manifest its presence, no evidence of any preternatural power was exhibited. The spirit was then seriously informed that the person to whom the promise was made of striking the coffin was about to visit the vault, and that the performance of the promise was now claimed. The company, at one in the morning, went into the church, and the gentleman to whom the promise was made, with one companion entered the vault: the spirit was solemnly required to perform her promise; but silence alone ensued. Mr. Kent himself went down with several others. Upon their return they examined the girl, but could draw no confession from her. Between two and three she desired to go home with her father, and was permitted to do so. And the whole assembly came to the sage conclusion, "That the child had some art of making or counterfeiting particular noises, and that there was no agency of any higher cause."

It was then given out that the coffin in which the body of the supposed ghost had been deposited, or, at least, the body

---

* The top joke of all, and what pleased me the most,
  Some wise ones and I sat up with the Ghost,
  With her nails and her knuckles she answer'd so nice,
  For yes she knock'd once, and for no she knock'd twice.
                                        Garrick's Farmer's Return.

itself, had been displaced or removed out of the vault. So on the afternoon of the 25th of February, Mr. Kent, a clergyman, the undertaker, the clerk, and sexton of the parish, and two or three gentlemen, went into the vault, when the undertaker presently knew the coffin, which, to complete the evidence, was opened before Mr. Kent, and the body found in it.

Other steps were then taken to find out where the fraud, if any, lay. The girl's bed was tied up like a hammock, about a yard and a half from the ground; and her arms were extended, and fastened with fillets, for two nights successively, during which no noises were heard. The day after, being pressed to confess, and being told that if the knockings and scratchings were not heard any more, she, her father and mother would be sent to Newgate, and half an hour being given her to consider, she desired she might be put to bed, and try whether the noises would come: she lay in bed that night much longer than usual, but no noises were heard. This was on a Saturday. Being told that the approaching night only would be allowed for a trial, she concealed a board about four inches broad and six long under her stays. This board was used to set the kettle upon. Having got into bed she told the gentlemen she would bring Fanny at six the next morning. The master of the house, and a friend of his, being informed by the maids that the girl had taken a board to bed with her, waited for the appointed hour, when she began to knock and scratch upon the board, remarking, however, what they themselves were convinced of, "that these noises were not like those which used to be made." She was then told that she had taken a board to bed, and on her denying it, was searched and detected. It was thought, however, that the girl had been frightened into this deception by the threats that had been held out on the preceding night.

At length Mr. Kent resolved to vindicate his character in a legal way. On the 10th of July the father and mother of the child; Mary Frazer, who, it seems, acted as an interpreter between the ghost and those who examined her; the Rev. Mr. Moore, minister of St. Sepulchre, and one James, a reputable tradesman, were tried at Guildhall, before Lord Mansfield and a special jury, and convicted of a conspiracy against the life and character of Mr. Kent. The court being desirous that Mr. Kent, who had been so much injured on this occasion, should receive some pecuniary reparation from the offenders, deferred giving sentence for seven or eight months, in the hope that the parties might in the meantime compromise.   Accordingly the clergyman and tradesman agreed to pay Mr. Kent about six hundred pounds to purchase their pardon, and were thereupon dismissed in February, 1763, by Mr. Justice Wilmot, with a severe reprimand and a fine of six shillings and eightpence each.   Parsons was ordered to be set on the pillory three times in one month, once at the end of Cock Lane, and after that to be imprisoned two years, Elizabeth his wife one year, and Mary Frazer six months, in Bridewell, and to be there kept to hard labour. Mr. Brown, of Amen Corner, for writing and publishing letters on the subject, was fined £50.

The father appearing to be out of his mind at the time he was first to stand on the pillory, the execution of that part of his sentence was deferred until 16 Feb. 1763, when, as well as on the succeeding days of his standing there, the populace considered him so much an object of compassion, that, instead of pelting and otherwise using him ill, they made a handsome collection for him.

Boswell mentions that Dr. Johnson expressed great indignation at the imposture of the Cock Lane Ghost, and related with much satisfaction how he had assisted in detecting the cheat, and had published an account of it in the newspapers.

There is no doubt now that the deception was carried on by means of ventriloquism, a faculty at that period little known and less understood.   The young woman afterwards confessed as much.   She lived till 1807.

THE GHOST.

BOOK I.*

WITH eager search to dart the soul,
Curiously vain, from pole to pole,
And from the planets' wandering spheres
To extort the number of our years,
And whether all those years shall flow
Serenely smooth, and free from woe,
Or rude misfortune shall deform
Our life with one continual storm ;
Or if the scene shall motley be,
Alternate joy and misery,   10
Is a desire which, more or less,
All men must feel, though few confess.
Hence, every place and every age
Affords subsistence to the sage
Who, free from this world and its cares,
Holds an acquaintance with the stars,
From whom he gains intelligence
Of things to come some ages hence,

---

* The greater part of the first book of this Poem was
written when the author was curate of Cadbury, in Somersetshire ; and was then intended to be published under the
title of "The Fortune Teller." It was the least popular of
all his productions. The metre is rugged, and on the whole
inferior to that of the "Duellist ;" and though some fine passages
occur, the rambling, digressive manner in which it is written,
and its general mediocrity, reuder it the least interesting of
Churchill's poems.

Which unto friends, at easy rates,
He readily communicates.   20
　At its first rise, which all agree on,
This noble science was Chaldean ;
That ancient people, as they fed
Their flocks upon the mountain's head,
Gazed on the stars, observed their motions,
And suck'd in astrologic notions,
Which they so eagerly pursue,
As folks are apt whate'er is new,
That things below at random rove,
Whilst they're consulting things above ;   30
And when they now so poor were grown,
That they'd no houses of their own,
They made bold with their friends the stars
And prudently made use of theirs.
　To Egypt from Chaldee it travell'd,
And fate at Memphis was unravell'd :
The exotic science soon struck root,
And flourished into high repute :
Each learned priest, O strange to tell !
Could circles make, and cast a spell ;   40
Could read and write, and taught the nation
The holy art of divination.
Nobles themselves, for at that time
Knowledge in nobles was no crime,
Could talk as learned as the priest,
And prophesy as much at least :
Hence all the fortune-telling crew,
Whose crafty skill mars nature's hue,
Who, in vile tatters, with smirch'd face,
Run up and down from place to place,   50
To gratify their friends' desires,

From Bampfield Carew, to Moll Squires,
Are rightly term'd Egyptians all
Whom we, mistaking, Gypsies call.
The Grecian sages borrow'd this,
As they did other sciences,
From fertile Egypt, though the loan
They had not honesty to own.
Dodona's oaks, inspired by Jove,
A learned and prophetic grove,   60
Turn'd vegetable necromancers,
And to all comers gave their answers.
At Delphos, to Apollo dear,
All men the voice of Fate might hear;
Each subtle priest on three-legg'd stool,
To take in wise men, play'd the fool;

[52] Bamfylde Moore Carew was the son of a clergyman at Bickley in Devonshire, and was educated at Tiverton school, with a view to his taking orders; but falling into the company of some gypsies near that town, young Carew grew so fond of his associates, that, at the age of fifteen, he resolved to " live a life of ease " with them, and ran away from school. After a short time spent with the fortune-telling fraternity, he returned home, to the great joy of his parents, who had given up all expectation of ever seeing him again. His love of roving, however, still remained, and after a time grew so strong that he quitted his father's habitation once more. His exploits in this course of life were wonderful, and the history of his shifts and impositions is still a part of our popular library. He was twice transported from Exeter to North America; but returned before the ship which carried him out. He was a man of retentive memory, and happy address. The fraternity to which he belonged elected him their king; and he remained faithful to his subjects to the last. It is supposed that he died about 1770, aged 77.

[52] Mary Squires, a gypsy, and one of Carew's subjects, was a principal agent in Elizabeth Canning's affair, some account of which will be given in a subsequent note.

A mystery, so made for gain,
E'en now in fashion must remain.
Enthusiasts never will let drop
What brings such business to their shop,   70
And that great saint, we Whitefield call,
Keeps up the humbug spiritual.

Among the Romans, not a bird
Without a prophecy, was heard;
Fortunes of empires often hung
On the magician magpie's tongue,
And every crow was to the state
A sure interpreter of fate.
Prophets, embodied in a college
(Time out of mind your seat of knowledge,   80
For genius never fruit can bear
Unless it first is planted there;

[71] George Whitefield, one of the apostles of methodism,
was born in Gloucester, in December, 1714, at the Bell Inn,
which was then kept by his mother, whom for some time he
assisted as a waiter. He was educated at the school of St.
Mary de Crypt, and admitted a Servitor at Oxford, where
he acquired the character on which his future eminence was
founded.   Struck by the young man's piety and austerity of
manner, Benson, Bishop of Gloucester, made him a voluntary offer of ordination, which Whitefield accepted, and in
June, 1736, began his work, preaching in the streets, in the
fields, and in prisons; and his labours proved eminently successful.

Whitefield erected two large places of worship, one in
Tottenham Court Road, and the other in Moorfields; he was
chaplain to the Countess of Huntingdon, and superintendent
of the various chapels erected under her patronage.   His
attention being engaged by America, he repeatedly went
there and prosecuted his mission with extraordinary success.
He died of a violent asthma, in 1770, when on his seventh
visit to America.

[79] The College of Augurs consisted for some time of three,
then of nine, and afterwards of fifteen persons.

And solid learning never falls
Without the verge of college walls)
Infallible accounts would keep
When it was best to watch or sleep,
To eat or drink, to go or stay,
And when to fight or run away;
When matters were for actions ripe,
By looking at a double tripe;   90
When emperors would live or die
They in an ass's skull could spy;
When generals would their station keep,
Or turn their backs, in hearts of sheep,
In matters, whether small or great,
In private families or state
As amongst us, the holy seer
Officiously would interfere;
With pious arts and reverend skill
Would bend lay bigots to his will;   100
Would help or injure foes or friends,
Just as it served his private ends.
Whether, in honest way of trade,
Traps for virginity were laid,
Or if, to make their party great,
Designs were form'd against the state,
Regardless of the common weal,
By interest led, which they call zeal,
Into the scale was always thrown
The will of Heaven to back their own.   110
    England, a happy land we know,
Where follies naturally grow,
Where without culture they arise,
And tower above the common size;
England, a fortune-telling host

As numerous as the stars, could boast;
Matrons, who toss the cup, and see
The grounds of fate in grounds of tea;
Who, versed in every modest lore,
Can a lost maidenhead restore,   120
Or, if their pupils rather choose it,
Can shew the readiest way to lose it.
Gypsies, who every ill can cure
Except the ill of being poor,
Who charms 'gainst love and agues sell
Who can in hen-roost set a spell,
Prepared by arts, to them best known
To catch all feet except their own,
Who as to fortune, can unlock it
As easily as pick a pocket;   130
Scotchmen, who, in their country's right,
Possess the gift of second sight,
Who, when their barren heaths they quit,
(Sure argument of prudent wit;—
Which reputation to maintain,
They never venture back again)
By lies prophetic heap up riches,
And boast the luxury of breeches.
    Amongst the rest, in former years,
Campbell, illustrious name! appears,   140
Great hero of futurity,
Who, blind, could every thing foresee,
Who, dumb, could every thing foretel,
Who, fate with equity to sell,
Always dealt out the will of Heaven
According to what price was given.

[140] Campbell, a deaf and dumb fortune-teller, who for
years traded on the credulity of the public.

Of Scottish race, in Highlands born,
Possess'd with native pride and scorn,
He hither came, by custom led,
To curse the hands that gave him bread.   150
With want of truth, and want of sense,
Amply made up by impudence,
(A succedaneum, which we find
In common use with all mankind)
Caress'd and favour'd too by those
Whose heart with patriot feelings glows,
Who foolishly, where'er dispersed,
Still place their native country first ;
(For Englishmen alone have sense
To give a stranger preference,   160
Whilst modest merit of their own
Is left in poverty to groan)
Campbell foretold just what he would,
And left the stars to make it good,
On whom he had impress'd such awe,
His dictates current pass'd for law ;
Submissive, all his empire own'd ;
No star durst smile, when Campbell frown'd.
    This sage deceased, for all must die,
And Campbell's no more safe than I,   170
No more than I can guard the heart,
When Death shall hurl the fatal dart,
Succeeded, ripe in art and years,
Another favourite of the spheres ;
Another and another came,
Of equal skill, and equal fame ;
As white each wand, as black each gown,
As long each beard, as wise each frown,
In every thing so like, you'd swear,

Campbell himself was sitting there :   180
To all the happy art was known,
To *tell* our fortunes, *make* their own.
    Seated in garret,—for you know
The nearer to the stars we go
The greater we esteem his art,—
Fools curious flock'd from every part :
The rich, the poor, the maid, the married ;
And those who could not walk were carried.
    The butler, hanging down his head,
By chambermaid, or cookmaid led,   190
Inquires, if from his friend the moon
He has advice of pilfer'd spoon ?
    The court-bred woman of condition,
(Who to approve her disposition
As much superior, as her birth
To those composed of common earth,
With double spirit must engage
In every folly of the age)
The honourable arts would buy,
To pack the cards, and cog a die.   200
    The hero (who for brawn and face
May claim right honourable place
Amongst the chiefs of Butcher-row ;
Who might some thirty years ago,
If we may be allow'd to guess

---

[201] Lines 201-320 first appeared in the 3rd ed. of this Poem.

[201-236] The brackets in these lines enclose a single parenthesis—" The Hero (. . . .) like Drugger comes, &c.

[202] Butcher-row, a very curious, narrow, timber-built, gable-ended street, that used to run alongside St. Clement's church in the Strand. It now forms a part of the site of Pickett Street.

At his employment by his dress,
Put medicines off from cart or stage,
The grand Toscano of the age ;
Or might about the country go
High steward of a puppet-show,   210
Steward and stewardship most meet,
For all know *puppets never eat;*
Who would be thought (though, save the mark,
That point is something in the dark)
The man of honour, one like those
Renown'd in story, who loved blows
Better than victuals, and would fight,
Merely for sport, from morn to night;
Who treads like Mavors firm ; whose tongue
Is with the triple thunder hung ;   220
Who cries to Fear—stand off—aloof—
And talks as he were cannon proof,
Would be deem'd ready, when you list,
With sword and pistol, stick and fist,
Careless of points, balls, bruises, knocks,
At once to fence, fire, cudgel, box,
But at the same time bears about
Within himself, some touch of doubt,
Of prudent doubt, which hints—that fame
Is nothing but an empty name ;   230
That life is rightly understood
By all to be a real good ;
That, even in a hero's heart
Discretion is the better part;
That this same honour may be won,   .
And yet no kind of danger run,)
Like Drugger comes, that magic powers

²³⁷ Abel Drugger, in Jonson's Alchymist.

May ascertain his lucky hours;
For at some hours the fickle dame,
Whom Fortune properly we name,   240
Who ne'er considers wrong or right,
When wanted most plays least in sight,
And, like a modern court-bred jilt,
Leaves her chief favourites in a tilt:
Some hours there are, when from the heart
Courage into some other part,
No matter wherefore, makes retreat,
And fear usurps the vacant seat,
Whence, planet-struck, we often find
Stuarts and Sackvilles of mankind.   250
 Farther, he'd know (and by his art
A conjurer can that impart)
Whether politer it is reckon'd

<hr>

[250] Lord George Sackville, commander of the British and of several brigades of German cavalry, by not advancing with them at the battle of Minden, pursuant to the orders of the commander-in-chief, Prince Ferdinand of Brunswick, rendered the success of the day infinitely less brilliant and complete than it would otherwise have been. A few days after the battle, his lordship resigned his command, and returned to London. On his arrival there he was deprived of all his military appointments, in which he was succeeded by the Marquess of Granby.

Under these circumstances, he applied for a court-martial, which, being granted, came to the conclusion " that Lord George Sackville is guilty of having disobeyed the orders of Prince Ferdinand of Brunswick, whom he was by his commission and instructions directed to obey, as commander-in-chief according to the rules of war; and it is the further opinion of the court that the said Lord George Sackville is, and he is hereby adjudged, unfit to serve his majesty in any military capacity whatever."

This sentence George the Second confirmed, and ordered the name of Lord George Sackville to be struck out of the list of Privy Counsellors.

To have or not to have a second ;
To drag the friends in, or, alone,
To make the danger all their own ;
Whether repletion is not bad,
And fighters with full stomachs mad ;
Whether, before he seeks the plain,
It were not well to breathe a vein ;   260
Whether a gentle salivation,
Consistently with reputation,
Might not of precious use be found,
Not to prevent indeed a wound,
But to prevent the consequence
Which oftentimes arises thence,
Those fevers which the patient urge on

Much surprise was excited when Lord Sackville was admitted to the honour of kissing George the Third's hand
immediately on his accession, and while his predecessor lay
dead in his palace. In 1765, he was restored to his rank of
Privy Counsellor and appointed one of the Vice Treasurers
of Ireland. In 1775, during Lord North's administration,
he was appointed, by the name of the Right Honourable Lord
George Sackville Germain, to be one of his majesty's principal Secretaries of State, and took the American department, in which situation he displayed considerable ability
as a statesman, and was the ablest supporter in parliament
of the measures of administration.

In 1782 he was created a peer by the title of Baron Bole-
brooke, Viscount Sackville. On the report of the intended
creation, a motion was made in the House of Lords by the
Marquis of Carmarthen, "that it is derogatory to the honour
of this house, that any person labouring under the censure
of a court-martial, whose sentence the crown had been pleased
to confirm, should be recommended to his majesty to be
raised to the dignity of the peerage." Upon this motion the
question of adjournment was put and carried by a majority
of 75 against 30. Lord Sackville died in 1785. He is one
of the many persons to whom the authorship of Junius's letters has been attributed.

To gates of death, by help of surgeon;
Whether a wind at east or west
Is for green wounds accounted best;   270
Whether (was he to choose) his mouth
Should point towards the north or south;
Whether more safely he might use,
On these occasions, pumps or shoes;
Whether it better is to fight
By sunshine or by candlelight;
Or (lest a candle should appear
Too mean to shine in such a sphere;
For who could of a candle tell
To light a hero into hell?   280
And lest the sun should partial rise
To dazzle one or t'other's eyes,
Or one or t'other's brains to scorch)
Might not Dame Luna hold a torch?

   These points with dignity discuss'd,
And gravely fix'd, a task which must
Require no little time and pains,
To make our hearts friends with our brains,
The man of war would next engage
The kind assistance of the sage,   290
Some previous method to direct,
Which should make these of none effect.

   Could he not, from the mystic school
Of art, produce some sacred rule,
By which a knowledge might be got
Whether men valiant were, or not;
So he that challenges, might write
Only to those who would not fight?

   Or could he not some way dispense
By help of which (without offence   300

To Honour, whose nice nature's such
She scarce endures the slightest touch)
When he for want of t'other rule
Mistakes his man, and like a fool,
With some vain fighting blade gets in,
He fairly may get out again?
Or should some demon lay a scheme
To drive him to the last extreme,
So that he must confess his fears,
In mercy to his nose and ears,   310
And, like a prudent recreant knight,
Rather do any thing than fight,
Could he not some expedient buy
To keep his shame from public eye?
For well he held, and, men review,
Nine in ten hold the maxim too,
That honour's like a maidenhead,
Which, if in private brought to bed,
Is none the worse, but walks the town,
Ne'er lost, until the loss be known.   320
The parson, too, (for now and then
Parsons are just like other men,
And here and there a grave divine
Has passions such as yours and mine)
Burning with holy lust to know
When fate preferment will bestow,
'Fraid of detection, not of sin,
With circumspection sneaking in
To conjurer, as he does to whore,
Through some bye alley, or back-door,   330
With the same caution orthodox
Consults the stars, and gets a p—.
The citizen in fraud grown old,

Who knows no deity but gold,
Worn out, and gasping now for breath,
A medicine wants to keep off death;
Would know, if that he cannot have,
What coins are current in the grave;
If, when the stocks (which, by his power,
Would rise or fall in half an hour,   340
For, though unthought of and unseen,
He work'd the springs behind the screen)
By his directions came about,
And rose to par, he should sell out,
Whether he safely might, or no,
Replace it in the funds below.

By all address'd, believed, and paid,
Many pursued the thriving trade,
And, great, in reputation grown,
Successive held the magic throne,   350
Favour'd by every darling passion,
The love of novelty and fashion,
Ambition, avarice, lust, and pride,
Riches pour'd in on every side.
But when the prudent laws thought fit
To curb this insolence of wit;
When senates wisely had provided,
Decreed, enacted, and decided
That no such vile and upstart elves
Should have more knowledge than themselves;
When fines and penalties were laid   361
To stop the progress of the trade,

---

[358] It was by stat. 17, Geo. 2. c. 5. s. 2. enacted that all persons pretending skill in palmistry, telling fortunes, &c. should be deemed rogues and vagabonds, and punished accordingly.

And stars no longer could dispense,
With honour, farther influence;
And wizards (which must be confessed
Was of more force than all the rest)
No certain way to tell had got
Which were informers and which not;
Affrighted sages were, perforce,
Obliged to steer some other course: 370
By various ways, these sons of Chance
Their fortunes labour'd to advance,
Well knowing, by unerring rules,
Knaves starve not in the land of fools.

Some, with high titles and degrees,
Which wise men borrow when they please,
Without or trouble or expense,
Physicians instantly commence,
And proudly boast an equal skill
With those who claim the *right* to kill.   380
Others about the country roam
(For not one thought of going home)
With pistol and adopted leg,
Prepared at once to rob or beg.
Some, the more subtle of their race,
Who felt some touch of coward grace,
Who Tyburn to avoid had wit,
But never fear'd deserving it,
Came to their brother Smollett's aid,
And carried on the critic trade.   290
Attach'd to letters and the Muse,
Some verses wrote, and some wrote news;
Those each revolving month are seen
The heroes of a magazine;
These every morning great appear

In Ledger or in Gazetteer,
Spreading the falsehoods of the day,
By turns, for Faden and for Say;
Like Swiss, their force is always laid
On that side where they best are paid: 400
Hence mighty prodigies arise,
And daily monsters strike our eyes;
Wonders, to propagate the trade,
More strange than ever Baker made
Are hawk'd about from street to street,
And fools believe, whilst liars eat.

   Now armies in the air engage,
To fright a superstitious age;
Now comets through the ether range,
In governments portending change;   410
Now rivers to the ocean fly
So quick, they leave their channels dry;
Now monstrous whales on Lambeth shore
Drink the Thames dry, and thirst for more;
And every now and then appears
An Irish savage, numbering years
More than those happy sages could
Who drew their breath before the flood;
Now, to the wonder of all people,
A church is left without a steeple;   420
A steeple now is left in lurch,
And mourns departure of the church,

---

³⁹⁸ The editors of the newspapers mentioned in the preceding couplet. Faden was particularly obnoxious on account of the share he took in procuring, at the instigation of
Kidgell, a copy of the Essay on Woman, with a view to the
prosecution of Wilkes. See The Author, l. 357, note.

⁴⁰⁴ Sir Richard Baker, the chronicler, who flourished towards the conclusion of the sixteenth century.

Which, borne on wings of mighty wind,
Removed a furlong off we find;
Now, wrath on cattle to discharge,
Hailstones as deadly fall, and large,
As those which were on Egypt sent,
At once their crime and punishment,
Or those which, as the prophet writes,
Fell on the necks of Amorites,   430
When, struck with wonder and amaze,
The sun suspended, stay'd to gaze,
And, from her duty longer kept,
In Ajalon his sister slept.

But if such things no more engage
The taste of a politer age,
To help them out in time of need
Another Tofts must rabbits breed:

[438] Mary Tofts, who became famous as the rabbit woman of Godalming, in 1727. The account this woman gave of herself was briefly this:—She had been weeding in a field, and seeing a rabbit spring up near her, tried to catch it, with another woman. Her companion charged her with longing for the rabbit, but she denied it. Soon after another rabbit sprang up, which she also endeavoured to catch. The same night she dreamt she had the two rabbits in her lap, and awakened with a sick fit which lasted till morning. For three months she had a constant and strong desire to eat rabbits; but being in indigent circumstances she could not procure any: at last she was marvellously brought to bed of them. This story excited a lively controversy in the medical world, particularly between Dr. Douglas and Sir Richard Manningham, knt. F.R.S. the latter of whom, in 1726, published "an exact diary of what was observed during a close attendance upon Mary Toft the pretended Rabbit breeder of Godalming in Surrey, from Monday, Nov. 28, to Wednesday, Dec. 7 following, together with an account of her confession of the fraud.

Mr. St. André, an eminent surgeon, at one time lent himself to the delusion, but afterwards published a recantation.

Each pregnant female trembling hears,
And, overcome with spleen and fears,   440
Consults her faithful glass no more
But madly bounding o'er the floor,
Feels hairs o'er all her body grow,
By fancy turn'd into a doe.

Now, to promote their private ends,
Nature her usual course suspends,
And varies from the stated plan
Observed e'er since the world began.
Bodies, (which foolishly we thought,
By custom's servile maxims taught,   450
Needed a regular supply,
And without nourishment must die)
With craving appetites, and sense
Of hunger easily dispense,
And, pliant to their wondrous skill,
Are taught, like watches, to stand still,
Uninjured, for a month or more,
Then go on as they did before.
The novel takes, the tale succeeds,
Amply supplies its author's needs,   460
And Betty Canning is at least,

[461] In the year 1753, an extraordinary affair attracted the notice and divided the opinion of the public. A girl of eighteen years of age, named Elizabeth Canning, who had been missing for some time, came home to her mother in a deplorable and emaciated condition. She declared upon oath that on the 1st of January, about nine in the morning, while walking from Rosemary Lane, she was seized by two men in Moorfields, who first robbed and then gagged her; that in consequence of their ill usage she fell into a fit, and so continued for some hours. On recovering she found herself in a kitchen with an old gypsy woman and two young women. The former took her by the hand and promised to give

With Gascoyne's help, a six months' feast.
   Whilst, in contempt of all our pains,
The tyrant Superstition reigns
Imperious in the heart of man,
And warps his thoughts from Nature's plan;
Whilst fond Credulity, who ne'er

her some fine clothes; but considering this as an invitation to become a prostitute, she utterly refused, whereupon the old woman almost stripped her and pushed her into a back room like a hayloft, without any furniture in it, and there locked her up, threatening to cut her throat if she made any disturbance. On looking about her in the morning she discovered a large jug filled with water, and several pieces of bread amounting to about a quartern loaf, and some hay scattered on the floor. In this room she said she remained for more than 27 days without any other sustenance than the bread and water mentioned and a minced pie she had in her pocket. She said also she left some of these provisions behind her when she made her escape by breaking out of the house, and that during her confinement not a creature had come near her to see or speak to her. Upon her return an investigation was set on foot, and she having fixed upon a house at Enfield Wash, on the Hertford road, as the place where she had been confined, one Mrs. Wills, who kept it, together with Mary Squires, the gypsy, and Virtue Hall, a young woman who lived with Wills, were taken up and committed. Upon the examination the young woman fully confirmed the statement of Canning. After a full and long trial, Wills and Squires were found guilty, and the latter sentenced to suffer death. Sir Crisp Gascoyne the Lord Mayor being dissatisfied with the evidence, took great pains to unravel what he suspected was a conspiracy, and succeeded to his utmost wish. An alibi was clearly made out, and a free pardon granted to Mary Squires. An indictment for perjury was preferred against Elizabeth Canning, who was convicted on the clearest evidence of wilful and corrupt perjury, and thereupon sentenced to be transported for seven years.

The public were inflamed to an incredible pitch of folly and injustice on the occasion. Betty Canning was a heroine and a martyr in the estimation of the mob, and was celebrated as such in several popular street ballads.

The weight of wholesome doubts could bear,
To reason and herself unjust,
Takes all things blindly upon trust;
Whilst Curiosity, whose rage
No mercy shews to sex or age,
Must be indulged at the expense
Of judgment, truth, and common sense;
Impostures cannot but prevail,
And when old miracles grow stale,
Jugglers will still the art pursue,
And entertain the world with new.
  For them, obedient to their will,
And trembling at their mighty skill,
Sad spirits, summon'd from the tomb,
Glide glaring, ghastly through the gloom
In all the usual pomp of storms,
In horrid, customary forms,   .
A wolf, a bear, a horse, an ape,
As fear and fancy give them shape;
Tormented with despair and pain,
They roar, they yell, and clank the chain.
Folly and Guilt (for Guilt, howe'er
The face of Courage it may wear,
Is still a coward at the heart)
At fear-created phantoms start.
The priest, that very word implies
That he's both innocent and wise,
Yet fears to travel in the dark,
Unless escorted by his clerk.
  But let not every bungler deem
Too lightly of so deep a scheme;   .
For reputation of the art
Each Ghost must act a proper part,

Observe decorum's needful grace,
And keep the laws of time and place;
Must change, with happy variation,
His manners with his situation ;
What in the country might pass down,
Would be impertinent in town.
No spirit of discretion here
Can think of breeding awe and fear,
'Twill serve the purpose more by half
To make the congregation laugh.   510
We want no ensigns of surprise,
Locks stiff with gore, and saucer eyes;
Give us an entertaining sprite,
Gentle, familiar, and polite,
One who appears in such a form
As might an holy hermit warm,
Or who on former schemes refines,
And only talks by sounds and signs,
Who will not to the eye appear,
But pays her visits to the ear,   520
And knocks so gently, 'twould not fright
A lady in the darkest night.
Such is our Fanny, whose good will,
Which cannot in the grave lie still,
Brings her on earth to entertain
Her friends and lovers in Cock Lane.

THE GHOST.

BOOK II.

 SACRED, standard rule we find,
By poets held time out of mind—
To offer at Apollo's shrine,
And call on one, or all the Nine.
This custom, through a bigot zeal
Which moderns of fine taste must feel
For those who wrote in days of yore,
Adopted stands like many more ;
Though every cause which then conspired
To make it practised and admired,   10
Yielding to Time's destructive course,
For ages past hath lost its force.
   With ancient bards, an invocation   .
Was a true act of adoration,
Of worship an essential part,
And not a formal piece of art,
Of paltry reading a parade,
A dull solemnity in trade,
A pious fever, taught to burn
An hour or two, to serve a turn.   20
   They talk'd not of Castalian springs,
By way of saying pretty things,

As we dress out our flimsy rhimes;
'Twas the religion of the times;
And they believed that holy stream
With greater force made fancy teem,
Reckon'd by all a true specific
To make the barren brain prolific:
Thus Romish church, (a scheme which bears
Not half so much excuse as theirs)   30
Since Faith implicitly hath taught her,
Reveres the force of holy water.

    The Pagan system, whether true
Or false, its strength, like buildings, drew
From many parts disposed to bear,
In one great whole, their proper share.
Each god of eminent degree
To some vast beam compared might be;
Each godling was a peg, or rather
A cramp, to keep the beams together: 40
And man as safely might pretend
From Jove the thunderbolt to rend,
As with an impious pride aspire
To rob Apollo of his lyre.

    With settled faith and pious awe,
Establish'd by the voice of Law,
Then poets to the Muses came,
And from their altars caught the flame.
Genius, with Phœbus for his guide,
The Muse ascending by his side,   50
With towering pinions dared to soar,
Where eye could scarcely strain before.

    But why should we, who cannot feel
These glowings of a Pagan zeal,
That wild enthusiastic force,

By which, above her common course,
Nature, in ecstasy upborne,
Look'd down on earthly things with scorn ;
Who have no more regard, 'tis known,
For their religion than our own,   60
And feel not half so fierce a flame
At Clio's as at Fisher's name ;
Who know these boasted sacred streams
Were mere romantic idle dreams,
That Thames has waters clear as those
Which on the top of Pindus rose,
And that the fancy to refine,
Water's not half so good as wine ;
Who know, if profit strikes our eye,
Should we drink Helicon quite dry,   70
The whole fountain would not thither lead
So soon as one poor jug from Tweed ;
Who, if to raise poetic fire
The power of Beauty we require,
In any public place can view
More than the Grecians ever knew ;
If wit into the scale is thrown,
Can boast a Lennox of our own ;
Why should we servile customs choose,

---

[62] Catherine Fisher, better known by the name of Kitty
Fisher, a courtezan of great beauty and celebrity.

[78] Mrs. Arabella Lennox, the author of some very pleasing
novels, was the daughter of a North American gentleman of
the name of Ramsay, and was born at New York. Sir John
Hawkins relates in his life of Johnson that the Doctor celebrated the birth of her "first literary child"—as he called
Mrs. Lennox's first work—by a night of festivity spent with
the authoress and about twenty other friends at the Devil's
Tavern. Mrs. Lennox's "first literary child" was "The Life
of Harriot Stuart," published in 1751.

And court an antiquated Muse? 80
No matter why—to ask a reason
In pedant bigotry is treason.
    In the broad, beaten turnpike-road
Of hacknied panegyric ode,
No modern poet dares to ride
Without Apollo by his side,
Nor in a sonnet take the air,
Unless his lady Muse be there;
She, from some amaranthine grove,
Where little Loves and Graces rove, 90
The laurel to my Lord must bear,
Or garlands make for whores to wear;
She, with soft elegiac verse,
Must grace some mighty villain's hearse,
Or for some infant, doom'd by fate
To wallow in a large estate,
With rhymes the cradle must adorn,
To tell the world a fool is born.
    Since, then, our critic Lords expect
No hardy poet should reject 100
Establish'd maxims, or presume
To place much better in their room,
By nature fearful, I submit,
And in this dearth of sense and wit,
With nothing done, and little said,
(By wild excursive Fancy led
Into a second Book thus far,
Like some unwary traveller,
Whom varied scenes of wood and lawn
With treacherous delight have drawn, 110
Deluded from his purposed way;
Whom every step leads more astray;

Who, gazing round, can nowhere spy
Or house or friendly cottage nigh,
And resolution seems to lack
To venture forward or go back)
Invoke some goddess to descend,
And help me to my journey's end;
Though conscious Arrow all the while
Hears the petition with a smile,   120
Before the glass her charms unfolds,
And in herself my Muse beholds.

   Truth, goddess of celestial birth,
But little loved or known on earth;
Whose power but seldom rules the heart;
Whose name, with hypocritic art,
An arrant stalking-horse is made,
A snug pretence to drive a trade,
An instrument, convenient grown
To plant, more firmly, Falsehood's throne,   130
As rebels varnish o'er their cause
With specious colouring of laws,
And pious traitors draw the knife
In the king's name against his life;
Whether, (from cities far away,
Where Fraud and Falsehood scorn thy sway)
The faithful nymph's and shepherd's pride,
With Love and Virtue by thy side,
Your hours in harmless joys are spent
Amongst the children of Content;   140
Or, fond of gaiety and sport,
You tread the round of England's court,
Howe'er my Lord may frowning go
And treat the stranger as a foe,
Sure to be found a welcome guest

In George's and in Charlotte's breast;
If, in the giddy hours of youth,
My constant soul adhered to truth;
If, from the time I first wrote Man,
I still pursued thy sacred plan,   154
Tempted by Interest in vain
To wear mean Falsehood's golden chain;
If, for a season drawn away,
Starting from virtue's path astray,
All low disguise I scorn'd to try,
And dared to sin, but not to lie;
Hither, O hither! condescend,
Eternal Truth! thy steps to bend,
And favour him, who, every hour,
Confesses and obeys thy power.   160
    But come not with that easy mien
By which you won the lively Dean,
Nor yet assume that strumpet air
Which Rab'lais taught thee first to wear,
Nor yet that arch, ambiguous face
Which with Cervantes gave thee grace;
But come in sacred vesture clad,
Solemnly dull, and truly sad!
    Far from thy seemly matron train
Be idiot Mirth, and Laughter vain!   170
For Wit and Humour, which pretend
At once to please us and amend,
They are not for my present turn;
Let them remain in France with Sterne.
    Of noblest City parents born,
Whom wealth and dignities adorn,
Who still one constant tenor keep,

---

154 See the Conference, ll. 213-236.

Not quite awake nor quite asleep,
With thee let formal Dulness come,
And deep Attention, ever dumb;   180
Who on her lips her fingers lays,
Whilst every circumstance she weighs,
Whose downcast eye is often found
Bent without motion to the ground,
Or, to some outward thing confined,
Remits no image to the mind,
No pregnant mark of meaning bears,
But, stupid, without vision stares:
Thy steps let Gravity attend,
Wisdom's and Truth's unerring friend;   190
For one may see with half an eye,
That gravity can never lie,
And his arch'd brow, pull'd o'er his eyes,
With solemn proof proclaims him wise.

    Free from all waggeries and sports,
The produce of luxurious courts,
Where sloth and lust enervate youth,
Come thou, a downright City Truth:
The City, which we ever find
A sober pattern for mankind,   200
Where man, *in equilibrio* hung,
Is seldom old, and never young,
And from the cradle to the grave,
Not Virtue's friend nor Vice's slave;
As dancers on the wire we spy,
Hanging between the earth and sky.

    She comes—I see her from afar
Bending her course to Temple-Bar:
All sage and silent is her train,
Deportment grave, and garments plain,   210

Such as may suit a parson's wear,
And fit the headpiece of a mayor.
  By truth inspired, our Bacon's force
Open'd the way to learning's source;
Boyle through the works of nature ran,
And Newton, something more than man,
Dived into nature's hidden springs,
Laid bare the principles of things,
Above the earth our spirits bore,
And gave us worlds unknown before.   220
By Truth inspired, when Lauder's spite
O'er Milton cast the veil of night,
Douglas arose, and through the maze
Of intricate and winding ways
Came where the subtle traitor lay,
And dragg'd him, trembling, to the day;
Whilst he, (O shame to noblest parts!
Dishonour to the liberal arts,

---

[221] William Lauder was by birth a Scotchman, and taught Latin at the university of Edinburgh, where, in 1739, he published *Poetarum Scotorum Musæ Sacræ*. From thence he came to London, where, in 1747, he made a memorable attack on Milton in a book entitled "An Essay on Milton's use and imitation of the Moderns in his Paradise lost." His quotations, consisting of purposely interpolated passages in old and obscure authors, passed as genuine for a time; but in 1751 the forgeries were detected by Dr. Douglas, afterwards Bishop of Salisbury. Lauder died in Barbadoes about 1771.

[227] Dr. Johnson, with an honest persuasion of Lauder's truthfulness, for a time believed the charge he brought against Milton, and so far promoted it as to assist him in writing or revising the preface to his book. Upon the detection of the forgeries by Douglas in a pamphlet, Dr. Johnson advised Lauder to subscribe an ample confession of his guilt, which was very ably penned by the Doctor, and published in the form of a letter from Lauder to Douglas.

To traffic in so vile a scheme!)
Whilst he, our letter'd Polypheme,   230
Who had confederate forces join'd,
Like a base coward skulk'd behind.
By Truth inspired, our critics go
To track Fingal in Highland snow,
To form their own and other's creed
From manuscripts they cannot read.
By Truth inspired, we numbers see
Of each profession and degree,
Gentle and simple, lord and cit,
Wit without wealth, wealth without wit,   240
When Punch and Sheridan have done,
To Fanny's ghostly lectures run.
By Truth and Fanny now inspired,
I feel my glowing bosom fired;
Desire beats high in every vein
To sing the spirit of Cock Lane;
To tell (just as the measure flows
In halting rhyme, half verse, half prose)
With more than mortal arts endued,
How she united force withstood,   250
And proudly gave a brave defiance
To Wit and Dulness in alliance.
    This apparition (with relation
To ancient modes of derivation,
This we may properly so call,
Although it ne'er appears at all,
As by the way of inuendo,
Lucus is made *à non lucendo*)
Superior to the vulgar mode,
Nobly disdains that servile road   260
Which coward Ghosts, as it appears,

Have walk'd in, full five thousand years,
And, for restraint too mighty grown,
Strikes out a method of her own.
    Others may meanly start away,
Awed by the herald of the day;
With faculties too weak to bear
The freshness of the morning air,
May vanish with the melting gloom,
And glide in silence to the tomb :   270
She dares the sun's most piercing light,
And knocks by day as well as night.
Others, with mean and partial view,
Their visits pay to one or two ;
She, great in reputation grown,
Keeps the best company in Town.
Our active, enterprising Ghost
As large and splendid routs can boast
As those, which, raised by Pride's command,
Block up the passage through the Strand.   280
    Great adepts in the fighting trade,
Who served their time on the parade ;
She-saints, who, true to pleasure's plan,
Talk about God, and lust for man ;
Wits who believe nor God nor Ghost,
And fools who worship every post ;
Cowards, whose lips with war are hung ;
Men truly brave, who hold their tongue ;
Courtiers, who laugh they know not why,
And cits, who for the same cause cry ;   290

279 The parties of the Duchess of Northumberland at
Charing Cross were much attended by persons of distinction. Her Grace was fond of seeing literary men at her
house, but was unfortunate in her selection of them; Sir
John Hill, Mallet, &c. being of the chosen few.

The canting tabernacle brother,
(For one rogue still suspects another)
Ladies, who to a spirit fly,
Rather than with their husbands lie ;
Lords, who as chastely pass their lives
With other women as their wives ;
Proud of their intellects and clothes,
Physicians, lawyers, parsons, beaus,
And, truant from their desks and shops,
Spruce Temple clerks and 'prentice fops,   300
To Fanny come, with the same view,
To find her false, or find her true.

Hark! something creeps about the house !
Is it a spirit or a mouse ?
Hark ! something scratches round the room !
A cat, a rat, a stubb'd birch broom.
Hark ! on the wainscot now it knocks !
" If thou'rt a Ghost," cried Orthodox,
With that affected, solemn air
Which hypocrites delight to wear,   310
And all those forms of consequence
Which fools adopt instead of sense ;
" If thou'rt a Ghost, who from the tomb
Stalk'st sadly silent through this gloom,
In breach of nature's stated laws,
For good, or bad, or for no cause,
Give now nine knocks ; like priests of old,
Nine we a sacred number hold."

" Psha," cried Profound, (a man of parts,
Deep read in all the curious arts,   320
Who, to their hidden springs had traced
The force of numbers rightly placed)
" As to the number, you are right;

As to the form, mistaken quite.
What's nine?—Your adepts all agree
The virtue lies in three times three."

He said; no need to say it twice,
For thrice she knock'd, and thrice, and thrice.

The crowd, confounded and amazed,
In silence at each other gazed :⁣⁣⁣⁣⁣⁣⁣⁣⁣⁣⁣⁣⁣⁣⁣⁣⁣⁣⁣⁣⁣⁣⁣⁣⁣⁣⁣⁣⁣ 330
From Celia's hand the snuff-box fell,
Tinsel, who ogled with the belle,
To pick it up attempts in vain,
He stoops, but cannot rise again.
Immane Pomposo was not heard
T' import one crabbed foreign word :
Fear seizes heroes, fools and wits,
And Plausible his prayers forgets.

At length, as people just awake,
Into wild dissonance they break ;⁣⁣⁣⁣⁣⁣⁣⁣⁣⁣⁣⁣⁣⁣⁣⁣⁣⁣⁣⁣⁣⁣⁣⁣⁣⁣⁣ 340
All talk'd at once, but not a word
Was understood or plainly heard.
Such is the noise of chattering geese,
Slow sailing on the summer breeze ;
Such is the language Discord speaks
In Welsh women o'er beds of leeks ;

[335] Dr. Johnson's diction and dictionary afforded to Wilkes
and his partisans a never-failing source of ridicule, which
occasionally was not misplaced, as the following extracts
will shew :—

Whig—the name of a faction.
Network—anything reticulated or decussated at equal dis-
tances, with interstices between the intersections.
Cough—A convulsion of the lungs vellicated by some sharp
serosity.
Excise—a hateful tax levied upon commodities, and adjudged not by the common judges of property; but
wretches hired by those to whom excise is paid.

Such the confused and horrid sounds
Of Irish in potato grounds.
   But tired, for even C——'s tongue
Is not on iron hinges hung,   350
Fear and Confusion sound retreat,
Reason and Order take their seat.
The fact confirm'd beyond all doubt,
They now would find the causes out.
For this a sacred rule we find
Among the nicest of mankind;
Which never might exception brook
From Hobbes e'en down to Bolingbroke,
To doubt of facts, however true,
Unless they know the causes too.   360
   Trifle, of whom 'twas hard to tell
When he intended ill or well;
Who, to prevent all farther pother,
Probably meant nor one nor t'other;
Who to be silent always loath,
Would speak on either side, or both;
Who led away by love of fame,
If any new idea came,
Whate'er it made for, always said it,
Not with an eye to truth, but credit,—   370
For orators profess'd 'tis known,
Talk not for our sake, but their own,—
Who always shew'd his talents best
When serious things were turn'd to jest,
And under much impertinence
Possess'd no common share of sense;
Who could deceive the flying hours
With chat on butterflies and flowers;
Could talk of powder, patches, paint,

With the same zeal as of a saint;   380
Could prove a Sibyl brighter far
Than Venus or the Morning Star;
Whilst something still so gay, so new,
The smile of approbation drew,
And females eyed the charming man,
Whilst their hearts flutter'd with their fan;
Trifle, who would by no means miss
An opportunity like this,
Proceeding on his usual plan,
Smiled, stroked his chin, and thus began :   390
    " With sheers or scissars, sword or knife,
When the Fates cut the thread of life,
(For if we to the grave are sent,
No matter with what instrument)
The body in some lonely spot,
On dunghill vile, is laid to rot,
Or sleep among more holy dead
With prayers irreverently read;
The soul is sent where Fate ordains,
To reap rewards, to suffer pains.   400
    " The virtuous, to those mansions go,
Where pleasures unembitter'd flow,
Where, leading up a jocund band,
Vigour and Youth dance hand in hand,
Whilst Zephyr, with harmonious gales,
Pipes softest music through the vales,
And Spring and Flora, gaily crown'd
With velvet carpet spread the ground;
With livelier blush where roses bloom,
And every shrub expires perfume,   410
Where crystal streams meandering glide,
Where warbling flows the amber tide,

Where other suns dart brighter beams,
And light through purer æther streams.
   " Far other seats, far different state,
The sons of wickedness await,
Justice, (not that old hag I mean
Who's nightly in the Garden seen,
Who lets no spark of mercy rise,
For crimes, by which men lose their eyes :   420
Nor her, who with an equal hand
Weighs tea and sugar in the Strand ;
Nor her, who, by the world deem'd wise,
Deaf to the widow's piercing cries,
Steel'd 'gainst the starving orphan's tears,
On pawns her base tribunal rears ;
But her, who after death presides,
Whom sacred truth unerring guides,
Who, free from partial influence,
Nor sinks nor raises evidence,   430
Before whom nothing's in the dark,
Who takes no bribe, and keeps no clerk)
Justice, with equal scale below,
In due proportion weighs out woe,
And always with such lucky aim
Knows punishments so fit to frame,
That she augments their grief and pain,
Leaving no reason to complain.
   " Old maids and rakes are join'd together,

----

[418] One of the greatest abuses that existed in Churchill's time was the administration of the police of London, which was intrusted to a set of vulgar, ignorant men called trading justices. These men, assisted by clerks taken from the lowest stations, levied fines and annual tributes on those offenders who were rich enough to purchase exemption from punishment. Their head quarters were in Covent Garden.

Coquettes and prudes, like April weather, 440
Wit's forced to chum with Common Sense,
And Lust is yoked to Impotence.
Professors (Justice so decreed)
Unpaid, must constant lectures read ;
On earth it often doth befal,
They're paid, and never read at all :
Parsons must practise what they teach,
And bishops are compell'd to preach.

  " She, who on earth was nice and prim,
Of delicacy full and whim ; 450
Whose tender nature could not bear
The rudeness of the churlish air,
Is doom'd, to mortify her pride,
The change of weather to abide,
And sells, whilst tears with liquor mix,
Burnt brandy on the shore of Styx.

  " Avaro,—by long use grown bold
In every ill which brings him gold,
Who his Redeemer would pull down,

---

457 In the Conclave (a poem written by Churchill, but
deemed too personal and virulent for publication) Dr. Pearce,
the prelate here vilified, was attacked under the name of
Longinus.   The poem opened with these lines :—
" The Conclave was met, and Longinus the Pope,
Who leads a great number of fools in a rope,
Who makes them get up, and who makes them sit still ;
Who makes them say yea or nay, just as he will ;
Who a critic profound does all critics defy,
And settles the difference 'twixt *Beta* and *Pi ;*
Who forgiveness of faults preaches up to another,
But forbids it to come near himself or his brother," &c.

459 A painted window representing the crucifixion was
put up over the altar in St. Margaret's Church, Westminster.
Dr. Pearce, then Bishop of Rochester and Dean of Westminster, thought it savoured of popery, and endeavoured
to have it removed.

And sell his God for half-a-crown ;   400
Who, if some blockhead should be willing
To lend him on his soul a shilling,
A well-made bargain would esteem it,
And have more sense than to redeem it,—
Justice shall in those shades confine,
To drudge for Plutus in the mine,
All the day long to toil and roar,
And, cursing, work the stubborn ore
For coxcombs here who have no brains,
Without a sixpence for his pains :   470
Thence, with each due return of night
Compell'd, the tall, thin, half-starved sprite
Shall earth re-visit, and survey
The place where once his treasure lay,
Shall view the stall where holy Pride,
With letter'd Ignorance allied,
Once hail'd him mighty and adored,
Descended to another lord :
Then shall he, screaming, pierce the air,
Hang his lank jaws and scowl despair ;   480
Then shall he ban at Heaven's decrees,
And, howling, sink to hell for ease.
    " Those, who on earth through life have past
With equal pace from first to last,
Nor vex'd with passions nor with spleen,
Insipid, easy, and serene ;
Whose heads were made too weak to bear
The weight of business or of care ;
Who, without merit, without crime,
Contrive to while away their time,   490
Nor good nor bad, nor fools nor wits,
· Mild Justice, with a smile, permits

Still to pursue their darling plan,
And find amusement how they can.
  " The beau, in gaudiest plumage drest
With lucky fancy, o'er the rest,
Of air a curious mantle throws,
And chats among his brother beaus;
Or, if the weather's fine and clear,
No sign of rain or tempest near,   500
Encouraged by the cloudless day,
Like gilded butterflies at play,
So lively all, so gay, so brisk,
In air they flutter, float and frisk.
  " The belle, (what mortal doth not know
Belles after death admire a beau?)
With happy grace renews her art
To trap the coxcomb's wandering heart;
And, after death as whilst they live,
A heart is all which beaux can give.   510
  " In some still, solemn, sacred shade,
Behold a group of authors laid,
Newspaper wits, and sonneteers,
Gentlemen bards, and rhyming peers;
Biographers, whose wondrous worth
Is scarce remember'd now on earth,
Whom Fielding's humour led astray,
And plaintive fops, debauch'd by Gray,
All sit together in a ring,
And laugh and prattle, write and sing.   520
  " On his own works, with laurel crown'd,
Neatly and elegantly bound,
(For this is one of many rules,
With writing lords and laureate fools,
And which for ever must succeed

With other lords who cannot read,—
However destitute of wit,
To make their works for bookcase fit)
Acknowledged master of those seats,
Cibber his Birth-day Odes repeats.   530
   " With triumph now possess that seat,
With triumph now thy Odes repeat;
Unrivall'd vigils proudly keep,
Whilst every hearer's lull'd to sleep;
But know, illustrious Bard! when Fate,
Which still pursues thy name with hate,
The regal laurel blasts, which now
Blooms on the placid Whitehead's brow,
Low must descend thy pride and fame,
And Cibber's be the second name."   540
   Here Trifle cough'd, (for coughing still
Bears witness to the speaker's skill,
A necessary piece of art,
Of rhetoric an essential part;
And adepts in the speaking trade
Keep a cough by them ready made,
Which they successfully dispense
When at a loss for words or sense)
Here Trifle cough'd, here paused—but while
He strove to recollect his smile,   550

<hr>

530 Colley Cibber, the hero of the Dunciad, and White-head's predecessor in the Laureate's chair. His plays for many seasons ranked high in the acting list, and his "Apology for his Life" is one of the most amusing specimens of autobiography in our language, and comprises the best history of the English stage during the long period he was connected with it. Some natural defects prevented his ever attaining high excellence as an actor. He died in 1757, at the age of 86.

That happy engine of his art,
Which triumph'd o'er the female heart,
Credulity, the child of Folly,
Begot on cloister'd Melancholy,
Who heard, with grief, the florid fool
Turn sacred things to ridicule,
And saw him, led by whim away,
Still farther from the subject stray,
Just in the happy nick, aloud,
In shape of Moore, address'd the crowd: 560
　" Were we with patience here to sit,
Dupes to the impertinence of wit,
Till Trifle his harangue should end,
A Greenland night we might attend,
Whilst he, with fluency of speech,
Would various mighty nothings teach;"
Here Trifle, sternly looking down,
Gravely endeavour'd at a frown,
But Nature unawares stept in,
And, mocking, turn'd it to a grin.   570
" And when, in Fancy's chariot hurl'd,
We had been carried round the world,
Involved in error still and doubt,
He'd leave us where we first set out.
Thus soldiers (in whose exercise
Material use with grandeur vies)
Lift up their legs with mighty pain,
Only to set them down again.
　" Believe ye not (yes, all I see
In sound belief concur with me)   580
That Providence, for worthy ends,

---

560 The Rev. Mr. Moore, curate of St. Sepulchre's. See
the preliminary note to the 1st Book of the Ghost.

To us unknown, this Spirit sends?
Though speechless lay the trembling tongue,
Your faith was on your features hung;
Your faith I in your eyes could see,
When all were pale and stared like me:
But scruples to prevent, and root
Out every shadow of dispute,
Pomposo, Plausible, and I,
With Fanny, have agreed to try   590
A deep concerted scheme—this night
To fix or to destroy her quite.
If it be true, before we've done,
We'll make it glaring as the sun;
If it be false, admit no doubt,
Ere morning's dawn we'll find it out.
Into the vaulted womb of death,
Where Fanny now, deprived of breath,
Lies festering, whilst her troubled sprite
Adds horror to the gloom of night,   600
Will we descend, and bring from thence
Proofs of such force to common sense,
Vain triflers shall no more deceive,
And Atheists tremble and believe."

   He said, and ceased; the chamber rung
With due applause from every tongue:
The mingled sound (now let me see—
Something by way of simile)
Was it more like Strymonian cranes,
Or winds low murmuring when it rains,   610
Or drowsy hum of clustering bees,
Or the hoarse roar of angry seas?
Or (still to heighten and explain,
For else our simile is vain)

Shall we declare it like all four,
A scream, a murmur, hum, and roar?
　Let Fancy now, in awful state,
Present this great triumvirate,
(A method which received we find
In other cases by mankind)　　　　　　620
Elected with a joint consent,
All fools in town to represent.
　The clock strikes twelve—Moore starts and
　　　swears;
In oaths, we know, as well as prayers,
Religion lies, and a church brother
May use at will or one or t'other;
Plausible from his cassock drew
A holy manual, seeming new;
A book it was of private prayer,
But not a pin the worse for wear;　　　630
For, as we by the bye may say,
None but small saints in private pray.
Religion, fairest maid on earth!
As meek as good, who drew her birth
From that bless'd union, when in heaven
Pleasure was bride to Virtue given;
Religion, ever pleased to pray,
Possess'd the precious gift one day;
Hypocrisy, of Cunning born,
Crept in and stole it ere the morn;　　　640
Whitefield, that greatest of all saints,　-
Who always prays and never faints,
(Whom she to her own brothers bore,
Rapine and Lust, on Severn's shore)
Received it from the squinting dame;
From him to Plausible it came,

Who, with unusual care opprest,
Now, trembling, pull'd it from his breast;
Doubts in his boding heart arise,
And fancied spectres blast his eyes ; 650
Devotion springs from abject fear,
And stamps his prayers for once sincere.
   Pomposo,—insolent and loud,
Vain idol of a scribbling crowd,
Whose very name inspires an awe,
Whose every word is sense and law;
For what his greatness hath decreed,
Like laws of Persia and of Mede,
Sacred through all the realm of Wit,
Must never of repeal admit ; 660
Who, cursing flattery, is the tool
Of every fawning, flattering fool ;
Who Wit with jealous eye surveys,
And sickens at another's praise ;
Who, proudly seized of learning's throne,
Now damns all learning but his own ;
Who scorns those common wares to trade in,
Reasoning, convincing, and persuading,
But makes each sentence current pass
With puppy, coxcomb, scoundrel, ass ; 670
For 'tis with him a certain rule,   .
The folly's proved when he calls fool ;

653 Dr. Johnson, whose Tory politics rendered him particularly obnoxious to Churchill, notwithstanding their common prejudices against the Scotch, affected to hold our
Author in great contempt. The character of Pomposo was
much extolled by Johnson's enemies; but the only reply
that the Doctor made to the satire was, that he " thought
Churchill a shallow fellow in the beginning, and had seen no
reason for altering his opinion."

Who to increase his native strength,
Draws words six syllables in length,
With which, assisted with a frown,
By way of club, he knocks us down;
Who 'bove the vulgar dares to rise,
And sense of decency defies;
For this same decency is made
Only for bunglers in the trade,   68■
And, like the cobweb laws, is still
Broke through by great ones when they will—
Pomposo, with strong sense supplied,
Supported, and confirm'd by Pride,
His comrades' terrors to beguile
" Grinn'd horribly a ghastly smile:"
Features so horrid, were it light,
Would put the devil himself to flight.

Such were the three in name and worth,
Whom Zeal and Judgment singled forth   690
To try the sprite on reason's plan,
Whether it was of God or man.

Dark was the night; it was that hour
When terror reigns in fullest power;
When, as the learn'd of old have said,
The yawning grave gives up her dead;
When Murder, Rapine by her side,
Stalks o'er the earth with giant stride:
Our Quixotes (for that knight of old
Was not in truth by half so bold;   700
Though Reason at the same time cries,
Our Quixotes are not half so wise,
Since they, with other follies, boast
An expedition 'gainst a Ghost)
Through the dull, deep surrounding gloom,
In close array, towards Fanny's tomb

Adventured forth; Caution before,
With heedful step, the lanthorn bore,
Pointing at graves; and in the rear,
Trembling, and talking loud, went Fear.   710
The church-yard teem'd; th' unsettled ground,
As in an ague, shook around;
While, in some dreary vault confined,
Or riding on the hollow wind,
Horror, which turns the heart to stone,
In dreadful sounds was heard to groan.
All staring, wild, and out of breath,
At length they reach the place of death.
     A vault it was, long time applied
To hold the last remains of Pride;   720
No beggar there, of humble race,
And humble fortunes, finds a place,
To rest in pomp as well as ease;
The only way's to pay the fees.
Fools, rogues, and whores, if rich and great,
Proud even in death, here rot in state.
No thieves disrobe the well-dressed dead;
No plumbers steal the sacred lead;
Quiet and safe the bodies lie;
No sextons sell; no surgeons buy.   730
     Thrice each the ponderous key applied,
And thrice to turn it vainly tried,
Till taught by Prudence to unite,
And straining with collected might,
The stubborn wards resist no more,
But open flies the growling door.
     Three paces back they fell amazed,
Like statues stood, like madmen gazed;
The frighted blood forsakes the face,
And seeks the heart with quicker pace;   740

The throbbing heart its fears declares,
And upright stand the bristled hairs;
The head in wild distraction swims,
Cold sweats bedew the trembling limbs;
Nature, whilst fears her bosom chill,
Suspends her powers, and life stands still.
　　Thus had they stood till now; but Shame
(An useful though neglected dame,
By Heaven design'd the friend of man,
Though we degrade her all we can,　　　　　750
And strive, as our first proof of wit,
Her name and nature to forget)
Came to their aid in happy hour,
And with a wand of mighty power
Struck on their hearts; vain fears subside,
And, baffled, leave the field to Pride.
　　Shall they, (forbid it, Fame!) shall they
The dictates of vile Fear obey?
Shall they, the idols of the Town,
To bugbears fancy-form'd bow down?　　　　760
Shall they, who greatest zeal exprest,
And undertook for all the rest,
Whose matchless courage all admire,
Inglorious from the task retire?
How would the wicked ones rejoice,
And infidels exalt their voice,
If Moore and Plausible were found,
By shadows awed, to quit their ground!
How would fools laugh, should it appear
Pomposo was the slave of fear!　　　　　770
" Perish the thought! though to our eyes
In all its terrors, hell should rise,
Though thousand Ghosts, in dread array,
With glaring eye-balls, cross our way;

Though Caution, trembling, stands aloof,
Still we will on, and dare the proof."
They said; and, without farther halt,
Dauntless march'd onward to the vault.
    What mortal men, who e'er drew breath,
Shall break into the house of Death   780
With foot unhallow'd, and from thence
The mysteries of that state dispense,
Unless they with due rights prepare
Their weaker sense such sights to bear,
And gain permission from the state,
On earth their journal to relate?
Poets themselves, without a crime,
Cannot attempt it e'en in rhyme,
But always, on such grand occasion,
Prepare a solemn invocation,   790
A posy for grim Pluto weave,
And in smooth numbers ask his leave.
But why this caution? why prepare
Rites needless now? for thrice in air
The spirit of the Night hath sneezed,
And thrice hath clapp'd his wings well-pleased.
    Descend then, Truth, and guard thy side,
My Muse, my patroness, and guide!
Let others at invention aim,
And seek by falsities for fame;   80
Our story wants not, at this time,
Flounces and furbelows in rhyme;
Relate plain facts; be brief and bold;
And let the poets, famed of old,
Seek, whilst our artless tale we tell,
In vain to find a parallel.
Silent all three went in; about
All three turn'd silent, and came out.

THE GHOST.

BOOK III.

IT was the hour, when housewife Morn
With pearl and linen hangs each thorn;
When happy bards, who can regale
Their Muse with country air and ale,
Ramble afield to brooks and bowers,
To pick up sentiments and flowers;
When dogs and squires from kennel fly,
And hogs and farmers quit their sty;
When my Lord rises to the chase,
And brawny chaplain takes his place.   10
  These images, or bad or good,
If they are rightly understood,
Sagacious readers must allow
Proclaim us in the country now;
For observations mostly rise
From objects just before our eyes,
And every lord in critic wit
Can tell you where the piece was writ;
Can point out, as he goes along,
(And who shall dare to say he's wrong?)   20
Whether the warmth (for bards, we know,
At present never more than glow)
Was in the town or country caught,
By the peculiar turn of thought.
  It was the hour,—though critics frown,

We now declare ourselves in Town,
Nor will a moment's pause allow
For finding when we came, or how.
The man who deals in humble prose,
Tied down by rule and method goes ;　　30
But they who court the vigorous Muse
Their carriage have a right to choose.
Free as the air, and unconfined,
Swift as the motions of the mind,
The poet darts from place to place,
And instant bounds o'er time and space ;
Nature (whilst blended fire and skill
Inflame our passions to his will)
Smiles at her violated laws,
And crowns his daring with applause.　　40

   Should there be still some rigid few
Who keep propriety in view ;
Whose heads turn round, and cannot bear
This whirling passage through the air,
Free leave have such at home to sit,
And write a regimen for wit ;
To clip our pinions let them try,
Not having heart themselves to fly.

   It was the hour, when devotees
Breathe pious curses on their knees ;　　50
When they with prayers the day begin
To sanctify a night of sin ;
When rogues of modesty, who roam
Under the veil of night, sneak home,
That free from all restraint and awe,
Just to the windward of the law,
Less modest rogues their tricks may play,
And plunder in the face of day.

But hold,—whilst thus we play the fool,
In bold contempt of every rule,   60
Things of no consequence expressing,
Describing now, and now digressing,
To the discredit of our skill
The main concern is standing still.
   In plays, indeed, when storms of rage
Tempestuous in the soul engage,
Or when the spirits, weak and low,
Are sunk in deep distress and woe,
With strict propriety we hear
Description stealing on the ear,   70
And put off feeling half an hour
To thatch a cot, or paint a flower;
But in these serious works, design'd
To mend the morals of mankind,
We must for ever be disgraced,
With all the nicer sons of taste,
If once, the shadow to pursue,
We let the substance out of view.
Our means must uniformly tend
In due proportion to their end,   80
And every passage aptly join
To bring about the one design.
Our friends themselves cannot admit
This rambling, wild, digressive wit;
No—not those very friends, who found
Their credit on the self-same ground.
   Peace, my good grumbling Sir; for once,
Sunk in the solemn, formal dunce,
This coxcomb shall your fears beguile;
We will be dull—that you may smile.   90
   Come, Method, come in all thy pride,

Dulness and Whitehead by thy side;
Dulness and Method still are one,
And Whitehead is their darling son:
Not he whose pen, above control,
Struck terror to the guilty soul,
Made Folly tremble through her state,
And villains blush at being great;
Whilst he himself, with steady face,
Disdaining modesty and grace,   100
Could blunder on through thick and thin,
Through every mean and servile sin,
Yet swear by Philip and by Paul
He nobly scorn'd to blush at all;
But he, who in the Laureate chair,
By grace, not merit, planted there,
In awkward pomp is seen to sit,
And by his patent proves his wit;
For favours of the great, we know,
Can wit as well as rank bestow;   110

[95] Paul Whitehead, a man of notoriously profligate
character. He was the author of several satires, now
deservedly forgotten, in which he unsparingly lashed the
vices and follies of the age, and carried his pseudo patriotism
almost to republicanism: they were intitled, "The State
Dunces;" "Honour;" and "Manners;" for the last of
which he was ordered by the House of Lords to be taken
into custody. He also wrote some other poems of little
merit. His companionable qualities or rather vices procured
him the friendship of Sir Francis Dashwood, who, when
Chancellor of the Exchequer, conferred on him a patent
place of £800 a year, which he enjoyed till his death in 1774,
and which gave him a most convincing proof of the
folly of his former principles. By his will, Paul Whitehead
bequeathed his heart to his patron Lord Le Despencer, who
caused it to be enclosed in an urn, and deposited in the
church he erected at High Wycombe.

And they who, without one pretension,
Can get for fools a place or pension,
Must able be supposed of course
(If reason is allow'd due force)
To give such qualities and grace
As may equip them for the place.
But he—who measures, as he goes,
A mongrel kind of tinkling prose,
And is too frugal to dispense,
At once, both poetry and sense ;   120
Who, from amidst his slumbering guards,
Deals out a charge to subject bards,
Where couplets after couplets creep
Propitious to the reign of sleep ;
Yet every word imprints an awe,
And all his dictates pass for law
With beaus, who simper all around,
And belles, who die in every sound :
For in all things of this relation,
Men mostly judge from situation,   130
Nor in a thousand find we one
Who really weighs what's said or done ;
They deal out censure, or give credit,
Merely from him who did or said it. ·
But he—who, happily serene,
Means nothing, yet would seem to mean,
Who rules and cautions can dispense
With all that humble insolence
Which impudence in vain would teach,
And none but modest men can reach ;   140
Who adds to sentiments the grace

¹²² William Whitehead, (for an account of whom see
"Prophecy of Famine," l. 256), published, in 1762, "A
Charge to the Poets."

Of always being out of place,
And drawls out morals with an air
A gentleman would blush to wear ;
Who, on the chastest, simplest plan,
As chaste, as simple, as the man,
Without or character, or plot,
Nature unknown, and art forgot,
Can, with much racking of the brains,
And years consumed in letter'd pains,   150
A heap of words together lay,
And, smirking, call the thing a play ;
Who, champion sworn in virtue's cause,
'Gainst vice his tiny bodkin draws,
But to no part of prudence stranger,
First blunts the point for fear of danger.
So nurses sage, as caution works,
When children first use knives and forks,
For fear of mischief, it is known,
To others' fingers or their own,   160
To take the edge off wisely choose,
Though the same stroke takes off the use.
    Thee, Whitehead, thee I now invoke,
Sworn foe to Satire's generous stroke,
Which makes unwilling conscience feel,
And wounds, but only wounds to heal.
Good-natured, easy creature, mild
And gentle as a new-born child,
Thy heart would never once admit
E'en wholesome rigour to thy wit ;   170
Thy head, if conscience should comply,
Its kind assistance would deny,

---

[153] Alluding to Whitehead's comedy of the School for
Lovers, a servile copy from " le Testament " of Fontenelle.

And lend thee neither force, nor art
To drive it onward to the heart.
O may thy sacred power control
Each fiercer working of my soul,
Damp every spark of genuine fire,
And languors, like thine own, inspire!
Trite be each thought, and every line
As moral, and as dull as thine! 180

    Poised in mid-air (it matters not
To ascertain the very spot,
Nor yet to give you a relation
How it eluded gravitation)
Hung a watch-tower, by Vulcan plann'd
With such rare skill, by Jove's command,
That every word, which whisper'd here
Scarce vibrates to the neighbour ear,
On the still bosom of the air
Is borne, and heard distinctly there; 190
The palace of an ancient dame,
Whom men as well as gods call Fame;
A prattling gossip, on whose tongue
Proof of "perpetual motion" hung,
Whose lungs in strength all lungs surpass,
Like her own trumpet made of brass;
Who with an hundred pair of eyes
The vain attacks of sleep defies;
Who with an hundred pair of wings
News from the farthest quarters brings, 200
Sees, hears, and tells, untold before,
All that she knows and ten times more.
    Not all the virtues which we find
Concenter'd in a Hunter's mind,

201 Miss Hunter, a young lady of family and fortune, and

Can make her spare the rancorous tale,
If, in one point she chance to fail;
Or if once in a thousand years
A perfect character appears,
Such as of late with joy and pride
My soul possess'd, ere Arrow died;   210
Or such as envy must allow
The world enjoys in Hunter now;
This hag, who aims at all alike,
At virtues e'en like theirs will strike,
And make faults in the way of trade,
When she can't find them ready made.

    All things she takes in, small and great,
Talks of a toyshop and a state;
Of wits and fools, of saints and kings,
Of garters, stars, and leading strings;   220
Of old lords fumbling for a clap,
And young ones full of prayer and pap;
Of courts, of morals, and tye-wigs,
Of bears and serjeants dancing jigs;
Of grave professors at the bar
Learning to thrum on the guitar,
Whilst laws are slubber'd o'er in haste,

maid of honour to Queen Charlotte, eloped on the day of the
coronation with Henry Herbert, tenth Earl of Pembroke.
On her table was found a paper containing the famous lines
from Pope:—

"How oft when pressed to marriage have I said,
Curse on all laws but those which love has made.
Love, free as air, at sight of human ties,
Spreads his light wings, and in a moment flies," &c.

The king immediately deprived Lord Pembroke of his
military commands, and with his own hand struck him out
of the list of privy counsellors. Miss Hunter, after the death
of Lord Pembroke, became the wife of General Clarke.

And judgment sacrificed to taste;
Of whited sepulchres, lawn sleeves,
And God's house made a den of thieves; 230
Of funeral pomps, where clamours hung,
And fix'd disgrace on every tongue,
Whilst Sense and Order blush'd to see
Nobles without humanity;
Of coronations, where each heart,
With honest raptures, bore a part;
Of city feasts, where Elegance
Was proud her colours to advance,
And Gluttony, uncommon case,
Could only get the second place; 240
Of new-raised pillars in the state,
Who must be good, as being great;
Of shoulders, on which honours sit
Almost as clumsily as wit;
Of doughty knights, whom titles please,
But not the payment of the fees;
Of lectures, whither every fool
In second childhood goes to school;
Of grey-beards, deaf to Reason's call,
From Inn of Court, or City Hall, 250
Whom youthful appetites enslave,

²³¹ Alluding to the interment of George II, which took
place the 11th of November, 1760.

²³⁵ The coronation of George the Third on the 22nd of
September, 1761. This solemnity is noticed in the next
book.

²³⁷ Their majesties were entertained by the city at Guild-
hall, according to custom, on the first Lord Mayor's day after
their coronation. The banquet was provided in a style then
unprecedented in the civic annals. It cost £6898 5s. 4d.

²⁴⁷ Macklin and Sheridan were at this time rival lec-
turers on elocution.

With one foot fairly in the grave,
By help of crutch, a needful brother,
Learning of Hart to dance with t'other;
Of doctors regularly bred
To fill the mansions of the dead;
Of quacks, (for quacks they must be still,
Who save when forms require to kill)
Who life, and health, and vigour give
To him not one would wish to live;   260
Of artists who, with noblest view,
Disinterested plans pursue,
For trembling worth the ladder raise,
And mark out the ascent to praise;
Of arts and sciences, where meet,
Sublime, profound, and all complete,
A set (whom at some fitter time
The Muse shall consecrate in rhyme)
Who, humble artists to out-do,
A far more liberal plan pursue,   270
And let their well-judged premiums fall
On those who have no worth at all;
Of sign-post exhibitions, raised
For laughter more than to be praised,

---

[254] An eminent professor of dancing.

[267] The Society for the Encouragement of Arts, Manufactures, and Commerce, founded in the year 1753. Previous to the institution of the Royal Academy, in 1765, the Society of Arts had an annual exhibition in its room of meeting, in Beaufort-buildings, of such paintings as had obtained the premiums offered within the year. From this Society have branched the Royal Academy and several literary and scientific Institutions, and numerous societies for improvements in agriculture.

[274] Bonnell Thornton, previous to the annual opening of the Society of Arts on the 20th of April, 1762, advertised

(Though by the way we cannot see
Why praise and laughter mayn't agree)
Where genuine humour runs to waste,
And justly chides our want of taste,
Censured, like other things, though good,
Because they are not understood. 280

    To higher subjects now she soars,
And talks of politics and whores ;
(If to your nice and chaster ears
That term indelicate appears,
Scripture politely shall refine
And melt it into concubine)
In the same breath spreads Bourbon's league ;
And publishes the grand intrigue ;
In Brussels', or our own Gazette
Makes armies fight which never met, 290
And circulates the pox or plague
To London by the way of Hague,—
For all the lies which there appear
Stamp'd with authority come here ;
Borrows as freely from the gabble
Of some rude leader of a rabble,
Or from the quaint harangues of those
Who lead a nation by the nose,

for the same day in the papers an exhibition by the society
of sign painters, of all the curious signs to be met with in
town or country. The public considering it as a mere
newspaper skit, enjoyed the joke; but the plan was actually
carried into execution in a room in Bow-street, Covent-
garden.

    [287] The league between France and Spain in 1761, which
led to Great Britain's declaring war against Spain in 1762.

    [289] The Brussels Gazette was a notorious vehicle for the
experiments of continental diplomatists on the credulity of
the public.

As from those storms which, void of art,
Burst from our honest patriot's heart,   300
When Eloquence and Virtue (late
Remark'd to live in mutual hate)
Fond of each other's friendship grown,
Claim every sentence for their own ;
And with an equal joy recites
Parade amours and half pay fights,
Perform'd by heroes of fair weather,
Merely by dint of lace and feather,
As those rare acts which Honour taught
Our daring sons where Granby fought,   310
Or those which, with superior skill,
Sackville achieved by standing still.

    This hag, (the curious, if they please,
May search, from earliest times, to these,
And poets they will always see
With gods and goddesses make free,
Treating them all, except the Muse,
As scarcely fit to wipe their shoes)

[300] The Earl of Chatham.
[310] The Marquess of Granby, eldest son of the third Duke
of Rutland, distinguished himself during the seven years
war, under Prince Ferdinand of Brunswick. He was second
to Lord Sackville (whom he succeeded) in the command of
the English troops at the battle of Minden; and when
the latter pretended not to comprehend Prince Ferdinand's
orders, the Prince directed them to be repeated to the
Marquess of Granby, as he was sure he would understand
them. The Marquess died in 1770, in the 50th year of
his age, leaving a son, Charles Manners, who succeeded
as fourth Duke in 1779. Walpole describes him as an honest
open-hearted man of undaunted spirit, but no capacity,
that he drank as profusely as a German, was honest and
affable, and of unbounded good nature and generosity.

Who had beheld, from first to last,
How our triumvirate had past   320
Night's dreadful interval, and heard,
With strict attention, every word,
Soon as she saw return of light,
On sounding pinions took her flight.
    Swift through the regions of the sky,
Above the reach of human eye,
Onward she drove the furious blast,
And rapid as a whirlwind past,
O'er countries, once the seats of taste,
By time and ignorance laid waste ;   336
O'er lands, where former ages saw
Reason and truth the only law ;
Where arts and arms, and public love,
In generous emulation strove ;
Where kings were proud of legal sway,
And subjects happy to obey,
Though now in slavery sunk, and broke
To superstition's galling yoke ;
Of arts, of arms, no more they tell,
Or freedom, which with science fell :   340
By tyrants awed, who never find
The passage to their people's mind ;
To whom the joy was never known
Of planting in the heart their throne ;
Far from all prospect of relief,
Their hours in fruitless prayers and grief
For loss of blessings they employ
Which we unthankfully enjoy.
    Now is the time (had we the will)
To amaze the reader with our skill,   3.0
To pour out such a flood of knowledge

As might suffice for a whole college,
Whilst with a true poetic force,
We traced the goddess in her course,
Sweetly describing, in our flight,
Each common and uncommon sight,
Making our journal gay and pleasant,
With things long past, and things now present.
   Rivers—once Nymphs—(a transformation
Is mighty pretty in relation)   360
From great authorities we know
Will matter for a tale bestow:
To make the observation clear
We give our friends an instance here.
   The day (that never is forgot)
Was very fine, but very hot;
The nymph (another general rule)
 Enflamed with heat, laid down to cool;
Her hair, (we no exceptions find)
Waved careless, floating in the wind;   370
Her heaving breasts, like summer seas,
Seem'd amorous of the playful breeze:
Should fond Description tune our lays
In choicest accents to her praise,
Description we at last should find,
Baffled and weak, would halt behind.
Nature had form'd her to inspire
In every bosom soft desire;
Passions to raise, she could not feel;
Wounds to inflict, she would not heal.   380
A god, (his name is no great matter,
Perhaps a Jove, perhaps a Satyr)

[365] These lines are a witty burlesque on the tale of Lodona
and Pan in Pope's Windsor Forest.

Raging with lust, a godlike flame,
By chance, as usual, thither came;
With gloating eye the fair one view'd,
Desired her first, and then pursued:
She, (for what other can she do?)
Must fly—or how can he pursue?
The Muse, (so custom hath decreed)
Now proves her spirit by her speed,   300
Nor must one limping line disgrace
The life and vigour of the race.
She runs, and he runs, till at length,
Quite destitute of breath and strength,
To Heaven (for there we all apply
For help, when there's no other nigh)
She offers up her virgin prayer,
(Can virgins pray unpitied there?)
And when the god thinks he has caught her,
Slips through his hands and runs to water,   400
Becomes a stream, in which the poet
If he has any wit may show it.

A city once for power renown'd,
Now levell'd even to the ground,
Beyond all doubt is a direction
To introduce some fine reflection.

Ah, woeful me! ah, woeful man!
Ah! woeful all, do all we can!
Who can on earthly things depend
From one to t'other moment's end?   410
Honour, wit, genius, wealth, and glory,
Good lack! good lack! are transitory;
Nothing is sure and stable found,
The very earth itself turns round:
Monarchs, nay ministers, must die,

Must rot, must stink—ah, me! ah, why!
Cities themselves in time decay;
If cities thus—ah! well-a-day!
If brick and mortar have an end,
On what can flesh and blood depend!   420
Ah, woeful me! ah, woeful man!
Ah! woeful all, do all we can!

    England, (for that's at last the scene,
Though worlds on worlds should rise between,
Whither we must our course pursue)
England should call into review
Times long since past indeed, but not
By Englishmen to be forgot,
Though England, once so dear to Fame,
Sinks in Great Britain's dearer name.   430

    Here could we mention chiefs of old,
In plain and rugged honour bold,
To virtue kind, to vice severe,
Strangers to bribery and fear,
Who kept no wretched clans in awe,
Who never broke or warp'd the law,
Patriots, whom, in her better days,
Old Rome might have been proud to raise;
Who, steady to their country's claim,
Boldly stood up in Freedom's name,   440
E'en to the teeth of tyrant Pride,
And, when they could no more, they died.

    There (striking contrast!) might we place
A servile, mean, degenerate race;
Hirelings, who valued nought but gold,
By the best bidder bought and sold;
Truants from honour's sacred laws,
Betrayers of their country's cause,

The dupes of party, tools of power,
Slaves to the minion of an hour,   450
Lackeys, who watch'd a favourite's nod,
And took a puppet for their god.
    Sincere and honest in our rhymes,
How might we praise these happier times !
How might the Muse exalt her lays,
And wanton in a monarch's praise !
Tell of a prince in England born,
Whose virtues England's crown adorn,
In youth a pattern unto age,
So chaste, so pious, and so sage   460
Who, true to all those sacred bands
Which private happiness demands,
Yet never lets them rise above
The stronger ties of public love.
    With conscious pride see England stand,
Our holy Charter in her hand ;
She waves it round, and o'er the isle
See Liberty and Courage smile.
No more she mourns her treasures hurl'd
In subsidies to all the world ;   470
No more by foreign threats dismay'd,
No more deceived with foreign aid,
She deals out sums to petty states,
Whom Honour scorns, and Reason hates ;
But, wiser by experience grown,
Finds safety in herself alone.
" Whilst thus," she cries, " my children stand,
An honest, valiant, native band,

---

457 " Born and educated in this country, I glory in the
name of Briton !"—George the Third's first Speech to his
parliament, 18th of November, 1760.

A train'd militia, brave and free,
True to their king, and true to me,   480
No foreign hirelings shall be known,
Nor need we hirelings of our own :
Under a just and pious reign
The statesman's sophistry is vain ;
Vain is each vile, corrupt pretence :
These are my natural defence ;
Their faith I know, and they shall prove
The bulwark of the king they love."
   These, and a thousand things beside,
Did we consult a poet's pride,   490
Some gay, some serious, might be said,
But ten to one they'd not be read ;
Or were they by some curious few,
Not even those would think them true ;
For, from the time that Jubal first
Sweet ditties to the harp rehearsed,
Poets have always been suspected
Of having truth in rhyme neglected,
That bard except, who from his youth
Equally famed for faith and truth,   500
By prudence taught, in courtly chime
To courtly ears brought truth in rhyme.
   But though to poets we allow,
No matter when acquired or how,
From truth unbounded deviation,
Which custom calls Imagination,
Yet can't they be supposed to lie
One half so fast as Fame can fly ;

[499] Mallet.   One of his pieces was called "Truth in
Rhyme," and was addressed to the celebrated Lord Chesterfield.

Therefore (to solve this Gordian knot,—
A point we almost had forgot)   510
To courteous readers be it known,
That, fond of verse and falsehood grown,
Whilst we in sweet digression sung,
Fame check'd her flight, and held her tongue,
And now pursues, with double force
And double speed, her destined course,
Nor stops till she the place arrives
Where Genius starves and Dulness thrives;
Where riches virtue are esteem'd,
And craft is truest wisdom deem'd;   520
Where Commerce proudly rears her throne,
In state to other lands unknown;
Where, to be cheated and to cheat,
Strangers from every quarter meet;
Where Christians, Jews, and Turks shake hands,
United in commercial bands;
All of one faith, and that to own
No god but Interest alone.
　　When gods and goddesses come down
To look about them here in Town,   530
(For change of air is understood
By sons of Physic to be good,
In due proportion, now and then,
For these same gods as well as men)
By custom ruled, and not a poet
So very dull but he must know it,
In order to remain *incog*,
They always travel in a fog.
For if we majesty expose
To vulgar eyes, too cheap it grows;   540

517 The Royal Exchange.

The force is lost, and, free from awe,
We spy and censure every flaw;
But well preserved from public view,
It always breaks forth fresh and new;
Fierce as the sun in all his pride
It shines, and not a spot's descried.
　　Was Jove to lay his thunder by,
And with his brethren of the sky
Descend to earth, and frisk about,
Like chattering N—— from rout to rout,　　550
He would be found, with all his host,
A nine days' wonder at the most.
Would we in trim our honours wear,
We must preserve them from the air;
What is familiar men neglect,
However worthy of respect.
Did they not find a certain friend
In Novelty to recommend,
(Such we, by sad experience, find
The wretched folly of mankind)　　560
Venus might unattractive shine,
And Hunter fix no eyes but mine.
　　But Fame, who never cared a jot
Whether she was admired or not,
And never blush'd to shew her face
At any time in any place,
In her own shape, without disguise,
And visible to mortal eyes,
On 'Change, exact at seven o'clock,
Alighted on the weathercock,　　570
Which, planted there time out of mind
To note the changes of the wind,
Might no improper emblem be

Of her own mutability.

Thrice did she sound her trump, (the same
Which from the first belong'd to Fame,
An old, ill-favour'd instrument,
With which the goddess was content,
Though under a politer race
Bagpipes might well supply its place)   580
And thrice, awaken'd by the sound,
A general din prevail'd around;
Confusion through the city pass'd,
And fear bestrode the dreadful blast.

Those fragrant currents which we meet,
Distilling soft through every street,
Affrighted from the usual course,
Ran murmuring upwards to their source:
Statues wept tears of blood, as fast
As when a Cæsar breathed his last: 590
Horses, which always used to go
A foot-pace in my Lord Mayor's show,
Impetuous from their stable broke,
And aldermen and oxen spoke.

Halls felt the force, towers shook around,
And steeples nodded to the ground;
St. Paul himself (strange sight!) was seen

---

585 The sanitary improvements effected in the metropolis
during the past century were hardly commenced in Churchill's
time. Swift's description is happily obsolete:—

" Now from all parts the swelling kennels flow,
And bear their trophies with them as they go;
Filth of all hues and odour seem to tell
What street they sailed from by their sight and smell.

 . . . .

Sweeping from butchers' stalls, dung, guts, and blood,
Drown'd puppies, stinking sprats, all drench'd in mud,
Dead cats and turnip-tops come tumbling down the flood."
      A Description of a City Shower.

To bow as humbly as the Dean :
The Mansion House, for ever placed
A monument of City taste,   600
Trembled, and seem'd aloud to groan
Through all that hideous weight of stone.

    To still the sound, or stop her ears,
Remove the cause or sense of fears,
Physic, in college seated high,
Would any thing but medicine try.
No more in Pewterers' Hall was heard

⁵⁹⁹ The following note occurs on the subject of the Mansion House in an ingenious pamphlet intitled " Critical Observations on the Buildings and Improvements of London," published in 1771. When it was first resolved in Common Council to build a Mansion House for the Lord Mayor, Lord Burlington, zealous in the cause of the arts, sent down an original design of Palladio, worthy of its author, for their approbation and adoption. The first question in court was not, whether the plan was proper, but whether this same Palladio was a freeman of the city or no. On this great debates ensued, and it is hard to say how it might have gone, had not a worthy deputy risen up, and observed gravely, that it was of little consequence to discuss this point, when it was notorious that Palladio was a papist, and incapable of course. Lord Burlington's proposal was then rejected *nem. con.* and the plan of a freeman and a protestant adopted in its room. Dance, the man pitched upon (who afterwards carried his plan into execution) was originally a shipwright, and, to do him justice, he appears never to have lost sight of his first profession. The front of the Mansion House has all the resemblance possible to a deep-laden Indiaman, with her stern galleries and gingerbread work. The stairs and passages within are all ladders and gangways, and the two bulkheads on the roof fore and aft, not unaptly represent the binnacle and windlass on the deck of a great north-country *Catt.*"

   ⁶⁰⁷ Macklin's recitations and his lectures on elocution were delivered at Pewterers' Hall in Lime Street. This hardy veteran evinced throughout his long life an extraordinary versatility of talent, as an actor, author, lecturer and tutor.

The proper force of every word ;
Those seats were desolate become,
And hapless Elocution dumb.　　　　610
Form, city-born and city-bred,
By strict Decorum ever led,
Who threescore years had known the grace
Of one dull, stiff, unvaried pace,
Terror prevailing over Pride,
Was seen to take a larger stride ;
Worn to the bone, and clothed in rags,
See Avarice closer hug his bags ;
With her own weight unwieldy grown,
See Credit totter on her throne ;　　620
Virtue alone, had she been there,
The mighty sound unmoved could bear.

　　Up from the gorgeous bed, where Fate
Dooms annual fools to sleep in state,
To sleep so sound that not one gleam
Of Fancy can provoke a dream,
Great Dulman started at the sound,
Gaped, rubb'd his eyes, and stared around.
Much did he wish to know, much fear,
Whence sounds so horrid struck his ear,　　630
So much unlike those peaceful notes,
That equal harmony, which floats
On the dull wing of city air,
Grave prelude to a feast or fair :
Much did he inly ruminate
Concerning the decrees of Fate,

[627] Sir Samuel Fludyer, Bart. M.P. for Chippenham, Deputy-Governor of the Bank of England, and Lord Mayor of London for 1761-2. He was originally a clothier at Frome in Somersetshire, in which business he acquired a considerable fortune. He died in 1768.

Revolving, though to little end,
What this same trumpet might portend.
    Could the French—no—that could not be
Under Bute's active ministry,   640
Too watchful to be so deceived—
Have stolen hither unperceived?
To Newfoundland, indeed, we know
Fleets of war unobserved may go;
Or, if observed, may be supposed,
At intervals when Reason dozed,
No other point in view to bear
But pleasure, health, and change of air;
But Reason ne'er could sleep so sound
To let an enemy be found   650
In our land's heart, ere it was known
They had departed from their own.
    Or could his successor (Ambition
Is ever haunted with suspicion)
His daring successor elect,
All customs, rules, and forms reject,
And aim, regardless of the crime,
To seize the chair before his time?
    Or (deeming this the lucky hour,
Seeing his countrymen in power,   660
Those countrymen who, from the first,
In tumults and rebellion nursed,
Howe'er they wear the mask of art,
Still love a Stuart in their heart)

[643] In May, 1762, a French squadron escaped out of Brest
in a fog, and captured the town of St. John's in Newfoundland. Ministry were much blamed for their negligence;
but in the September following, the settlement was recap-
tured by a British force under the command of Lord Colville
and Colonel Amherst.
[657] Beckford was the Lord Mayor elect for 1762-3.

Could Scottish Charles ?—
               Conjecture thus,
That mental *ignis fatuus*,
Led his poor brains a weary dance
From France to England, hence to France,
Till Information (in the shape
Of chaplain learned, good Sir Crape,   670
A lazy, lounging, pamper'd priest,
Well known at every City feast,
For he was seen much oftener there
Than in the house of God at prayer;
Who, always ready in his place,
Ne'er let God's creatures wait for grace,
Though, as the best historians write,
Less famed for faith than appetite ;
His disposition to reveal,
The grace was short, and long the meal;   680
Who always would excess admit,
If haunch or turtle came with it,
And ne'er engaged in the defence
Of self-denying Abstinence,
When he could fortunately meet
With anything he liked to eat ;
Who knew that wine, on Scripture plan,
Was made to cheer the heart of man ;
Knew too, by long experience taught,
That cheerfulness was kill'd by thought;   690
And from those premises collected,
(Which few perhaps would have suspected)
That none who, with due share of sense,
Observed the ways of Providence,
Could with safe conscience leave off drinking
Till they had lost the power of thinking ;)

With eyes half closed came waddling in,
And, having stroked his double chin,
(That chin, whose credit to maintain
Against the scoffs of the profane,   700
Had cost him more than ever state
Paid for a poor electorate,
Which, after all the cost and rout
It had been better much without)
Briefly (for breakfast, you must know,
Was waiting all the while below)
Related, bowing to the ground,
The cause of that uncommon sound;
Related, too, that at the door
Pomposo, Plausible, and Moore,   710
Begg'd that Fame might not be allow'd
Their shame to publish to the crowd;
That some new laws he would provide,
(If old could not be misapplied
With as much ease and safety there
As they are misapplied elsewhere)
By which it might be construed treason
In man to exercise his reason;
Which might ingeniously devise
One punishment for truth and lies,   720
And fairly prove, when they had done,
That truth and falsehood were but one;

702 The electorate of Hanover was the favourite possession of the first two Georges, who were in reality Germans
by birth, education, and tastes; and the many expensive
wars in which the country was engaged during their reigns
were the result of their partiality.

710 Application was made on behalf of these gentlemen to
the Lord Mayor, for a prohibition against the hawking
through the streets of London " a full, true, and particular
account" of their midnight visit to Fauny's tomb.

Which juries must indeed retain,
But their effect should render vain,
Making all real power to rest
In one corrupted, rotten breast,
By whose false gloss the very Bible
Might be interpreted a libel.

Moore (who, his reverence to save,
Pleaded the fool to screen the knave,   730
Though all who witness'd on his part
Swore for his head against his heart)
Had taken down, from first to last,
A just account of all that pass'd ;
But, since the gracious will of Fate,
Who mark'd the child for wealth and state
E'en in the cradle, had decreed
The mighty Dulman ne'er should read,
That office of disgrace to bear
The smooth-lipp'd Plausible was there ;   740
From Holborn e'en to Clerkenwell,
Who knows not smooth-lipp'd Plausible ?
A preacher deem'd of greatest note

[726] Lord Mansfield's interpretation of the law of libel,
though founded upon precedents made in the worst of times,
was universally adhered to by the bench, with the exception
of Lord Camden. Juries were browbeaten and insulted, if
they dared to find a verdict beyond the mere fact of publication ; and that most absurd maxim, " the greater the truth,
the greater the libel," influenced the discretion of the judge
in the sentence he pronounced. We are indebted to the patriotic exertions of Mr. Fox for the explanatory bill passed in
1791, which restored to the jury the power of deciding upon
the law, as well as the fact, by returning a general verdict.

[740] The Rev. W. Sellon, in 1763, ostentatiously published
a sermon which he had preached at St. Andrew's, Holborn,
at Clerkenwell, and at St. Giles's. On its publication, the
critics discovered it to be as gross a piece of plagiarism as
ever issued from the press.

For preaching that which others wrote.
   Had Dulman now, (and fools, we see,
Seldom want curiosity)
Consented (but the mourning shade
Of Gascoyne hasten'd to his aid,
And in his hand, what could he more?
Triumphant Canning's picture bore)   750
That our three heroes should advance
And read their comical romance,
How rich a feast, what royal fare,
We for our readers might prepare!
So rich and yet so safe a feast,
That no one foreign, blatant beast,
Within the purlieus of the law,
Should dare thereon to lay his paw,
And, growling, cry, with surly tone,
Keep off—this feast is all my own.   760
   Bending to earth the downcast eye,
Or planting it against the sky,
As one immersed in deepest thought,
Or with some holy vision caught,
His hands, to aid the traitor's art,
Devoutly folded o'er his heart;
Here Moore in fraud well skill'd, should go,
All saint, with solemn step and slow.
O that Religion's sacred name,
Meant to inspire the purest flame,   770
A prostitute should ever be
To that arch-fiend Hypocrisy,
Where we find every other vice
Crown'd with damn'd sneaking cowardice.
Bold sin reclaim'd is often seen;
Past hope that man who dares be mean.

There, full of flesh, and full of grace,
With that fine, round, unmeaning face
Which Nature gives to sons of earth
Whom she designs for ease and mirth,   78.
Should the prim Plausible be seen ;
Observe his stiff affected mien ;
'Gainst Nature arm'd by gravity,
His features too in buckle see ;
See with what sanctity he reads,
With what devotion tells his beads !
Now, Prophet, shew me, by thine art,
What's the religion of his heart :
Shew there, if truth thou canst unfold,
Religion centred all in gold ;   790
Shew him, nor fear correction's rod,
As false to friendship as to God.

Horrid, unwieldy, without form,
Savage as ocean in a storm,
Of size prodigious, in the rear,
That post of honour, should appear
Pomposo ; Fame around should tell
How he a slave to interest fell ;
How, for integrity renown'd,
Which booksellers have often found,   800
He for subscribers baits his hook,

784 " His features too in *buckle* see." In the Spectator
to be " in buckle" means, to be in close, stiff curl. " The
wearer of it (a wig) goes, it seems, in his own hair when he
is at home, and lets his wig be *in buckle* for a whole half
year, that he may put it on upon occasion to meet the judges
in it."—No. 129. The word is here used metaphorically, to
convey the idea of features as stiff as the curls of a wig—a
contorted, unnatural, fixed expression of countenance.

801 This passage reminded Dr. Johnson of the necessity of

And takes their cash—but where's the book
No matter where—wise fear, we know,
Forbids the robbing of a foe;
But what, to serve our private ends,
Forbids the cheating of our friends?
No man alive, who would not swear
All's safe, and therefore honest there:
For, spite of all the learned say,
If we to truth attention pay,   910
The word dishonesty is meant
For nothing else but punishment.
Fame, too, should tell, nor heed the threat
Of rogues, who brother rogues abet,
Nor tremble at the terrors hung
Aloft, to make her hold her tongue,
How to all principles untrue,
Not fix'd to old friends nor to new,
He damns the pension which he takes,
And loves the Stuart he forsakes.   920
Nature (who, justly regular,
Is very seldom known to err,
But now and then in sportive mood,
As some rude wits have understood,
Or through much work required in haste,
Is with a random stroke disgraced)
Pomposo form'd on doubtful plan,
Not quite a beast, nor quite a man;
Like—God knows what—for never yet
Could the most subtle human wit   930
Find out a monster which might be
The shadow of a simile.

publishing his edition of Shakespeare, subscriptions for
which had been received by him upwards of twenty years.

These three, these great, these mighty three—
Nor can the poet's truth agree,
Howe'er report hath done him wrong
And warp'd the purpose of his song,
Amongst the refuse of their race,
The sons of Infamy, to place
That open, generous, manly mind,
Which we, with joy, in Aldrich find—   840
These three, who now are faintly shown,
Just sketch'd, and scarcely to be known,
If Dulman their request had heard,
In stronger colours had appear'd,
And friends, though partial, at first view,
Shuddering, had own'd the picture true.

But had the journal been display'd,
And their whole process open laid,
What a vast, unexhausted field
For mirth must such a journal yield!   850
In her own anger strongly charm'd,
'Gainst hope, 'gainst fear, by conscience arm'd,
Then had bold Satire made her way,
Knights, lords and dukes her destined prey.

But Prudence, ever sacred name
To those who feel not virtue's flame,
Or only feel it, at the best,
As the dull dupes of Interest,
Whisper'd aloud (for this we find
A custom current with mankind,   860
So loud to whisper, that each word

---

840 The Reverend Stephen Aldrich, Rector of St. John's, Clerkenwell, had too much good sense to be imposed upon by the Cock Lane Ghost, and actively contributed to its exposure.

May all around be plainly heard ;
And Prudence sure would never miss
A custom so contrived as this
Her candour to secure, yet aim
Sure death against another's fame)
" Knights, lords, and dukes—mad wretch, forbear!
Dangers unthought of ambush there ;
Confine thy rage to weaker slaves,
Laugh at small fools, and lash small knaves,   870
But never, helpless, mean, and poor,
Rush on, where laws cannot secure ;
Nor think thyself, mistaken youth !
Secure in principles of truth :
Truth ! why, shall every wretch of letters
Dare to speak truth against his betters !
Let ragged Virtue stand aloof,
Nor mutter accents of reproof ;
Let ragged Wit a mute become,   879
When wealth and power would have her dumb ;
For who the devil doth not know
That titles and estates bestow
An ample stock, where'er they fall,
Of graces which we mental call !
Beggars, in every age and nation,
Are rogues and fools by situation ;
The rich and great are understood
To be of course both wise and good ;
Consult then interest more than pride,
Discreetly take the stronger side ;   890
Desert, in time, the simple few
Who Virtue's barren path pursue ;
Adopt my maxims—follow me—
To Baal bow the prudent knee ;

Deny thy God, betray thy friend,
At Baal's altars hourly bend,
So shalt thou rich and great be seen;
To be great now, you must be mean."
   Hence, tempter, to some weaker soul,
Which fear and interest control;   900
Vainly thy precepts are address'd
Where Virtue steels the steady breast.
Through meanness wade to boasted power,
Through guilt repeated every hour;
What is thy gain, when all is done?
What mighty laurels hast thou won?
Dull crowds, to whom the heart's unknown,
Praise thee for virtues not thy own:
But will, at once man's scourge and friend,
Impartial Conscience too commend?   910
From her reproaches canst thou fly?
Canst thou with worlds her silence buy?
Believe it not—her stings shall find
A passage to thy coward mind:
There shall she fix her sharpest dart;
There shew thee truly, as thou art,
Unknown to those, by whom thou'rt prized,
Known to thyself, to be despised.
   The man who weds the sacred Muse
Disdains all mercenary views;   920
And he who Virtue's throne would rear
Laughs at the phantoms raised by fear.
Though Folly, robed in purple, shines,
Though Vice exhausts Peruvian mines,
Yet shall they tremble, and turn pale,
When Satire wields her mighty flail;
Or should they, of rebuke afraid,

With Melcombe seek hell's deepest shade,
Satire, still mindful of her aim,
Shall bring the cowards back to shame.   93ა
    Hated by many, loved by few,
Above each little private view,
Honest, though poor, (and who shall dare
To disappoint my boasting there?)
Hardy, and resolute though weak
The dictates of my heart to speak,
Willing I bend at Satire's throne;
What power I have be all her own.
    Nor shall yon lawyer's specious art,
Conscious of a corrupted heart,   940
Create imaginary fear
To damp us in our bold career.
Why should we fear; and what? the laws?
They all are arm'd in virtue's cause;
And aiming at the self-same end,
Satire is always virtue's friend;
Nor shall that Muse whose honest rage,
In a corrupt, degenerate age,—
When, dead to every nicer sense,
Deep sunk in vice and indolence,   950
The spirit of old Rome was broke

929 George Bubb Doddington, the son of an apothecary at Weymouth, by his address in the electioneering management of that and its sister borough, raised himself to the peerage under the title of Lord Melcombe. He was a retainer of the court of Frederick Prince of Wales, and on the accession of George the Third, became a devoted supporter of the measures of Lord Bute. Lord Melcombe was a man of shrewd sense and observation, and his diary of events, published by Mr. Penruddocke Wyndham, reveals an amount of gross venality and low intrigue, which illustrates strongly the influence of petty occurrences on the administration of public affairs.

Beneath the tyrant fiddler's yoke,—
Banish'd the rose from Nero's cheek,
Under a Brunswick fear to speak.

Drawn by conceit from reason's plan,
How vain is that poor creature, man!
How pleased is every paltry elf
To prate about that thing himself!
After my promise made in rhyme,
And meant in earnest at that time,   960
To jog, according to the mode,
In one dull pace, in one dull road,
What but that curse of heart and head
To this digression could have led?
Where plunged, in vain I look about,
And can't stay in, nor well get out.

Could I, whilst Humour held the quill,
Could I digress with half that skill;
Could I with half that skill return,
Which we so much admire in Sterne,   970
Where each digression, seeming vain,
And only fit to entertain,
Is found, on better recollection,
To have a just and nice connexion,
To help the whole with wondrous art,
Whence it seems idly to depart;
Then should our readers ne'er accuse
These wild excursions of the Muse;
Ne'er backward turn dull pages o'er
To recollect what went before;   980
Deeply impress'd, and ever new,
Each image past should start to view,
And we to Dulman now come in,
As if we ne'er had absent been.

Have you not seen, when danger's near,
The coward cheek turn white with fear ?
Have you not seen, when danger's fled,
The self-same cheek with joy turn red ?
These are low symptoms which we find
Fit only for a vulgar mind,   990
Where honest features, void of art,
Betray the feelings of the heart :
Our Dulman with a face was bless'd,
Where no one passion was express'd ;
His eye, in a fine stupour caught,
Implied a plenteous lack of thought ;
Nor was one line that whole face seen in
Which could be justly charged with meaning.

To Avarice by birth allied,
Debauch'd by marriage into pride,   1000
In age grown fond of youthful sports,
Of pomps, of vanities, and courts,
And by success too mighty made
To love his country or his trade ;
Stiff in opinion, (no rare case
With blockheads in or out of place)
Too weak and insolent of soul
To suffer reason's just control,
But bending, of his own accord,
To that trim, transient toy, My Lord ;   1010
The dupe of Scots, (a fatal race,
Whom God in wrath contrived to place,
To scourge our crimes, and gall our pride,
A constant thorn in England's side ;
Whom first, our greatness to oppose,
He in his vengeance mark'd for foes ;
Then, more to serve His wrathful ends,

And more to curse us, mark'd for friends);
Deep in the state, if we give credit
To him, for no one else e'er said it;   1020
Sworn friend of great ones not a few,
Though he their titles only knew,
And those, (which, envious of his breeding,
Book-worms have charged to want of reading)
Merely to shew himself polite,
He never would pronounce aright;
An orator with whom a host
Of those which Rome and Athens boast,
In all their pride might not contend;
Who, with no powers to recommend,   1030
Whilst Jackey Home and Billy Whitehead,
And Dicky Glover sat delighted,
Could speak whole days in Nature's spite,
Just as those able versemen write,—
Great Dulman from his bed arose;
Thrice did he spit—thrice wiped his nose—

[1032] Richard Glover was an eminent merchant in the
city of London, and distinguished himself by a remarkable
speech he delivered at the bar of the House of Commons on
behalf of the mercantile interest, previous to the breaking
out of the Spanish war, in 1740. His zeal for the public
interfering with his private concerns, his business decayed,
and he was, in 1751, an unsuccessful candidate for the city
chamberlainship. For some years afterwards he lived in
perfect obscurity; but having surmounted his immediate
difficulties, he reappeared in public life in 1761, as M.P. for
Weymouth, under the patronage of Lord Melcombe and
Frederick Prince of Wales. He, however, took no active
part in political affairs, but confined himself to his literary
pursuits. Of his principal performance, an epic poem intitled Leonidas, extravagant expectations were entertained;
but though told in language highly classical and elegant,
the fate of the Spartan hero excited only a transient interest.
Glover died in 1785.

Thrice strove to smile—thrice strove to frown—
And thrice look'd up—and thrice look'd down—
Then silence broke—" Crape, who am I ?"
Crape bow'd, and smiled an arch reply.   1040
" Am I not, Crape ?—I am, you know,
Above all those who are below.
Have I not knowledge ? and for wit,
Money will always purchase it:
Nor, if it needful should be found,
Will I grudge ten, or—twenty pound,
For which the whole stock may be bought
Of scoundrel wits not worth a groat.
But lest I should proceed too far,
I'll feel my friend the Minister   1050
(Great Men, Crape, must not be neglected)
How he in this point is affected ;
For, as I stand a magistrate
To serve him first, and next the state,
Perhaps he may not think it fit
To let his magistrates have wit.   .
    " Boast I not, at this very hour,
Those large effects which troop with power ?
Am I not mighty in the land ?
Do not I sit, while others stand ?   1060
Am I not, with rich garments graced,
In seat of honour always placed ?
And do not Cits of chief degree,
Though proud to others, bend to me ?
    " Have I not, as a Justice ought,
The laws such wholesome rigour taught,
That Fornication, in disgrace,
Is now afraid to shew her face,
And not one whore these walls approaches

1039 The Rev. Dr. Bruce, Sir S. Fludyer's Chaplain.

Unless they ride in our own coaches? 1070
And shall this Fame, an old, poor strumpet,
Without our license sound her trumpet;
And, envious of our City's quiet,
In broad day-light blow up a riot?
If insolence like this we bear,
Where is our state? our office where?
Farewell all honours of our reign,
Farewell the neck-ennobling chain,
Freedom's known badge o'er all the globe;
Farewell the solemn-spreading robe, 1080
Farewell the sword, farewell the mace,
Farewell all title, pomp, and place;
Removed from men of high degree,
(A loss to them, Crape, not to me)
Banish'd to Chippenham or to Frome,
Dulman once more shall ply the loom."

Crape, lifting up his hands and eyes,
" Dulman—the loom—at Chippenham "—cries;
" If there be powers which greatness love,
Which rule below, but dwell above, 1090
Those powers united all shall join
To contradict the rash design.
" Sooner shall stubborn Will lay down
His opposition with his gown;
Sooner shall Temple leave the road
Which leads to Virtue's mean abode;
Sooner shall Scots this country quit,

[1093] William Beckford, Esq. elected an Alderman June 1752, and twice Lord Mayor of London, in 1762 and 1769. He was a West India merchant, possessed a princely fortune, and became highly popular by his strenuous opposition to the court. Mr. Beckford died in the year 1770, during his second mayoralty. His son was the author of Vathek.

And England's foes be friends to Pitt,
Than Dulman, from his grandeur thrown,
Shall wander outcast, and unknown.   1100
    "Sure as that cane, (a cane there stood
Near to a table made of wood,
Of dry, fine wood a table made,
By some rare artist in the trade,
Who had enjoy'd immortal praise
If he had lived in Homer's days)
Sure as that cane, which once was seen
In pride of life all fresh and green,
The banks of Indus to adorn,
Then, of its leafy honours shorn,   1110
According to exactest rule,
Was fashion'd by the workman's tool,
And which at present we behold
Curiously polish'd, crown'd with gold,
With gold well wrought; sure as that cane
Shall never on its native plain
Strike root afresh, shall never more
Flourish in tawny India's shore,
So sure shall Dulman and his race
To latest times this station grace."   1120
    Dulman, who all this while had kept
His eyelids closed as if he slept,
Now looking steadfastly on Crape,
As at some god in human shape—
"Crape, I protest, you seem to me
To have discharged a prophecy:
Yes—from the first it doth appear
Planted by Fate, the Dulmans here
Have always held a quiet reign,
And here shall to the last remain.   1130

" Crape, they're all wrong about this Ghost—
Quite on the wrong side of the post—
Blockheads! to take it in their head
To be a message from the dead,—
For that by mission they design,
A word not half so good as mine.
Crape—here it is—start not one doubt—
A plot—a plot—I've found it out."
" O God!" cries Crape, " how bless'd the nation,
Where one son boasts such penetration!"   1140

 " Crape, I've not time to tell you now
When I discover'd this, or how;
To Stentor go—if he's not there,
His place let Bully Norton bear—
Our citizens to council call—
Let all meet—'tis the cause of all:
Let the three witnesses attend,
With allegations to befriend,
To swear just so much, and no more,
As we instruct them in before.   1150

 " Stay—Crape—come back—what, don't you see
The effects of this discovery?
Dulman all care and toil endures—
The profit, Crape, will all be yours.
A mitre, (for, this arduous task
Perform'd, they'll grant whate'er I ask)
A mitre (and perhaps the best)
Shall, through my interest, make thee blest:
And at this time, when gracious fate
Dooms to the Scot the reins of state,   1160
Who is more fit, (and for your use
We could some instances produce)

 1149 One of the law officers of the city of London.

Of England's church to be the head,
Than you, a Presbyterian bred?
But when thus mighty you are made,
Unlike the brethren of thy trade,
Be grateful, Crape, and let me not,
Like old Newcastle, be forgot.

"But an affair, Crape, of this size   1170
Will ask from conduct vast supplies;
It must not, as the vulgar say,
Be done in hugger-mugger way:
Traitors, indeed, (and that's discreet)
Who hatch the plot, in private meet:
They should in public go, no doubt,
Whose business is to find it out.

"To-morrow—if the day appear
Likely to turn out fair and clear—
Proclaim a grand processionado;

1165 Thomas Secker, Archbishop of Canterbury, was bred
a Presbyterian, but was converted to the established church
by Bishop Talbot, whose relation he had married.   The good
Bishop made him prebend of Durham, whence he was removed by Queen Caroline to the Rectory of St. James, on
the death of the celebrated Dr. Samuel Clarke.   He then
successively filled the sees of Bristol and Oxford.   He was
translated to the Primacy in 1758, and died in 1768.

1168 The Duke of Newcastle, who died in 1768, had for
more than fifty years filled high offices in the state.   In the
year following the resignation of Pitt and Temple the Duke
of Newcastle was compelled by repeated insults to retire in
favour of the Earl of Bute—whom he had himself introduced
into the ministry.   It was then observed that though the
whole bench of bishops were of his appointment, Warburton
was the only one of the number who had the gratitude to
visit a fallen patron.

1170 The purpose of this solemn preparation was for the
address of thanks to his majesty on the conclusion of the
peace with France.

Bo all the City-pomp display'd ;   1180
Let the Train-bands"—Crape shook his head ;
They heard the trumpet, and were fled—
"Well"—cries the Knight—"if that's the case,
My servants shall supply their place—
My servants—mine alone—no more
Than what my servants did before—
Dost not remember, Crape, that day,
When, Dulman's grandeur to display,
As all too simple and too low,
Our City friends were thrust below,   1190
Whilst, as more worthy of our love,
Courtiers were entertain'd above ?
Tell me, who waited then ? and how ?
My servants—mine—and why not now ?
In haste then, Crape, to Stentor go—
But send up Hart, who waits below ;
With him, till you return again,
(Reach me my spectacles and cane)
I'll make a proof how I advance in
My new accomplishment of dancing."   1200
    Not quite so fast as lightning flies,
Wing'd with red anger, through the skies ;
Not quite so fast as, sent by Jove,
Iris descends on wings of love ;
Not quite so fast as Terror rides
When he the chasing winds bestrides,
Crape hobbled—but his mind was good—
Could he go faster than he could ?
    Near to that tower, which, as we're told,
The mighty Julius raised of old ;   1210
Where, to the block by Justice led,
The rebel Scot hath often bled ;

Where arms are kept so clean, so bright,
'Twere sin they should be soil'd in fight;
Where brutes of foreign race are shown
By brutes much greater of our own;
Fast by the crowded Thames, is found
An ample square of sacred ground,
Where artless eloquence presides,
And nature every sentence guides.　　　1220

　Here female parliaments debate
About religion, trade, and state;
Here every Naiad's patriot soul,
Disdaining foreign, base control,
Despising French, despising Erse,
Pours forth the plain old English curse,
And bears aloft, with terrors hung,
The honours of the vulgar tongue.

　Here Stentor, always heard with awe,
In thund'ring accents deals out law:　　　1230
Twelve furlongs off each dreadful word
Was plainly and distinctly heard,
And every neighbour hill around
Return'd and swell'd the mighty sound.
The loudest virgin of the stream,
Compared with him would silent seem;
Thames, who, enraged to find his course
Opposed, rolls down with double force,
Against the bridge indignant roars,
And lashes the resounding shores,　　　1240
Compared with him, at lowest tide
In softest whispers seems to glide.

　Hither directed by the noise,
Swell'd with the hope of future joys,
Through too much zeal and haste made lame,

The reverend slave of Dulman came.
"Stentor"—with such a serious air,
With such a face of solemn care,
As might import him to contain
A nation's welfare in his brain—   1250
"Stentor"—cries Crape—" I'm hither sent
On business of most high intent,
Great Dulman's orders to convey;
Dulman commands, and I obey.
Big with those throes which patriots feel,
And labouring for the commonweal,
Some secret, which forbids him rest,
Tumbles and tosses in his breast;
Tumbles and tosses to get free,
And thus the Chief commands by me: 1260
"To-morrow—if the day appear
Likely to turn out fair and clear—
Proclaim a grand processionade;
Be all the city-pomp display'd;
Our citizens to council call—
Let all meet—'tis the cause of all!"

THE GHOST.*

BOOK IV.

COXCOMBS, who vainly make pretence
To something of exalted sense
'Bove other men, and, gravely wise,
Affect those pleasures to despise,
Which, merely to the eye confined,
Bring no improvement to the mind,
Rail at all pomp; they would not go
For millions to a puppet-show,
Nor can forgive the mighty crime
Of countenancing pantomime;   10
No, not at Covent Garden, where,
Without a head for play or player,
Or, could a head be found most fit.
Without one player to second it,
They must, obeying Folly's call,

* This fourth book of the Ghost is at once the most careless and the longest of Churchill's compositions. It is also
the most obscure and indistinct in its allusions, the minute
elucidation of which would not repay the labour of the investigation, nor the perusal of its results.

Thrive by mere shew, or not at all.
With these grave fops, who (bless their brains!)
Most cruel to themselves, take pains
For wretchedness, and would be thought
Much wiser than a wise man ought   20
For his own happiness, to be;
Who what they hear, and what they see,
And what they smell, and taste, and feel,
Distrust, till Reason sets her seal,
And, by long trains of consequences
Ensured, gives sanction to the senses;
Who would not, Heaven forbid it! waste
One hour in what the world calls Taste,
Nor fondly deign to laugh or cry,
Unless they know some reason why,—   30
With these grave fops, whose system seems
To give up certainty for dreams
The eye of man is understood
As for no other purpose good
Than as a door, through which, of course,
Their passage crowding objects force;
A downright usher, to admit
New-comers to the court of Wit:
(Good Gravity! forbear thy spleen,
When I say wit, I wisdom mean)   40
Where, (such the practice of the court,
Which legal precedents support)
Not one idea is allow'd
To pass unquestion'd in the crowd,
But ere it can obtain the grace
Of holding in the brain a place,
Before the chief in congregation
Must stand a strict examination.

Not such as those, who physic twirl,
Full fraught with death, from every curl ;   50
Who prove, with all becoming state,
Their voice to be the voice of Fate,
Prepared with essence, drop, and pill,
To be another Ward or Hill,
Before they can obtain their ends,
To sign death-warrants for their friends,
And talents vast as theirs employ,
Secundum artem to destroy,
Must pass (or laws their rage restrain)
Before the chiefs of Warwick Lane :   60
Thrice happy Lane, where, uncontroll'd,
In power and lethargy grown old,
Most fit to take, in this bless'd land,
The reins which fell from Wyndham's hand,
Her lawful throne great Dulness rears,
Still more herself, as more in years ;
Where she, (and who shall dare deny

---

[54] Joshua Ward. He began life in partnership with his brother William, a dry salter, in Thames Street. About the year 1733, on returning from a long residence abroad, he began to practise physic, and in time was called in to attend King George the Second, whose hand he cured. The king was so highly satisfied with his conduct, that he gave him a suite of apartments at Whitehall for his residence, that he might always be near the royal person. He died in 1761, at a very advanced age.

[60] Warwick Lane, Newgate Street, was the seat of the College of Physicians, who, by their charter, are empowered to examine candidates for, and to confer, the privilege of practising medicine.

[64] Charles Wyndham, Earl of Egremont, who, in conjunction with the Earl of Halifax, issued the general warrant. He died suddenly in 1763, and was succeeded in his office by Lord Sandwich.

Her right, when Reeves and Chauncy's by)
Calling to mind, in ancient time,
One Garth, who err'd in wit and rhyme,   70
Ordains, from henceforth, to admit
None of the rebel sons of Wit,
And makes it her peculiar care
That Schomberg never shall be there.

  Not such as those, whom Folly trains
To letters, though unbless'd with brains;
Who, destitute of power and will
To learn, are kept to learning still;
Whose heads, when other methods fail,
Receive instruction from the tail,   80
Because their sires, a common case
Which brings the children to disgrace,
Imagine it a certain rule

---

[68] Dr. Reeves was a physician of considerable practice in the city.

[68] Dr. Chauncy, descended of a good family, and possessed of a competent estate, did not seek practice, but amused himself with the pursuits of a black-letter collector.

[70] Sir Samuel Garth, the celebrated poet and physician. His benevolent scheme for establishing a charitable foundation to supply the sick poor with medicines at prime cost, being warmly opposed by the apothecaries and some of the college, gave rise to his admirable satire the Dispensary. Dr. Garth was a staunch whig, and attached himself to the great Duke of Marlborough, whom he accompanied in his voluntary exile to Ostend, in the latter days of Queen Anne, when the Tories had obtained a complete ascendancy. On the accession of King George he was appointed his majesty's physician, and knighted with the Duke of Marlborough's sword. He died in 1718.

[74] Dr. Isaac Schomberg, an eminent and learned physician, the friend of Garrick, who in his dying moments recognized his services, and affectionately hailed him as "last not least in our dear love." Schomberg died in 1780.

They never could beget a fool,
Must pass, or must compound for, ere
The chaplain, full of beef and prayer,
Will give his reverend permit
Announcing them for orders fit;
So that the prelate (what's a name?
All prelates now are much the same)   90
May, with a conscience safe and quiet,
With holy hands lay on that Fiat
Which doth all faculties dispense,
All sanctity, all faith, all sense;
Makes Madan quite a saint appear,
And makes an oracle of Cheere.

　　Not such as in that solemn seat,
Where the Nine Ladies hold retreat—
The Ladies Nine, who, as we're told,
Scorning those haunts they loved of old,   100
The banks of Isis now prefer,
Nor will one hour from Oxford stir—
Are held for form, which Balaam's ass
As well as Balaam's self might pass,
And with his master take degrees
Could he contrive to pay the fees.

　　Men of sound parts, who, deeply read,
O'erload the storehouse of the head
With furniture they ne'er can use,
Cannot forgive our rambling Muse   110
This wild excursion; cannot see
Why Physic and Divinity,
To the surprise of all beholders,
Are lugg'd in by the head and shoulders;

[95] Martin Madan, a celebrated English preacher, many
years chaplain to the Lock Hospital.   He died in 1790.

Or how, in any point of view,
Oxford hath any thing to do:
But men of nice and subtle learning,
Remarkable for quick discerning,
Through spectacles of critic mould,
Without instruction, will behold   120
That we a method here have got
To shew what is, by what is not;
And that our drift (parenthesis
For once apart) is briefly this.
  Within the brain's most secret cells
A certain Lord Chief Justice dwells,
Of sovereign power, whom, one and all,
With common voice, we Reason call,
Though, for the purposes of satire,
A name, in truth, is no great matter: 130
Jefferies or Mansfield, which you will,
It means a Lord Chief Justice still.
Here, so our great projectors say,
The senses all must homage pay;
Hither they all must tribute bring,
And prostrate fall before their king.
Whatever unto them is brought
Is carried on the wings of thought
Before his throne, where, in full state,
He on their merits holds debate,   140
Examines, cross-examines, weighs
Their right to censure or to praise:
Nor doth his equal voice depend
On narrow views of foe and friend,
Nor can or flattery or force
Divert him from his steady course;
The channel of inquiry's clear;

No sham examination's here.
He, upright Justicer, no doubt,
Ad libitum puts in and out,   151
Adjusts and settles in a trice
What virtue is, and what is vice;
What is perfection, what defect;
What we must choose, and what reject;
He takes upon him to explain
What pleasure is, and what is pain;
Whilst we, obedient to the whim,
And resting all our faith on him,
True members of the Stoic weal,
Must learn to think and cease to feel.   160
This glorious system form'd for man
To practise when and how he can,
If the five senses in alliance
To Reason hurl a proud defiance,
And, though oft conquer'd, yet unbroke,
Endeavour to throw off that yoke
Which they a greater slavery hold
Than Jewish bondage was of old;
Or if they, something touch'd with shame,
Allow him to retain the name   170
Of Royalty, and, as in sport,
To hold a mimic formal court,
Permitted (no uncommon thing)
To be a kind of puppet-king,
And suffer'd, by the way of toy,
To hold a globe, but not employ;
Our system-mongers, struck with fear,
Prognosticate destruction near;
All things to anarchy must run;
The little world of man's undone.   180

Nay, should the eye, that nicest sense,
Neglect to send intelligence
Unto the brain distinct and clear,
Of all that passes in her sphere;
Should she presumptuous joy receive
Without the understanding's leave,
They deem it rank and daring treason
Against the monarchy of Reason,
Not thinking, though they're wondrous wise,
That few have reason, most have eyes;   190
So that the pleasures of the mind
To a small circle are confined,
Whilst those which to the senses fall
Become the property of all.
Besides, (and this is sure a case
Not much at present out of place)
Where nature reason doth deny,
No art can that defect supply;
But if (for it is our intent
Fairly to state the argument)   200
A man shall want an eye or two,
The remedy is sure, though new;
The cure's at hand—no need of fear—
For proof—behold the Chevalier—
As well prepared, beyond all doubt,
To put eyes in as put them out.
But, argument apart, which tends
To embitter foes and separate friends,
(Nor, turn'd apostate from the Nine,

---

204 The chevalier John Taylor, a quack oculist of much
notoriety in his day, who advertised himself as Opthalmiator
Pontifical, Imperial, and Royal. In 1761, he published his
adventures,—one of the strangest rhapsodies that ever appeared. He died in 1788.

Would I, though bred up a divine,   210
And foe, of course, to Reason's weal,
Widen that breach I cannot heal)
By his own sense and feelings taught,
In speech as liberal as in thought,
Let every man enjoy his whim ;
What's he to me, or I to him ?
Might I, though never robed in ermine,
A matter of this weight determine,
No penalties should settled be
To force men to hypocrisy,   220
To make them ape an awkward zeal,
And, feeling not, pretend to feel.
I would not have, might sentence rest
Finally fix'd within my breast,
E'en Annet censured and confined,
Because we're of a different mind.

Nature who, in her act most free,
Herself delights in liberty,
Profuse in love, and without bound,
Pours joy on every creature round ;   230
Whom yet, was every bounty shed
In double portions on our head,
We could not truly bounteous call,
If freedom did not crown them all.

By Providence forbid to stray,
Brutes never can mistake their way ;
Determined still, they plod along

[225] Peter Annet having been convicted of blasphemy for
writing a paper intitled the " Free Inquirer," in which he
impugned the authority of the books of Moses, and denied
the miracles related in the New Testament, was sentenced to
one year's imprisonment in Bridewell with hard labour,
and to stand twice in the pillory.

By instinct, neither right nor wrong;
But man, had he the heart to use
His freedom, hath a right to choose;   240
Whether he acts or well, or ill,
Depends entirely on his will.
To her last work, her favourite man,
Is given on Nature's better plan,
A privilege in power to err!
Nor let this phrase resentment stir
Amongst the grave ones, since indeed,
The little merit man can plead
In doing well, dependeth still
Upon his power of doing ill.   250
  Opinions should be free as air;
No man, whate'er his rank, whate'er
His qualities, a claim can found
That my opinion must be bound,
And square with his; such slavish chains
From foes the liberal soul disdains;
Nor can, though true to friendship, bend
To wear them even from a friend.
Let those who rigid judgment own
Submissive bow at Judgment's throne,   260
And if they of no value hold
Pleasure, till pleasure is grown cold,
Pall'd and insipid, forced to wait
For Judgment's regular debate
To give it warrant, let them find
Dull subjects suited to their mind.
Theirs be slow wisdom; be my plan,
To live as merry as I can,
Regardless as the fashions go,
Whether there's reason for't or no: 270

Be my employment here on earth
To give a liberal scope to mirth,
Life's barren vale with flowers t'adorn,
And pluck a rose from every thorn.
　　But if, by error led astray,
I chance to wander from my way,
Let no blind guide observe, in spite,
I'm wrong, who cannot set me right.
That doctor could I ne'er endure
Who found disease, and not a cure ;　　　280
Nor can I hold that man a friend
Whose zeal a helping hand shall lend
To open happy Folly's eyes,
And, making wretched, make me wise :
For next (a truth which can't admit
Reproof from Wisdom or from Wit)
To being happy here below,
Is to believe that we are so.
　　Some few in knowledge find relief ;
I place my comfort in belief.　　　290
Some for reality may call ;
Fancy to me is all in all.
Imagination, through the trick
Of doctors, often makes us sick,
And why, let any sophist tell,
May it not likewise make us well ?
This I am sure, whate'er our view,
Whatever shadows we pursue—
For our pursuits, be what they will,
Are little more than shadows still—　　　300
Too swift they fly, too swift and strong,
For man to catch or hold them long ;
But joys which in the fancy live,

Each moment to each man may give :
True to himself, and true to ease,
He softens Fate's severe decrees,
And (can a mortal wish for more ?)
Creates, and makes himself new o'er,
Mocks boasted, vain reality,
And is whate'er he wants to be.   310

   Hail, Fancy—to thy power I owe
Deliverance from the gripe of woe ;
To thee I owe a mighty debt,
Which Gratitude shall ne'er forget,
Whilst Memory can her force employ
A large increase of every joy.
When at my doors, too strongly barr'd,
Authority had placed a guard,
A knavish guard, ordain'd by law
To keep poor Honesty in awe ;   320
Authority severe and stern,
To intercept my wish'd return ;
When foes grew proud, and friends grew cool,
And laughter seized each sober fool ;
When Candour started in amaze,
And, meaning censure, hinted praise ;
When Prudence, lifting up her eyes
And hands, thank'd Heaven that she was wise ;
When all around me, with an air
Of hopeless sorrow, look'd despair ;   330
When they or said, or seem'd to say
" There is but one, one only way :
Better, and be advised by us,
Not be at all, than to be thus ;"
When Virtue shunn'd the shock, and Pride,
Disabled, lay by Virtue's side,

Too weak my ruffled soul to cheer,
Which could not hope, yet would not fear;—
Health in her motion, the wild grace
Of pleasure speaking in her face,   340
Dull regularity thrown by,
And comfort beaming from her eye,
Fancy, in richest robes array'd,
Came smiling forth, and brought me aid;
Came smiling o'er that dreadful time,
And, more to bless me, came in rhyme.

    Nor is her power to me confined;
It spreads; it comprehends mankind.

    When (to the spirit-stirring sound
Of trumpets, breathing courage round,   350
And fifes, well-mingled to restrain
And bring that courage down again;
Or to the melancholy knell
Of the dull, deep, and doleful bell,
Such as of late the good Saint Bride
Muffled, to mortify the pride
Of those, who, England quite forgot,
Paid their vile homage to the Scot,
Where Asgill held the foremost place,

[344] The profits resulting from the publication of Churchill's Poems relieved the author from all his pecuniary difficulties.

[355] On the signing, under Lord Bute's administration, of the Treaty of Paris which terminated the war that had been conducted with such brilliant success by Pitt, an address of congratulation having been wrung from the city of London, it was carried up to St. James's, 12th of May, 1763, by Sir Charles Asgill as locum tenens, accompanied by other civic officers. The procession was throughout received with hootings by the mob, and as it passed Fleet-street the great bell of St. Bride's began to toll, and then a dumb peal struck up; at its return it received a similar salutation from Bow bells.

Whilst my Lord figured at a race) 360
Processions ('tis not worth debate
Whether they are of stage or state)
Move on, so very, very slow,
'Tis doubtful if they move or no ;
When the performers all the whiie
Mechanically frown or smile,
Or, with a dull and stupid stare,
A vacancy of sense declare,
Or, with down-bending eye, seem wrought
Into a labyrinth of thought, 370
Where Reason wanders still in doubt,
And, once got in, cannot get out,
What cause sufficient can we find,
To satisfy a thinking mind
Why, duped by such vain farces, man
Descends to act on such a plan ?
Why they, who hold themselves divine,
Can in such wretched follies join,
Strutting like peacocks, or like crows,
Themselves and Nature to expose? 380
What cause, but that (you'll understand
We have our remedy at hand,
That if perchance we start a doubt,
Ere it is fix'd, we wipe it out;
As surgeons, when they lop a limb,
Whether for profit, fame, or whim,
Or mere experiment to try,
Must always have a styptic by)
Fancy steps in, and stamps that real,
Which, *ipso facto*, is ideal. 390
    Can none remember? yes, I know,
All must remember that rare show

When to the country Sense went down,
And fools came flocking up to town;
When knights (a work which all admit
To be for knighthood much unfit)
Built booths for hire; when parsons play'd,
In robes canonical array'd,
And, fiddling, join'd the Smithfield dance,
The price of tickets to advance;   40:
Or, unto tapsters turn'd, dealt out,
Running from booth to booth about,
To every scoundrel, by retail,
True pennyworths of beef and ale,
Then first prepared, by bringing beer in,
For present grand electioneering;
When heralds, running all about
To bring in order, turn'd it out;
When, by the prudent Marshal's care,
Lest the rude populace should stare,   410
And with unhallow'd eyes profane
Gay puppets of Patrician strain,
The whole procession, as in spite,
Unheard, unseen, stole off by night;
When our loved monarch, nothing loath,
Solemnly took that sacred oath
Whence mutual firm agreements spring
Betwixt the subject and the king;
By which, in usual manner crown'd,
His head, his heart, his hands, he bound,   42C
Against himself, should passion stir
The least propensity to err,

[406] A new parliament was summoned at the accession of
George the Third, and met in November, 1761; the can-
vassing was consequently at its height at the time of the
coronation.

Against all slaves, who might prepare
Or open force, or hidden snare,
That glorious Charter to maintain,
By which we serve, and he must reign;
Then Fancy, with unbounded sway,
Revell'd sole mistress of the day,
Ana wrought such wonders, as might make
Egyptian sorcerers forsake   430
Their baffled mockeries, and own
The palm of magic hers alone.
    A knight (who in the silken lap
Of lazy Peace, had lived on pap;
Who never yet had dared to roam
'Bove ten or twenty miles from home,
Nor even that, unless a guide
Was placed to amble by his side,
And troops of slaves were spread around
To keep his Honour safe and sound;   440
Who could not suffer, for his life,
A point to sword, or edge to knife,
And always fainted at the sight
Of blood, though 'twas not shed in fight;
Who disinherited one son
For firing off an alder gun,
And whipt another, six years old,
Because the boy, presumptuous, bold
To madness, likely to become
A very Swiss, had beat a drum,   450
Though it appear'd an instrument
Most peaceable and innocent,.
Having, from first, been in the hands
And service of the City bands)
Graced with those ensigns, which were meant

To further Honour's dread intent,
The minds of warriors to inflame,
And spur them on to deeds of fame:
With little sword, large spurs, high feather,
Fearless of every thing but weather,   460
(And all must own, who pay regard
To charity, it had been hard
That in his very first campaign
His honours should be soil'd with rain)
A hero all at once became,
And (seeing others much the same
In point of valour as himself,
Who leave their courage on a shelf
From year to year, till some such rout
In proper season calls it out)   470
Strutted, look'd big, and swagger'd more
Than ever hero did before:
Look'd up, look'd down, look'd all around,
Like Mavors, grimly smiled and frown'd;
Seem'd heaven, and earth, and hell to call
To fight, that he might rout them all,
And personated valour's style
So long, spectators to beguile,
That passing strange, and wondrous true,
Himself at last believed it too;   480
Nor for a time could he discern,
Till truth and darkness took their turn,
So well did Fancy play her part,
That coward still was at the heart.
    Whiffle (who knows not Whiffle's name,
By the impartial voice of Fame
Recorded first through all this land
In Vanity's illustrious band?)

Who, by all bounteous Nature meant
For offices of hardiment,   490
A modern Hercules at least
To rid the world of each wild beast,
Of each wild beast which came in view
Whether on four legs or on two,
Degenerate, delights to prove
His force on the parade of Love,
Disclaims the joys which camps afford,
And for the distaff quits the sword;
Who fond of women would appear
To public eye and public ear,   500
But, when in private, let's them know
How little they can trust to show;
Who sports a woman, as of course,
Just as a jockey shews a horse,
And then returns her to the stable,
Or, vainly plants her at his table,
Where he would rather Venus find,
(So pall'd, and so depraved his mind)
Than, by some great occasion led,
To seize her panting in her bed,   510
Burning with more than mortal fires,
And melting in her own desires;
Who, ripe in years, is yet a child,
Through fashion, not through feeling, wild;
Whate'er in others, who proceed
As Sense and Nature have decreed,
From real passion flows, in him
Is mere effect of mode and whim;
Who laughs, a very common way,
Because he nothing has to say,   520
As your choice spirits oaths dispense

To fill up vacancies of sense;
Who having some small sense defies it,
Or, using, always misapplies it;
Who now and then brings something forth
Which seems indeed of sterling worth;
Something, by sudden start and fit,
Which at a distance looks like wit,
But, on examination near,
To his confusion will appear,   530
By truth's fair glass, to be at best
A threadbare jester's threadbare jest;
Who frisks and dances through the street,
Sings without voice, rides without seat,
Plays o'er his tricks, like Æsop's ass,
A *gratis* fool to all who pass;
Who riots, though he loves not waste,
Whores without lust, drinks without taste,
Acts without sense, talks without thought,
Does every thing but what he ought;   540
Who, led by forms, without the power
Of vice, is vicious; who one hour,
Proud without pride, the next will be
Humble without humility:
Whose vanity we all discern,
The spring on which his actions turn;
Whose aim in erring, is to err,
So that he may be singular,
And all his utmost wishes mean
Is, though he's laugh'd at, to be seen: 550
Such (for when Flattery's soothing strain
Had robb'd the Muse of her disdain,
And found a method to persuade
Her art to soften every shade,

Justice, enraged, the pencil snatch'd
From her degenerate hand, and scratch'd
Out every trace, then, quick as thought,
From life this striking likeness caught)
In mind, in manners, and in mien,
Such Whiffle came, and such was seen   560
In the world's eye; but (strange to tell!)
Misled by Fancy's magic spell,
Deceived, not dreaming of deceit,
Cheated, but happy in the cheat,
Was more than human in his own.
O bow, bow all at Fancy's throne,
Whose power could make so vile an elf
With patience bear that thing *himself*.

But, mistress of each art to please,
Creative Fancy, what are these,   570
These pageants of a trifler's pen,
To what thy power effected then?
Familiar with the human mind,
And swift and subtle as the wind,
Which we all feel, yet no one knows
Or whence it comes, or where it goes,
Fancy at once in every part
Possess'd the eye, the head, the heart;
And in a thousand forms array'd,
A thousand various gambols play'd.   580
Here, in a face which well might ask
The privilege to wear a mask
In spite of law, and justice teach
For public good t'excuse the breach,
Within the furrow of a wrinkle
'Twixt eyes, which could not shine, but twinkle
Like centinels i' th' starry way,

Who wait for the return of day,
Almost burnt out, and seem to keep
Their watch, like soldiers, in their sleep ;   590
Or like those lamps, which, by the power
Of law, must burn from hour to hour,
(Else they, without redemption, fall
Under the terrors of that Hall
Which, once notorious for a hop,
Is now become a justice shop)
Which are so managed, to go out
Just when the time comes round about,
Which yet, through emulation, strive
To keep their dying light alive,   600
And (not uncommon, as we find
Amongst the children of mankind)
As they grow weaker, would seem stronger,
And burn a little, little longer :
Fancy, betwixt such eyes enshrined,
No brush to daub, no mill to grind,
Thrice waved her wand around, whose force
Changed in an instant Nature's course,
And, hardly credible in rhyme,
Not only stopp'd, but call'd back time ;   610
The face of every wrinkle clear'd,
Smooth as the floating stream appear'd,
Down the neck ringlets spread their flame,

591 By an act of parliament then lately past, for the more
effectually lighting, &c. the liberty of Westminster, the
sitting magistrate at Bow Street was armed with very strin-
gent powers for punishing such lamplighters as neglected
their duties.
594 The Westminster Session-house was then held at a
house in King Street, which had probably been a low place
of public entertainment.

The neck admiring whence they came ;
On the arch'd brow the Graces play'd ;
On the full bosom Cupid laid ;
Suns, from their proper orbits sent,
Became for eyes a supplement ;
Teeth, white as ever teeth were seen,
Deliver'd from the hand of Green,   620
Started, in regular array,
Like train-bands on a grand field-day,
Into the gums, which would have fled,
But, wond'ring, turn'd from white to red ;
Quite alter'd was the whole machine,
And Lady —— was fifteen.

    Here she made lordly temples rise
Before the pious Dashwood's eyes,
Temples which, built aloft in air,
May serve for show, if not for prayer ;   630
In solemn form herself, before,
Array'd like Faith, the Bible bore :
There, over Melcombe's feather'd head,—
Who, quite a man of gingerbread,
Savour'd in talk, in dress, and phiz,
More of another world than this,
To a dwarf Muse a giant page,
The last grave fop of the last age,
In a superb and feather'd hearse,
Bescutcheon'd and betagg'd with verse,   640
Which, to beholders from afar,
Appear'd like a triumphal car,

---

[629] See Gotham, Book i. l. 463, note.
[633] In Hogarth's " Five orders of Periwigs," the first
head in the second row was designed to represent Lord
Melcombe.

She rode, in a east rainbow clad ;
There, throwing off the hallow'd plaid,
Naked, as when (in those drear cells
Where self-bless'd, self-cursed Madness dwells)
Pleasure, on whom, in Laughter's shape,
Frenzy had perfected a rape,
First brought her forth, before her time,
Wild witness of her shame and crime ;   656.
Driving before an idol band
Of drivelling Stuarts, hand in hand ;
Some who, to curse mankind, had wore
A crown they ne'er must think of more ;
Others, whose baby brows were graced
With paper crowns, and toys of paste ;
She jigg'd, and playing on the flute,
Spread raptures o'er the soul of Bute.

    Big with vast hopes, some mighty plan,
Which wrought the busy soul of man   660
To her full bent, the Civil Law,
(Fit code to keep a world in awe)
Bound o'er his brows, fair to behold,
As Jewish frontlets were of old ;
The famous Charter of our land
Defaced, and mangled in his hand ;
As one whom deepest thoughts employ,
But deepest thoughts of truest joy,
Serious and slow he strode, he stalk'd ;
Before him troops of heroes walk'd,   670
Whom best he loved, of heroes crown'd,
By Tories guarded all around ;
Dull, solemn pleasure in his face,
He saw the honours of his race,
He saw their lineal glories rise,

And touch'd, or seem'd to touch the skies;
Not the most distant mark of fear,
No sign of axe, or scaffold near,
Not one cursed thought, to cross his will,
Of such a place as Tower Hill.   680
    Curse on this Muse, a flippant jade!
A shrew; like every other maid
Who turns the corner of nineteen,
Devour'd with peevishness and spleen:
Her tongue, (for as when bound for life,
The husband suffers for the wife,
So if in any works of rhyme
Perchance there blunders out a crime,
Poor culprit bards must always rue it,
Although 'tis plain the Muses do it)   690
Sooner or later cannot fail
To send me headlong to a jail.
Whate'er my theme, (our themes we choose
In modern days without a Muse,
Just as a father will provide
To join a bridegroom and a bride,
As if, though they must be the players,
The game was wholly his, not theirs)
Whate'er my theme, the Muse, who still
Owns no direction but her will,   700
Flies off, and ere I could expect,
By ways oblique and indirect,
At once quite over head and ears
In fatal politics appears.
Time was, and, if I aught discern
Of fate, that time shall soon return,
When, decent and demure at least,
As grave and dull as any priest,

I could see Vice in robes array'd,
Could see the game of Folly play'd   710
Successfully in fortune's school,
Without exclaiming rogue or fool :
Time was, when nothing loth or proud,
I lackeyed with the fawning crowd
Scoundrels in office, and would bow
To cyphers great in place ; but now
Upright I stand, as if wise Fate,
To compliment a shatter'd state,
Had me, like Atlas, hither sent
To shoulder up the firmament,   720
And if I stoop'd, with general crack,
The heavens would tumble from my back :
Time was, when rank and situation
Secured the great ones of the nation
From all control ; satire and law
Kept only little knaves in awe ;
But now, decorum lost, I stand
Bemused, a pencil in my hand,
And, dead to every sense of shame,
Careless of safety and of fame,   730
The names of scoundrels minute down,
And libel more than half the town.
    How can a statesman be secure
In all his villanies, if poor
And dirty authors thus shall dare
To lay his rotten bosom bare ?
Muses should pass away their time
In dressing out the poet's rhyme
With bills and ribands, and array
Each line in harmless taste, though gay.   740
When the hot burning fit is on,

They should regale their restless son
With something to allay his rage,
Some cool Castalian beverage,
Or some such draught (though they, 'tis plain,
Taking the Muse's name in vain,
Know nothing of their real court,
And only fable from report)
As makes a Whitehead's ode go down,
Or slakes the Feverette of Brown :   750
But who would in his senses think
Of Muses giving gall to drink,
Or that their folly should afford
To raving poets gun or sword?
Poets were ne'er design'd by fate
To meddle with affairs of state,
Nor should (if we may speak our thought
Truly as men of honour ought)
Sound policy their rage admit,
To launch the thunderbolts of wit   760
About those heads which, when they're shot,
Can't tell if 'twas by Wit or not.

[750] The Rev. John Brown, D.D., born in 1715, was author of an " Estimate of the Manners and Principles of the Times." Though only remembered now by Cowper's line—

" The inestimable estimate of Brown,"

—this publication excited uncommon attention, and ran through seven editions in one year. His insatiable vanity, dogmatism, and arrogance, rendered him disgusting to others, and a torment to himself; prevented by ill health from accepting an invitation from the Empress of Russia, to superintend an enlarged plan of education in that country, and highly irritated by the slights and mortifications he received in this, he in 1766 became insane, and put an end to his own life in the 50th year of his age.

These things well known, what devil in spite
Can have seduced me thus to write
Out of that road, which must have led
To riches, without heart or head,
Into that road, which had I more
Than ever poet had before
Of wit and virtue, in disgrace
Would keep me still, and out of place ;   770
Which, if some judge (you'll understand
One famous, famous through the land
For making law) should stand my friend
At last may in a pillory end ;
And all this, I myself admit,
Without one cause to lead to it ?

    For instance now—this book—the Ghost—
Methinks I hear some critic Post
Remark most gravely—" The first word
Which we about the Ghost have heard."   780
Peace, my good Sir !—not quite so fast—
What is the first, may be the last,
Which is a point, all must agree,
Cannot depend on you or me.
Fanny, no Ghost of common mould,
Is not by forms to be controll'd
To keep her state, and shew her skill ;
She never comes but when she will.
I wrote and wrote—perhaps you doubt,
And shrewdly, what I wrote about ;   790

773 Alluding to Lord Mansfield's scheme of successive
judicial decisions, which now constitute a third division
or code generally designated as Judge-made law; Churchill's animadversions, however, only apply to the use Lord
Mansfield made of this code with reference to the law of
libel.

Believe me, much to my disgrace,
I, too, am in the self-same case;
But still I wrote, till Fanny came
Impatient, nor could any shame
On me, with equal justice, fall,
If she had never come at all.
An underling, I could not stir
Without the cue thrown out by her,
Nor from the subject aid receive
Until she came and gave me leave.   800
So that, (ye sons of Erudition,
Mark, this is but a supposition,
Nor would I to so wise a nation
Suggest it as a revelation)
If henceforth, dully turning o'er
Page after page, ye read no more
Of Fanny, who, in sea or air,
May be departed God knows where,
Rail at jilt Fortune, but agree
No censure can be laid on me;   810
For sure (the cause let Mansfield try)
Fanny is in the fault, not I.
  But, to return—and this I hold
A secret worth its weight in gold
To those who write, as I write now,
Not to mind where they go, or how;
Through ditch, through bog, o'er hedge and stile,
Make it but worth the reader's while,
And keep a passage fair and plain
Always to bring him back again.   820
Through dirt who scruples to approach,
At Pleasure's call, to take a coach?
But we should think the man a clown,

Who in the dirt should set us down.
　　But, to return—If Wit, who ne'er
The shackles of restraint could bear,
In wayward humour should refuse
Her timely succour to the Muse,
And, to no rules and orders tied,
Roughly deny to be her guide,　　　　　　　　830
She must renounce decorum's plan,
And get back when, and how she can;
As parsons, who, without pretext,
As soon as mention'd, quit their text,
And, to promote sleep's genial power,
Grope in the dark for half an hour,
Give no more reason (for we know
Reason is vulgar, mean, and low)
Why they come back (should it befal
That ever they come back at all)　　　　　　840
Into the road, to end their rout,
Than they can give why they went out.
　　But to return—this book—the Ghost—
A mere amusement at the most;
A trifle, fit to wear away
The horrors of a rainy day;
A slight shot silk, for summer wear,
Just as our modern statesmen are,—
If rigid honesty permit
That I for once purloin the wit　　　　　　850
Of him, who, were we all to steal,
Is much too rich the theft to feel;
Yet in this book, where ease should join
With mirth to sugar every line;
Where it should all be mere chit-chat,
Lively, good-humour'd, and all that;

Where honest Satire, in disgrace,
Should not so much as show her face,
The shrew, o'erleaping all due bounds,
Breaks into laughter's sacred grounds,⠀⠀860
And, in contempt, plays o'er her tricks
In science, trade, and politics.
⠀⠀But why should the distemper'd scold
Attempt to blacken men enroll'd
In power's dread book, whose mighty skill
Can twist an empire to their will;
Whose voice is fate, and on their tongue
Law, liberty, and life, are hung;
Whom on inquiry, truth shall find,
With Stuarts link'd; time out of mind⠀⠀870
Superior to their country's laws,
Defenders of a tyrant's cause;
Men, who the same damn'd maxims hold,
Darkly, which they avow'd of old;
Who, though by different means, pursue
The end which they had first in view,
⠀And, force found vain, now play their part
With much less honour, much more art?
Why, at the corners of the streets,
To every patriot drudge she meets,⠀⠀880
Known or unknown, with furious cry
Should she wild clamours vent? or why,
The minds of groundlings to inflame,
A Dashwood, Bute, and Wyndham name?
Why, having not, to our surprise,
The fear of death before her eyes,
Bearing, and that but now and then,
No other weapon but her pen,
Should she an argument afford

For blood, to men who wear a sword?　890
Men, who can nicely trim and pare
A point of honour to a hair;
(Honour—a word of nice import,
A pretty trinket in a court,
Which my Lord, quite in rapture, feels
Dangling and rattling with his seals;
Honour—a word which all the Nine
Would be much puzzled to define;
Honour—a word which torture mocks,
And might confound a thousand Lockes;　900
Which (for I leave to wiser heads,
Who fields of death prefer to beds
Of down, to find out, if they can,
What Honour *is*, on their wild plan)
Is *not*,—to take it in their way,
And this we sure may dare to say
Without incurring an offence,—
Courage, law, honesty, or sense)
Men, who all spirit, life, and soul,
Neat butchers of a buttonhole,　910
Having more skill, believe it true
That they must have more courage too;
Men who, without a place or name,
Their fortunes speechless as their fame,
Would by the sword new fortunes carve,
And rather die in fight than starve.
At coronations, a vast field,
Which food of every kind might yield,
Of good, sound food, at once most fit
For purposes of health and wit,　920
Could not ambitious Satire rest,
Content with what she might digest?

Could she not feast on things of course,
A champion, or a champion's horse?
A champion's horse—no better say,
Though better figured on that day—
A horse, which might appear to us
Who deal in rhyme, a Pegasus;
A rider, who, when once got on,
Might pass for a Bellerophon   930
Dropt on a sudden from the skies,
To catch and fix our wondering eyes,
To witch, with wand instead of whip;
The world with noble horsemanship;
To twist and twine, both horse and man,
On such a well-concerted plan,
That, Centaur-like, when all was done,
We scarce could think they were not one.
Could she not to our itching ears
Bring the new names of new-coin'd peers,   940
Who walk'd, nobility forgot,
With shoulders fitter for a knot
Than robes of honour; for whose sake
Heralds, in form, were forced to make,—
To make, because they could not find,—
Great predecessors to their mind?
Could she not (though 'tis doubtful since,
Whether he plumber is, or prince)

[926] Alluding to the horse which Lord Talbot mounted as high-steward at the coronation. His performance was so ludicrously described in No. 12 of the North Briton, as with other provocations to occasion the duel between his lordship and Mr. Wilkes, at Bagshot.

[940] Lord Bute created sixteen peerages during the first two years of George the Third's reign, in order to obtain a decided majority in the House of Lords.

Tell of a simple knight's advance   950
To be a doughty peer of France?
Tell how he did a dukedom gain,
And Robinson was Aquitaine?
Tell how her city chiefs, disgraced,
Were at an empty table placed?
A gross neglect, which, whilst they live,
They can't forget, and won't forgive,
A gross neglect of all those rights
Which march with city appetites,
Of all those canons, which we find
By Gluttony, time out of mind   960
Established, which they ever hold
Dearer than any thing but gold.

    Thanks to my stars—I now see shore—
Of courtiers, and of courts no more—
Thus stumbling on my city friends,
Blind Chance my guide, my purpose bends
In line direct, and shall pursue
The point which I had first in view,
Nor more shall with the reader sport
Till I have seen him safe in port.   970
Hush'd be each fear—no more I bear

[952] At the coronation of George the Third, the Duke of
Normandy (not Aquitaine) was represented by Sir Thomas
Robinson, elder brother of the first Lord Rokeby. In allu-
sion to his great height the well-known epigram was written ·

    "Unlike my subject now shall be my song,
    It shall be witty and it shan't be long."

[953] The Lord Mayor, Aldermen, and a deputation of the
Common Council, were invited to the coronation dinner at
Whitehall; by some mistake no table had been set for them,
and, consequently, they got but a scanty meal, and returned
to the city, late in the evening in their barge, much displeased with their part in the ceremony.

Through the wide regions of the air
The reader, terrified; no more
Wild ocean's horrid paths explore.
Be the plain track from henceforth mine—
Cross-roads to Allen I resign;
Allen, the honour of this nation;
Allen, himself a corporation;
Allen, of late notorious grown
For writings none, or all his own;　　980
Allen, the first of letter'd men,
Since the good Bishop holds his pen,
And at his elbow takes his stand
To mend his head, and guide his hand.
But hold—once more, Digression, hence!
Let us return to common sense;
The car of Phœbus I discharge,
My carriage now a Lord Mayor's barge.

　Suppose we now (we may suppose
In verse, what would be sin in prose)　　990
The sky with darkness overspread,
And every star retired to bed;
The gewgaw robes of Pomp and Pride
In some dark corner thrown aside,
Great lords and ladies giving way
To what they seem to scorn by day,
The real feelings of the heart,
And Nature taking place of Art;
Desire triumphant through the night,

---

[980] Warburton was suspected of having assisted Mr. Allen in his correspondence with the Earl of Chatham, about the address of thanks from the city of Bath, on the peace of 1763. Mr. Allen was the inventor and farmer of cross posts, by which he acquired a large fortune.

And Beauty panting with delight; 1000
Chastity, woman's fairest crown,
Till the return of morn laid down,
Then to be worn again as bright
As if not sullied in the night;
Dull Ceremony, business o'er,
Dreaming in form at Cottrell's door
Precaution trudging all about
To see the candles safely out;
Bearing a mighty master-key,
Habited like Economy, 1010
Stamping each lock with triple seals,
Mean Avarice creeping at her heels.
　　Suppose we too, like sheep in pen,
The Mayor and Court of Aldermen
Within their barge, which through the deep,
The rowers more than half asleep,
Moved slow, as overcharged with state;
Thames groan'd beneath the mighty weight,
And felt that bawble heavier far
Than a whole fleet of men of war. 1020
Sleep o'er each well-known, faithful head
With liberal hand his poppies shed,
Each head, by Dulness render'd fit
Sleep and his empire to admit.
Through the whole passage not a word,
Not one faint, weak half-sound was heard;
Sleep had prevail'd to overwhelm
The steersman nodding o'er the helm;
The rowers, without force or skill,

---

[100] Sir Clement Cottrell, master of the ceremonies; who
was succeeded in office by Sir Robert Chester.

Left the dull barge to drive at will;   1030
The sluggish oars suspended hung,
And even Beardmore held his tongue.
Commerce, regardful of a freight
On which depended half her state,
Stepp'd to the helm; with ready hand
She safely clear'd that bank of sand,
Where, stranded, our west-country fleet
Delay and danger often meet,
Till Neptune, anxious for the trade,
Comes in full tides, and brings them aid.   1040
Next (for the Muses can survey
Objects by night as well as day;
Nothing prevents their taking aim,
Darkness and light to them the same)
They pass'd that building which of old
Queen-mothers was design'd to hold;
At present a mere lodging-pen,
A palace turn'd into a den,
To barracks turn'd; and soldiers tread
Where dowagers have laid their head.   1050
Why should we mention Surrey Street,
Where every week grave judges meet
All fitted out with hum and ha,
In proper form to drawl out law,
To see all causes duly tried

1032 Beardmore, the under-sheriff, was an occasional writer
in the Monitor, an opposition paper, and was employed by
Wilkes as his solicitor in his contest with government.

1045 The Savoy and Old Somerset House, formerly the re-
sidences of the Queens of England, were purchased by parliament for national uses, and the more convenient palace of
Buckingham House became the residence of Queen Charlotte
instead.

'Twixt knaves who drive, and fools who ride?
Why at the Temple should we stay?
What of the Temple dare we say?
A dangerous ground we tread on there,
And words perhaps may actions bear;   1060
Where, as the brethren of the seas
For fares, the lawyers ply for fees.
What of that Bridge most wisely made
To serve the purposes of trade,
In the great mart of all this nation,
By stopping up the navigation,
And to that sand bank adding weight,
Which is already much too great?
What of that Bridge, which, void of sense,
But well supplied with impudence,   1070
Englishmen, knowing not the Guild,
Thought they might have a claim to build,
Till Paterson, as white as milk,
As smooth as oil, as soft as silk,
In solemn manner had decreed
That on the other side the Tweed,
Art, born and bred, and fully grown,
Was with one Mylne, a man unknown,

[1061] A hackney coach office was established in 1696, in Surrey Street, Strand, and five Commissioners were appointed to regulate the fares and settle disputes.

[1063] A senseless clamour was excited by various interested persons against the erection of a bridge over the Thames at Blackfriars. Perhaps Churchill opposed it because Mr. Paterson, the chief promoter of the scheme, was the leader of the Anti-Wilkite party in the city; and Mr. Mylne, the architect, was a Scotchman. The bridge was opened for carriages on the 18th November, 1769, and the toll imposed for defraying the expense of building, and which produced about £8000 a year was continued twenty years.

But grace, preferment, and renown
Deserving, just arrived in town ;   1080
One Mylne, an artist perfect quite
Both in his own and country's right,
As fit to make a bridge as ho,
With glorious Patavinity,
To build inscriptions, worthy found
To lie for ever underground.
  Much more, worth observation too,
Was this a season to pursue
The theme, our Muse might tell in rhyme:
The will she hath, but not the time;   1090
For, swift as shaft from Indian bow,
(And when a goddess comes, we know
Surpassing Nature acts preva'l,
And boats want neither oar nor sail)
The vessel pass'd, and reach'd the shore
So quick, that thought was scarce before
  Suppose we now our city court
Safely deliver'd at the port,
And, of their state regardless quite,   ·
Landed, like smuggled goods, by night.   1100
The solemn magistrate laid down,
The dignity of robe and gown,
With every other ensign gone,
Suppose the woollen nightcap on ;
The flesh-brush used, with decent state,
To make the spirits circulate,
(A form which, to the senses true,
The lickerish chaplain uses too,

[1084] The inscription on the bridge was ascribed to Paterson,
and was much ridiculed in a witty pamphlet called " City
Latin."

Though, something to improve the plan,
He takes the maid instead of man)   1110
Swathed, and with flannel cover'd o'er,
To shew the vigour of threescore,
The vigour of threescore and ten
Above the proof of younger men,
Suppose, the mighty Dulman led
Betwixt two slaves, and put to bed;
Suppose, the moment he lies down,
No miracle in this great Town,
The drone as fast asleep, as he
Must in the course of nature be,   1120
Who, truth for our foundation take,
When up, is never half awake.

    There let him sleep, whilst we survey
The preparations for the day;
That day on which was to be shown
Court pride by City pride outdone.

    The jealous mother sends away,
As only fit for childish play,
That daughter who, to gall her pride,
Shoots up too forward by her side.   1130

    The wretch, of God and man accurst,
Of all hell's instruments the worst,
Draws forth his pawns, and for the day
Struts in some spendthrift's vain array;
Around his awkward doxy shine
The treasures of Golconda's mine;
Each neighbour, with a jealous glare,
Beholds her folly publish'd there.

    Garments well saved, (an anecdote
Which we can prove, or would not quote)   1140

    [1113] Sir Samuel Fludyer, Lord Mayor in 1761.

Garments well saved, which first were made
When tailors, to promote their trade,
Against the Picts in arms arose,
And drove them out, or made them clothes;
Garments immortal, without end,
Like names and titles, which descend
Successively from sire to son;
Garments, unless some work is done
Of note, not suffer'd to appear
'Bove once at most in every year,   1150
Were now, in solemn form, laid bare,
To take the benefit of air,
And, ere they came to be employ'd
On this solemnity, to void
That scent, which Russia's leather gave,
From vile and impious moth to save.
    Each head was busy, and each heart
In preparation bore a part;
Running together all about
The servants put each other out,   1160
Till the grave master had decreed,
The more haste, ever the worst speed.
Miss, with her little eyes half-closed,
Over a smuggled toilette dosed:
The waiting-maid, whom story notes
A very Scrub in petticoats,
Hired for one work, but doing all,
In slumbers lean'd against the wall.
Milliners, summon'd from afar,
Arrived in shoals at Temple Bar,   1170
Strictly commanded to import
Cart loads of foppery from court
With labour'd, visible design

Art strove to be superbly fine ;
Nature, more pleasing, though more wild,
Taught otherwise her darling child,
And cried, with spirited disdain,
Be Hunter elegant and plain.

    Lo ! from the chambers of the East,
A welcome prelude to the feast,   1183
In saffron-colour'd robe array'd,
High in a car by Vulcan made,
Who work'd for Jove himself, each steed
High-mettled, of celestial breed,
Pawing and pacing all the way,
Aurora brought the wish'd-for day,
And held her empire, till out-run
By that brave, jolly groom the Sun.

    The trumpet—hark ! it speaks—it swells
The loud, full harmony ; it tells   1190
The time at hand when Dulman, led
By Form, his citizens must head,
And march those troops, which at his call
Were now assembled, to Guildhall,
On matters of importance great,
To court and city, church and state.

    From end to end the sound makes way,
All hear the signal and obey ;
But Dulman, who, his charge forgot,
By Morpheus fetter'd, heard it not ;   1200
Nor could, so sound he slept and fast,
Hear any trumpet, but the last.

    Crape, ever true and trusty known,
Stole from the maid's bed to his own ;
Then in the spirituals of pride,
Planted himself at Dulman's side.

Thrice did the ever-faithful slave,
With voice which might have reach'd the grave,
And broke death's adamantine chain,
On Dulman call, but call'd in vain. 1210
Thrice with an arm, which might have made
The Theban boxer curse his trade,
The drone he shook, who rear'd the head,
And thrice fell backward on his bed.
What could be done ? Where force hath fail'd
Policy often hath prevail'd,
And what, an inference most plain,
Had been, Crape thought might be again.

Under his pillow (still in mind
The proverb kept, Fast bind, fast find) 1220
Each blessed night the keys were laid,
Which Crape to draw away assay'd.
What not the power of voice or arm
Could do, this did, and broke the charm;
Quick started he with stupid stare,
For all his little soul was there.

Behold him, taken up, rubb'd down,
In elbow-chair, and morning-gown;
Behold him, in his latter bloom, 1229
Stripp'd, wash'd, and sprinkled with perfume;
Behold him bending with the weight
Of robes, and trumpery of state;
Behold him (for the maxim's true,
Whate'er we by another do
We do ourselves, and chaplain paid,
Like slaves in every other trade,
Had mutter'd over God knows what,
Something which he by heart had got)
Having, as usual, said his prayers,

Go titter, totter, to the stairs: 1240
Behold him for descent prepare
With one foot trembling in the air;
He starts, he pauses on the brink,
And, hard to credit! seems to think;
Through his whole train (the chaplain gave
The proper cue to every slave)
At once, as with infection caught,
Each started, paused, and aim'd at thought;
He turns, and they turn; big with care,
He waddles to his elbow-chair,   1250
Squats down, and, silent for a season,
At last with Crape begins to reason:
But first of all he made a sign,
That every soul but the divine
Should quit the room; in him, he knows,
He may all confidence repose.
    "Crape—though I'm yet not quite awake—
Before this awful step I take,
On which my future all depends,
I ought to know my foes and friends.   1260
My foes and friends—observe me still—
I mean not those who well or ill
Perhaps may wish me, but those who
Have't in their power to do it too.
Now if, attentive to the state,
In too much hurry to be great,
Or through much zeal,—a motive, Crape,
Deserving praise,—into a scrape
I, like a fool, am got, no doubt
I, like a wise man should get out: 1270
Not that (remark without replies)
I say that to get out is wise,

Or by the very self-same rule
That to get in was like a fool.
The marrow of this argument
Must wholly rest on the event;
And therefore, which is really hard,
Against events too I must guard.
   "Should things continue as they stand,
And Bute prevail through all the land   1280
Without a rival, by his aid
My fortunes in a trice are made;
Nay, honours, on my zeal may smile,
And stamp me Earl of some great Isle:
But if, a matter of much doubt,
The present minister goes out,
Fain would I know on what pretext
I can stand fairly with the next.
For as my aim, at every hour,
Is to be well with those in power,   1290
And my material point of view,
Whoever's in, to be in too,
I should not, like a blockhead, choose
To gain these so as those to lose:
'Tis good in every case, you know,
To have two strings unto our bow."
   As one in wonder lost, Crape view'd
His lord, who thus his speech pursued:
   "This, my good Crape, is my grand point;
And as the times are out of joint,   1300
The greater caution is required

1284 The Isle of Bute, situate in the Frith of Clyde, is
about twelve miles in length, and five in breadth. A ludicrous statement was made of the sum contributed by it to
the revenue, amounting to thirteen shillings and nine-pence
three-farthings, subject to some deductions.

To bring about the point desired.
What I would wish to bring about
Cannot admit a moment's doubt;
The matter in dispute, you know,
Is what we call the *quomodo*.
That be thy task"—The reverend slave
Becoming in a moment grave,
Fix'd to the ground and rooted, stood
Just like a man cut out of wood,   1310
Such as we see (without the least
Reflection glancing on the priest)
One or more, planted up and down,
Almost in every church in town;   ·
He stood some minutes, then, like one
Who wish'd the matter might be done,
But could not do it, shook his head,
And thus the man of sorrow said:
    "Hard is this task, too hard I swear,
By much too hard for me to bear;   1320
Beyond expression hard my part,
Could mighty Dulman see my heart,
When he, alas! makes known a will
Which Crape's not able to fulfil.
Was ever my obedience barr'd
By any trifling, nice regard
To sense and honour? could I reach
Thy meaning without help of speech,
At the first motion of thy eye
Did not thy faithful creature fly?   1330
Have I not said, not what I ought,
But what my earthly master taught?
Did I e'er weigh, through duty strong,
In thy great biddings, right and wrong?

Did ever Interest, to whom thou
Canst not with more devotion bow,
Warp my sound faith, or will of mine
In contradiction run to thine?
Have I not, at thy table placed,
When business call'd aloud for haste, 1340
Torn myself thence, yet never heard
To utter one complaining word,
And had, till thy great work was done,
All appetites, as having none?
Hard is it, this great plan pursued
Of voluntary servitude,
Pursued, without or shame or fear,
Through the great circle of the year,
Now to receive, in this grand hour,
Commands which lie beyond my power, 1350
Commands which baffle all my skill,
And leave me nothing but my will:
Be that accepted; let my Lord
Indulgence to his slave afford:
This task, for my poor strength unfit,
Will yield to none but Dulman's wit."
　　With such gross incense gratified,
And turning up the lip of pride,
" Poor Crape"—and shook his empty head—
" Poor puzzled Crape!"—wise Dulman said, 1361
" Of judgment weak, of sense confined,
For things of lower note design'd;
For things within the vulgar reach,
To run of errands, and to preach;
Well hast thou judg'd that heads like mine
Cannot want help from heads like thine;
Well hast thou judged thyself unmeet

Of such high argument to treat ;
'Twas but to try thee that I spoke,
And all I said was but a joke.   1370
     " Nor think a joke, Crape, a disgrace
Or to my person or my place ;
The wisest of the sons of men
Have deign'd to use them now and then.
The only caution, do you see,
Demanded by our dignity,
From common use and men exempt,
Is that they may not breed contempt.
Great use they have, when in the hands
Of one like me, who understands,   1380
Who understands the time and place
The person, manner, and the grace
Which fools neglect ; so that we find,
If all the requisites are join'd
From whence a perfect joke must spring,
A joke's a very serious thing.
     " But to our business—my design,
Which gave so rough a shock to thine,
To my capacity is made
As ready as a fraud in trade ;   1390
Which, like broad-cloth, I can, with ease
Cut out in any shape I please.
     " Some, in my circumstance, some few,
Aye, and those men of genius too,
Good men, who, without love or hate,
Whether they early rise or late,
With names uncrack'd, and credit sound,
Rise worth a hundred thousand pound,
By threadbare ways and means would try
To bear their point—so will not I.   1400

New methods shall my wisdom find
To suit these matters to my mind,
So that the infidels at court,
Who make our City wits their sport,
Shall hail the honours of my reign,
And own that Dulman bears a brain.
" Some, in my place, to gain their ends,
Would give relations up, and friends ;
Would lend a wife, who they might swear
Safely, was none the worse for wear ;   1410
Would see a daughter, yet a maid,
Into a statesman's arms betray'd ;
Nay, should the girl prove coy, nor know
What daughters to a father owe,
Sooner than schemes so nobly plann'd
Should fail, themselves would lend a hand ;
Would vote on one side, whilst a brother,
Properly taught, would vote on t'other ;
Would every petty band forget ;
To public eye be with one set,   1420
In private with a second herd,
And be by proxy with a third ;
Would (like a queen, of whom I read
The other day—her name is fled—
In a book where, together bound,
Whittington and his Cat I found—
A tale most true, and free from art,
Which all Lord Mayors should have by heart—
A queen (O might those days begin
Afresh, when queens would learn to spin)   1430
Who wrought, and wrought, but, for some plot
The cause of which I've now forgot,
During the absence of the sun

Undid what she by day had done)
While they a double visage wear,
What's sworn by day, by night unswear.
  " Such be their arts, and such perchance,
May happily their ends advance ;
From a new system mine shall spring,
A *Locum tenens* is the thing.   1440
That's your true plan—to obligate
The present ministers of state,
My shadow shall our court approach,
And bear my power, and have my coach ;
My fine state-coach, superb to view,
A fine-state coach, and paid for too.
To curry favour, and the grace
Obtain of those who're out of place ;
In the mean time I—that's to say
I proper, I myself—here stay.   1450
  " But hold—perhaps unto the nation,
Who hate the Scot's administration,
To lend my coach may seem to be
Declaring for the ministry ;
For where the City-coach is, there
Is the true essence of the Mayor:
Therefore (for wise men are inten
Evils at distance to prevent,
Whilst fools the evils first endure,
And then are plagued to seek a cure)   1460
No coach—a horse—and free from fear
To make our Deputy appear,
Fast on his back shall he be tied,
With two grooms marching by his side ;
Then—for a horse—through all the land,
To head our solemn city-band,

Can any one so fit be found
As he, who in Artillery ground,
Without a rider, noble sight!
Led on our bravest troops to fight?   1470
    "But first, Crape, for my honour's sake—
A tender point—inquiry make
About that horse, if the dispute
Is ended, or is still in suit:
For whilst a cause (observe this plan
Of justice) whether horse or man
The parties be, remains in doubt,
Till 'tis determined out and out,
That power must tyranny appear
Which should, prejudging, interfere,   1480
And weak, faint judges overawe
To bias the free course of law.
    "You have my will—now quickly run,
And take care that my will be done.
In public, Crape, you must appear,
Whilst I in privacy sit here;
Here shall great Dulman sit alone,
Making this elbow-chair my throne,
And you, performing what I bid,
Do all, as if I nothing did."   1490
    Crape heard, and speeded on his way;
With him to hear was to obey;
Not without trouble, be assured,
A proper proxy was procured
To serve such infamous intent,
And such a lord to represent;
Nor could one have been found at all
On t'other side of London Wall.
    The trumpet sounds—solemn and slow

Behold the grand procession go,   1500
All moving on, cat after kind,
As if for motion ne'er design'd.
    Constables, whom the laws admit
To keep the peace by breaking it ;
Beadles, who hold the second place
By virtue of a silver mace,
Which every Saturday is drawn,
For use of Sunday, out of pawn ;
Treasurers, who with empty key
Secure an empty treasury ;   1516
Churchwardens, who their course pursue
In the same state, as to their pew
Churchwardens of St. Margaret go,
Since Peirson taught them pride and show ;
Who in short, transient pomp appear,
Like almanacks changed every year ;
Behind whom, with unbroken locks,
Charity carries the poor's box,
Not knowing that with private keys
They ope and shut it when they please ;   1520
Overseers, who by frauds ensure
The heavy curses of the poor ;
Unclean came flocking, bulls and bears,
Like beasts into the ark, by pairs.
    Portentous, flaming in the van,

1514 Mr. Peirson was a leading man in the parish committee for repairing and beautifying St. Margaret's church,
and the contest of that committee with Dr. Pearce, Dean of
Westminster, and Bishop of Rochester, about the beautifully
painted eastern window purchased by them for 400 guineas,
excited much attention. The Dean insisted upon its being
Popish and idolatrous, and demanded its removal, but without effect.

Stalk'd the Professor Sheridan,
A man of wire, a mere pantine,
A downright animal machine;
He knows alone in proper mode
How to take vengeance on an ode,   1530
And how to butcher Ammon's son
And poor Jack Dryden both in one:
On all occasions next the chair
He stands for service of the Mayor,
And to instruct him how to use
His A's and B's, and P's and Q's:
O'er letters, into tatters worn,
O'er syllables, defaced and torn,
O'er words disjointed, and o'er sense,
Left destitute of all defence,   1640
He strides; and all the way he goes
Wades, deep in blood, o'er Criss-cross-rows:
Before him every consonant
In agonies is seen to pant;
Behind, in forms not to be known,
The ghosts of tortured vowels groan.

    Next Hart and Duke, well worthy grace
And City favour, came in place:
No children can their toils engage;
Their toils are turn'd to reverend age;   1550
When a court dame, to grace his brows

[1527] A paste-board figure with movable limbs, invented by Mad. Pantini, one of Marshal Saxe's mistresses, which was much in vogue at the commencement of the last century.

[1530] Mr. Sheridan recited an ode of Dryden's at his own benefit.

[1542] Criss-cross-row, *The Alphabet.*

[1547] Dancing-masters.

Resolved, is wed to City-spouse,
Their aid with Madam's aid must join,
The awkward dotard to refine,
And teach (whence truest glory flows)
Grave sixty to turn out his toes.
Each bore in hand a kit; and each—
To show how fit he was to teach
A Cit, an Alderman, a Mayor—
Led in a string a dancing bear.   1560
    Since the revival of Fingal,
Custom—and custom's all in all—
Commands that we should have regard,
On all high seasons, to the bard.
Great acts like these, by vulgar tongue
Profaned, should not be said, but sung.
This place to fill, renown'd in fame,
The high and mighty Lockman came;
And—ne'er forgot in Dulman's reign,
With proper order to maintain   1570
The uniformity of pride,—
Brought Brother Whitehead by his side.
    On horse, who proudly paw'd the ground,
And cast his fiery eyeballs round,
Snorting, and champing the rude bit,
As if, for warlike purpose fit,
His high and generous blood disdain'd,
To be for sports and pastimes rein'd,
Great Dymoke, in his glorious station,

[1568] John Lockman, secretary to the British herring fishery, was an amiable, inoffensive man. In conversation he had some humour, but his attempts to excite merriment on paper were wretchedly unsuccessful.

[1579] Mr. Dymoke, the king's champion.

Paraded at the coronation. 1580
Not so our city Dymoke came,
Heavy, dispirited, and tame ;
No mark of sense, his eyes half-closed,
He on a mighty dray-horse dozed:
Fate never could a horse provide
So fit for such a man to ride,
Nor find a man with strictest care,
So fit for such a horse to bear.
Hung round with instruments of death,
The sight of him would stop the breath 1590
Of braggart Cowardice, and make
The very court Drawcansir quake ;
With dirks, which, in the hands of Spite,
Do their damn'd business in the night,
From Scotland sent, but here display'd
Only to fill up the parade ;
With swords, unflesh'd, of maiden hue,
Which rage or valour never drew;
With blunderbusses, taught to ride
Like pocket-pistols by his side, 1600
In girdle stuck, he seem'd to be
A little moving armoury.
One thing much wanting to complete
The sight, and make a perfect treat,
Was, that the horse, (a courtesy
In horses found of high degree)
Instead of going forward on,
All the way backward should have gone.
Horses, unless they breeding lack,
Some scruple make to turn their back, 1610
Though riders, which plain truth declares,
No scruple make of turning theirs.

Far, far apart from all the rest,
Fit only for a standing jest,
The independent, (can you get
A better suited epithet!)
The independent Amyand came,
All burning with the sacred flame
Of liberty, which well he knows
On the great stock of slavery grows.   1620
Like sparrow, who, deprived of mate
Snatch'd by the cruel hand of Fate,
From spray to spray no more will hop,
But sits alone on the house-top;
Or like himself, when all alone
At Croydon, he was heard to groan,
Lifting both hands in the defence
Of interest, and common sense;
Both hands, for as no other man
Adopted and pursued his plan,   1630
The left hand had been lonesome quite,
If he had not held up the right,—
Apart he came, and fix'd his eyes
With rapture on a distant prize,
On which, in letters worthy note,
There, twenty thousand pounds, was wrote.
False trap, for credit sapp'd is found

[1617] George and Claudius Amyand were at this period among the most eminent merchants in the city of London; the former was M.P. for Barnstaple, was created a baronet in 1764, and died in 1766. His title then descended to his son, who afterwards took the name of Cornwall. The latter was joint under-secretary of state with Henry Digby to Mr. Fox, afterwards Lord Holland. The Amyands uniformly gave the weight of their influence to administration, and took the lead in all the money negociations of the times.

By getting twenty thousand pound:
Nay, look not thus on me, and stare,
Doubting the certainty—to swear   1640
In such a case I should be loath—
But Perry Cust may take his oath.

   In plain and decent garb array'd
With the prim Quaker, Fraud, came Trade;
Connivance, to improve the plan
Habited like a juryman,
Judging as interest prevails,
Came next, with measures, weights, and scales;
Extortion next, of hellish race,
A cub most damn'd, to shew his face   1650
Forbid by fear but not by shame,
Turn'd to a Jew, like Gideon came;
Corruption, Midas-like, behold
Turning whate'er she touch'd to gold;
Impotence, led by Lust, and Pride,
Strutting with Ponton by her side;

[1642] Mr. Peregrine Cust, an eminent merchant, published an affidavit in defence of his own conduct and motives against the imputations of the "North Briton," and other popular organs.

[1652] Sampson Gideon, a Jew broker of immense wealth, who having been a staunch supporter of Sir Robert Walpole, in all his financial operations in the city, considered himself entitled to a baronetage, which Sir Robert was quite willing to concede; but strong prejudices then existing in consequence of the Jews' naturalization bill, George the Second declined conferring it; it was, however, afterwards bestowed on his son, a christian, and M.P. for Worcester, whose steady adherence to government was ultimately rewarded by an Irish peerage under the title of Lord Eardley.

[1656] Daniel Ponton, a gentleman of fortune, who had served the office of sheriff, and was in the magistracy for the county of Surrey. The warmth with which Mr. Ponton

Hypocrisy, demure and sad,
In garments of the priesthood clad,
So well disguised, that you might swear,
Deceived, a very priest was there ;   1660
Bankruptcy, full of ease and health,
And wallowing in well-saved wealth,
Came sneering through a ruin'd band,
And bringing B—— in her hand ;
Victory, hanging down her head,
Was by a Highland stallion led ;
Peace, clothed in sables, with a face
Which witness'd sense of huge disgrace,
Which spake a deep and rooted shame
Both of herself and of her name,   1670
Mourning creeps on, and, blushing, feels
War, grim War, treading on her heels ;
Pale Credit, shaken by the arts
Of men with bad heads and worse hearts,
Taking no notice of a band
Which near her were ordain'd to stand,
Well nigh destroy'd by sickly fit,
Look'd wistful all around for Pitt :
Freedom—at that most hallow'd name
My spirits mount into a flame,   1680
Each pulse beats high, and each nerve strains
Even to the cracking ; through my veins
The tides of life more rapid run,
And tell me I am Freedom's son—
Freedom came next, but scarce was seen,
When the sky, which appear'd serene
And gay before, was overcast ;

supported the cause of administration, rendered him obnoxious to the opposition. He died in 1777.

Horror bestrode a foreign blast,
And from the prison of the North,
To Freedom deadly, storms burst forth. 1690
   A car like those, in which, we're told,
Our wild forefathers warr'd of old,
Loaded with death, six horses bear
Through the blank region of the air.
Too fierce for time or art to tame,
They pour'd forth mingled smoke and flame
From their wide nostrils; every steed
Was of that ancient savage breed
Which fell Geryon nursed; their food
The flesh of man, their drink his blood. 1700
   On the first horses, ill-match'd pair,
This fat and sleek, that lean and bare,
Came ill-match'd riders side by side,
And Poverty was yoked with Pride;
Union most strange it must appear,
Till other Unions make it clear.
   Next in the gall of bitterness,
With rage, which words can ill-express,
With unforgiving rage, which springs
From a false zeal for holy things, 1710
Wearing such robes as prophets wear,
False prophets placed in Peter's chair,
On which, in characters of fire,
Shapes antic, horrible, and dire
Inwoven flamed; where, to the view,
In groups appear'd a rabble crew
Of sainted devils; where, all round,
Vile relics of vile men were found,
Who, worse than devils, from the birth
Perform'd the work of hell on earth, 1720

Jugglers, Inquisitors, and Popes,
Pointing at axes, wheels, and ropes,
And engines, framed on horrid plan,
Which none but the destroyer, man
Could, to promote his selfish views,
Have head to make or heart to use ;
Bearing, to consecrate her tricks,
In her left hand a crucifix—
Remembrance of our dying Lord ;
And in her right a two-edged sword ;   1736
Having her brows, in impious sport,
Adorn'd with words of high import,
" On earth peace, amongst men, good will ;
Love bearing, and forbearing still,"
All wrote in the heart's blood of those
Who rather death than falsehood chose ;
On her breast, (where, in days of yore,
When God loved Jews, the High Priest wore
Those oracles which were decreed
To instruct and guide the chosen seed)   1740
Having with glory clad and strength,
The Virgin pictured at full length,
Whilst at her feet, in small pourtray'd,
As scarce worth notice, Christ was laid,
Came Superstition, fierce and fell,
An imp detested, e'en in hell ;
Her eye inflamed, her face all o'er
Foully besmear'd with human gore,
O'er heaps of mangled saints she rode ;
Fast at her heels Death proudly strode,   1750

[1738] The *Rational*, a plate composed of precious stones,
which the High Priest of the Jews wore on his breast. See
Exodus, ch. **xxviii**.

And grimly smiled, well pleased to see
Such havoc of mortality:
Close by her side, on mischief bent,
And urging on each bad intent,
To its full bearing, savage, wild,
The mother fit of such a child,
Striving the empire to advance
Of Sin and Death, came Ignorance.

With looks, where dread command was placed,
And sovereign power by pride disgraced; 1760
Where, loudly witnessing a mind
Of savage, more than human kind;
Not choosing to be loved, but fear'd;
Mocking at right, Misrule appear'd,
With eyeballs glaring fiery red,
Enough to strike beholders dead:
Gnashing his teeth, and in a flood
Pouring corruption forth and blood
From his chafed jaws; without remorse
Whipping, and spurring on his horse, 1770
Whose sides, in their own blood embay'd,
E'en to the bone were open laid,
Came Tyranny, disdaining awe,
And trampling over sense and law.
One thing, and only one, he knew,
One object only would pursue;
Though less (so low doth passion bring)
Than man, he would be more than king.

With every argument and art
Which might corrupt the head and heart, 1780
Soothing the frenzy of his mind,
Companion meet, was Flattery join'd
Winning his carriage, every look

Employ'd, whilst it conceal'd, a hook;
When simple most, most to be fear'd;
Most crafty, when no craft appear'd;
His tales no man like him could tell;
His words, which melted as they fell,
Might even a hypocrite deceive,
And make an infidel believe,   1790
Wantonly cheating o'er and o'er
Those who had cheated been before.
Such Flattery came, in evil hour,
Poisoning the royal ear of power;
And, grown by prostitution great,
Would be first minister of state.

Within the chariot, all alone,
High seated on a kind of throne,
With pebbles graced, a figure came,
Whom Justice would, but dare not, name.   1800
Hard times when Justice without fear
Dare not bring forth to public ear
The names of those who dare offend
'Gainst justice, and pervert her end!
But, if the Muse afford me grace,
Description shall supply the place.

In foreign garments he was clad;
Sage ermine o'er the glossy plaid
Cast reverend honour; on his heart,
Wrought by the curious hand of Art,   1810
In silver wrought, and brighter far
Than heavenly or than earthly star,

[1812] Alluding to the Earl of Mansfield's original predilection for the Pretender. His brother was in the immediate service of the exiled family, and took an active part, with others of his clan, in measures for their restoration.

Shone a White Rose, the emblem dear
Of him he ever must revere,
Of that dread lord, who, with his host
Of faithful native rebels lost,
Like those black spirits doom'd to hell,
At once from power and virtue fell:
Around his clouded brows was placed
A bonnet, most superbly graced   1820
With mighty thistles, nor forgot
The sacred motto—"Touch me not."
   In the right hand a sword he bore
Harder than adamant, and more
Fatal than winds which from the mouth
Of the rough North invade the South;
The reeking blade to view presents
The blood of helpless innocents,
And on the hilt, as meek become
As lambs before the shearers dumb,   1830
With downcast eye, and solemn show
Of deep, unutterable woe,
Mourning the time when Freedom reign'd,
Fast to a rock was Justice chain'd.
   In his left hand, in wax imprest,
With bells and gewgaws idly drest,
An image, cast in baby mould,
He held, and seem'd o'erjoy'd to hold:
On this he fix'd his eyes; to this
Bowing, he gave the loyal kiss,   1840
And, for rebellion fully ripe,
Seem'd to desire the antitype.
What if to that Pretender's foes
His greatness, nay, his life, he owes?
Shall common obligations bind,

And shake his constancy of mind ?
Scorning such weak and petty chains,
Faithful to James he still remains
Though he the friend of George appear :
Dissimulation's virtue here.   1850
    Jealous and mean, he with a frown
Would awe, and keep all merit down ;
Nor would to truth and justice bend,
Unless out-bullied by his friend :
Brave with the coward, with the brave
He is himself a coward slave :
Awed by his fears, he has no heart
To take a great and open part :
Mines in a subtle train he springs,
And, secret, saps the ears of kings ;   1860
But not e'en there continues firm
'Gainst the resistance of a worm :
Born in a country, where the will
Of one is law to all, he still
Retain'd the infection, with full aim
To spread it wheresoe'er he came ;
Freedom he hated, law defied,
The prostitute of power and pride ;
Law he with ease explains away,
And leads bewilder'd Sense astray ;   1870
Much to the credit of his brain,
Puzzles the cause he can't maintain,
Proceeds on most familiar grounds,
And where he can't convince confounds :
Talents of rarest stamp and size,
To Nature false, he misapplies,
And turns to poison what was sent
For purposes of nourishment.

Paleness, not such as on his wings
The messenger of sickness brings,   1880
But such as takes its coward rise
From conscious baseness, conscious vice,
O'erspread his cheeks; disdain and pride,
To upstart fortunes ever tied,
Scowl'd on his brow; within his eye,
Insidious, lurking like a spy,
To caution principled by fear,
Not daring open to appear,
Lodged covert mischief: passion hung
On his lip quivering: on his tongue   1890
Fraud dwelt at large: within his breast
All that makes villain found a nest;
All that, on hell's completest plan,
E'er join'd to damn the heart of man.

    Soon as the car reach'd land, he rose,
And with a look which might have froze
The heart's best blood; which was enough
Had hearts been made of sterner stuff
In cities than elsewhere, to make
The very stoutest quail and quake,   1900
He cast his baleful eyes around:
Fix'd without motion to the ground,
Fear waiting on surprise, all stood,
And horror chill'd their curdled blood;
No more they thought of pomp, no more
(For they had seen his face before)
Of law they thought; the cause forgot,
Whether it was or Ghost, or plot,
Which drew them there: they all stood more
Like statues than they were before.   1910

    What could be done? Could art, could force,

Or both, direct a proper course
To make this savage monster tame,
Or send him back the way he came?
   What neither art, nor force, nor both,
Could do, a Lord of foreign growth,
A Lord to that base wretch allied
In country, not in vice and pride,
Effected; from the self-same land,
(Bad news for our blaspheming band   1920
Of scribblers, but deserving note)
The poison came and antidote.
Abash'd, the monster hung his head,
And like an empty vision fled;
His train, like virgin snows, which run,
Kiss'd by the burning, bawdy sun,
To lovesick streams, dissolved in air;
Joy, who from absence seem'd more fair,
Came smiling, freed from slavish awe;
Loyalty, Liberty, and Law,   1930
Impatient of the galling chain,
And yoke of power, resumed their reign;
And, burning with the glorious flame
Of public virtue, Mansfield came.

[1934] This clever artifice, by which the discomfiture of a man whom Churchill has just been vilifying in one of his most ferocious diatribes, is attributed to Lord Mansfield, the very object of his previous abuse, may have been designed by the poet to screen himself from the law. It certainly adds point to his satire.

THE CANDIDATE.

THIS Poem was written in 1764, on the contest between the Earls of Hardwicke and Sandwich for the High-stewardship of the University of Cambridge, vacant by the death of the Lord Chancellor Hardwicke. The spirit of party ran high in the University, and no means were left untried by either candidate to obtain a majority. The election was fixed for the 30th of March, when, after much altercation, the votes appearing equal, a scrutiny was demanded; whereupon the Vice-Chancellor adjourned the senate *sine die*. On appeal to the Lord High-Chancellor, he determined in favour of the Earl of Hardwicke, and a mandamus was issued accordingly.

Among the sketches of characters attributed to the Earl of Chesterfield, is one of Lord Sandwich, in which the following passage occurs:—

"The art of robbing vice of its disgust, and throwing around it the mantle of convivial pleasure, belongs in a very peculiar manner to this nobleman. I understand, that from his youth to the present time, he has proceeded in one uniform, unblushing course of debauchery and dissipation. His conversation is chiefly tinctured with unchaste expressions and indecent allusions; and some have assured me that if these were to be omitted by him, much of his wit, or, at least, what is called his wit, would be lost."

It will be remembered that it was Lord Sandwich who, in conjunction with the Earl of March (afterwards Duke of Queensbury), called the attention of the House of Lords to Wilkes' Essay on Woman, which he condemned in a speech full of virtuous horror and indignation. It began thus:—

"I have a paper in my hand, whose contents are of such a horrible and detestable nature, that I almost wonder it did not draw down the immediate vengeance of heaven upon this nation."

THE CANDIDATE.

ENOUGH of Actors—let them play the
   player,
   And, free from censure, fret, sweat,
   strut, and stare.
Garrick abroad, what motives can engage
To waste one couplet on a barren stage?
Ungrateful Garrick! when these tasty days,
In justice to themselves, allow'd thee praise;
When, at thy bidding, Sense, for twenty years
Indulged in laughter, or dissolved in tears;
When, in return for labour, time, and health,
The town had given some little share of wealth, 10
Couldst thou repine at being still a slave?
Darest thou presume to enjoy that wealth she gave?

---

[3] Garrick, in September, 1763, determined to visit the
Continent. He rightly judged that during a temporary absence the town would, upon comparison with other actors,
appreciate his superiority, and greet his return with re-
doubled pleasure. In this he was not disappointed; when
he returned in April, 1765, his first appearance was honoured
by the presence of the king. The joy of the audience was
expressed by unbounded acclamations, repeated at intervals
during his recitation of a prologue written by himself for the
occasion. His foreign tour had been of considerable service
in improving his manner and style of acting.

Couldst thou repine at laws ordain'd by those
Whom nothing but thy merit made thy foes?
Whom, too refined for honesty and trade,
By need made tradesmen, pride had bankrupts made;
Whom fear made drunkards, and, by modern rules,
Whom drink made wits, though Nature made
      them fools.
With such, beyond all pardon is thy crime,
In such a manner, and at such a time,   20
To quit the stage; but men of real sense,
Who neither lightly give, nor take offence,
Shall own thee clear, or pass an act of grace,
Since thou hast left a Powell in thy place.

    Enough of Authors—why, when scribblers fail,
Must other scribblers spread the hateful tale?
Why must they pity, why contempt express,
And why insult a brother in distress?
Let those, who boast the uncommon gift of brains
The laurel pluck, and wear it for their pains;   30

[24] William Powell, a pupil of Garrick's, and next to him and Barry, the most popular performer on the stage. His first appearance in Philaster captivated the public, and this theatrical phenomenon (for so he was called) helped to supply the chasm occasioned by his master's absence, and during two years was the great pillar of the theatre. He was endowed with great sensibility. If ever he displeased, it was from want of judgment. He occasionally ranted and blustered; would sometimes whine and blubber, and so excite ridicule when he meant to be pathetic.

Sterne, in a letter to Garrick, thus writes of Powell, "Give me some one with less smoke and more fire. There are who, like the Pharisees, still think that they shall be heard for much speaking: come, come away, my dear Garrick, and teach us another lesson."

Powell purchased a share in the patent of Covent Garden Theatre, and died at Bristol, July, 1769, at the age of 33.

Fresh on their brows for ages let it bloom,
And, ages past, still flourish round their tomb.
Let those who without genius write, and write,
Versemen or prosemen, all in Nature's spite,
The pen laid down, their course of folly run
In peace, unread, unmention'd be undone.
Why should I tell, to cross the will of Fate,
That Francis once endeavour'd to translate?
Why, sweet oblivion winding round his head,
Should I recal poor Murphy from the dead?   40
Why may not Langhorne, simple in his lay,
Effusion on effusion pour away,
With Friendship and with Fancy trifle here,
Or sleep in Pastoral at Belvidere?
Sleep let them all, with Dulness on her throne,
Secure from any malice but their own.
    Enough of Critics—let them, if they please,
Fond of new pomp, each month pass new decrees;
Wide and extensive be their infant state,
Their subjects many, and those subjects great, 50
Whilst all their mandates as sound law succeed
With fools who write, and greater fools who read.
What though they lay the realms of Genius waste,
Fetter the fancy and debauch the taste;
Though they, like doctors, to approve their skill,
Consult not how to cure, but how to kill;
Though by whim, envy, or resentment led,
They damn those authors whom they never read;

[38] The Rev. Philip Francis, the translator of Horace, often
attacked by Churchill.

[41] John Langhorne, D.D. still remembered as the popular
translator of Plutarch. He was also the author of a mixture
of prose and verse called "Effusions of Friendship and
Fancy," and of several pastoral poems

Though, other rules unknown, one rule they hold,
To deal out so much praise for so much gold: 60
Though Scot with Scot, in damnëd close intrigues,
Against the commonwealth of letters leagues;
Uncensured let them pilot at the helm,
And rule in letters, as they ruled the realm:
Ours be the curse, the mean, tame coward's curse,
(Nor could ingenious Malice make a worse,
To do our sense, and honour deep despite)
To credit what they say, read what they write.

    Enough of Scotland—let her rest in peace;   69
The cause removed, effects of course should cease.
Why should I tell how Tweed, too mighty grown,
And proudly swell'd with waters not his own,
Burst o'er his banks, and, by destruction led,
O'er our faint England desolation spread,
Whilst, riding on his waves, Ambition, plumed
In tenfold pride, the port of Bute assumed,
Now that the river god, convinced, though late,
And yielding, though reluctantly, to Fate,
Holds his fair course, and with more humble tides,
In tribute to the sea, as usual, glides?   80

    Enough of States, and such like trifling things;
Enough of kinglings, and enough of kings;
Henceforth, secure let ambush'd statesmen lie,
Spread the court web, and catch the patriot fly;
Henceforth, unwhipt of Justice, uncontroll'd
By fear or shame, let Vice, secure and bold,
Lord it with all her sons, whilst Virtue's groan
Meets with compassion only from the throne.

    Enough of Patriots—all I ask of man
Is only to be honest as he can: 90
Some have deceived, and some may still deceive;

'Tis the fool's curse at random to believe.
Would those, who, by opinion placed on high,
Stand fair and perfect in their country's eye,
Maintain that honour, let me in their ear
Hint this essential doctrine—Persevere.
Should they (which Heaven forbid) to win the grace
Of some proud courtier, or to gain a place,
Their king and country sell, with endless shame
The avenging Muse shall mark each trait'rous name;
But if, to honour true, they scorn to bend,   101
And, proudly honest, hold out to the end,
Their grateful country shall their fame record,
And I myself descend to praise a lord.

Enough of Wilkes—with good and honest men
His actions speak much stronger than my pen,
And future ages shall his name adore,
When he can act and I can write no more.
England may prove ungrateful and unjust,   109
But fostering France shall ne'er betray her trust:
'Tis a brave debt which gods on men impose,
To pay with praise the merit e'en of foes.
When the great warrior of Amilcar's race
Made Rome's wide empire tremble to her base,
To prove her virtue, though it gall'd her pride,
Rome gave that fame which Carthage had denied.

Enough of Self—that darling, luscious theme,

---

[110] Wilkes, at this time, had withdrawn to France, to avoid
the double prosecution hanging over him for No. 45 of the
North Briton, and the Essay on Woman.   A tolerably ac-
curate delineation of Wilkes' character may be found in
Charles Johnson's " Chrysal."   It is true that in pursuing
his own ends Wilkes did good service to the public, but even
his political life was very far from deserving Churchill's exaggerated panegyrics.

O'er which philosophers in raptures dream;
Of which with seeming disregard they write, 119
Then prizing most, when most they seem to slight;
Vain proof of folly tinctured strong with pride!
What man can from himself himself divide?
For me, (nor dare I lie) my leading aim
(Conscience first satisfied) is love of fame;
Some little fame derived from some brave few,
Who prizing Honour, prize her votaries too.
Let all (nor shall resentment flush my cheek)
Who know me well, what they know, freely speak,
So those (the greatest curse I meet below)
Who know me not, may not pretend to know. 130
Let none of those, whom, bless'd with parts
        above
My feeble genius, still I dare to love,
Doing more mischief than a thousand foes,
Posthumous nonsense to the world expose,
And call it mine, for mine, though never known,
Or which, if mine, I living blush'd to own.
Know all the world, no greedy heir shall find,
Die when I will, one couplet left behind.
Let none of those, whom I despise though great,
Pretending friendship to give malice weight, 140
Publish my life; let no false, sneaking peer,
(Some such there are) to win the public ear,
Hand me to shame with some vile anecdote,

138 Churchill, before his death, destroyed all his manu-
scripts, excepting the Dedication to his Sermons, and the
Journey, though he had completed neither of these poems.
141 John Boyle, Earl of Cork and Orrery, the translator of
Pliny's Letters, was also the author of Observations on the
Life of Swift, whose memory is not treated in them either
with candour or impartiality.

Nor soul-gall'd bishop damn me with a note.
Let one poor sprig of bay around my head
Bloom whilst I live, and point me out when dead ;
Let it, (may Heaven, indulgent, grant that prayer)
Be planted on my grave, nor wither there ;
And when, on travel bound, some rhyming guest
Roams through the Churchyard, whilst his dinner's
      drest,   150
Let it hold up this comment to his eyes—
Life to the last enjoy'd, here Churchill lies ;
Whilst (O, what joy that pleasing flattery gives !)
Reading my Works, he cries—Here Churchill lives.
    Enough of Satire—in less harden'd times
Great was her force, and mighty were her rhymes.
I've read of men, beyond man's daring brave,
Who yet have trembled at the strokes she gave ;
Whose souls have felt more terrible alarms
From her one line, than from a world in arms : 160
When in her faithful and immortal page
They saw transmitted down from age to age
Recorded villains, and each spotted name
Branded with marks of everlasting shame,
Succeeding villains sought her as a friend,
And, if not really mended, feign'd to mend.
But in an age, when actions are allow'd
Which strike all honour dead, and crimes avow'd
Too terrible to suffer the report,
Avow'd and praised by men who stain a court, 170
Propp'd by the arm of Power; when Vice, high-born,

    [144] The reader hardly requires a prompter to remind him
that Warburton is the person alluded to in this line.
    [152] This line is still to be read on the tombstone of
Churchill—not the original stone, but a more modern one—
in the churchyard of St. Martin's, Dover.

High-bred, high-station'd, holds rebuke in scorn;
When she is lost to every thought of fame;
And, to all virtue dead, is dead to shame;
When Prudence a much easier task must hold
To make a new world, than reform the old,
Satire throws by her arrows on the ground,
And if she cannot cure, she will not wound.

Come, Panegyric—though the Muse disdains,
Founded on truth, to prostitute her strains   180
At the base instance of those men, who hold
No argument but power, no god but gold,
Yet, mindful that from heaven she drew her birth,
She scorns the narrow maxims of this earth;
Virtuous herself, brings Virtue forth to view,
And loves to praise, where praise is justly due.

Come, Panegyric—in a former hour,
My soul with pleasure yielding to thy power;
Thy shrine I sought; I pray'd; but wanton air,
Before it reach'd thy ears, dispersed my prayer;
E'en at thy altars whilst I took my stand,   191
The pen of truth and honour in my hand,
Fate, meditating wrath 'gainst me and mine,
Chid my fond zeal, and thwarted my design,
Whilst, Hayter brought too quickly to his end,
I lost a subject and mankind a friend.

[195] Dr. Thomas Hayter, Bishop of Norwich, was the
natural son of Blackbourn, Archbishop of York. In Sept.
1761, he was translated to the See of London, when his
powers both of mind and body were still in their full vigour;
but he had no opportunity of displaying them in that station,
as he died the year after. He was the intimate friend
of Jortin and of Clarke, and had been appointed, in 1759,
Governor to George the Third, then Prince of Wales, but
was abruptly dismissed by the Princess Dowager and Lord
Bute.

Come, Panegyric—bending at thy throne,
Thee and thy power my soul is proud to own:
Be thou my kind protector, thou my guide,
And lead me safe through passes yet untried.
Broad is the road, nor difficult to find,,   200
Which to the house of Satire leads mankind;
Narrow, and unfrequented, are the ways,
Scarce found out in an age, which lead to Praise.

What though no theme I choose of vulgar note,
Nor wish to write as brother bards have wrote,
So mild, so meek in praising, that they seem
Afraid to wake their patrons from a dream?
What though a theme I choose, which might demand
The nicest touches of a master's hand?   210
Yet, if the inward workings of my soul
Deceive me not, I shall attain the goal,
And Envy shall behold, in triumph raised,
The poet praising, and the patron praised.

What patron shall I choose? shall public voice,
Or private knowledge, influence my choice?
Shall I prefer the grand retreat of Stowe,
Or, seeking patriots, to friend Wildman's go?
"To Wildman's!" cried Discretion, (who had heard,
Close standing at my elbow, every word)   220
"To Wildman's! art thou mad? canst thou be sure

²¹⁷ Then the magnificent seat of Earl Temple, and afterwards of the Duke of Buckingham.
²¹⁸ The minority, with the Duke of Devonshire at their
head, established a society at a tavern kept by one Wildman,
a brother-in-law of Mr. J. H. Tooke. This institution was
intended merely to keep the party together, without entering
into any political discussions. On the apostacy of many of
the members, the association dwindled away; and the death
of the Duke of Devonshire occasioned the dissolution of the
society.

One moment there to have thy head secure ?
Are they not all (let observation tell)
All mark'd in characters as black as hell ;
In Doomsday book, by ministers set down,
Who style their pride the honour of the crown ?
Make no reply—let reason stand aloof—
Presumptions here must pass as solemn proof.
That settled faith, that love which ever springs
In the best subjects, for the best of kings,   230
Must not be measured now, by what men think,
Or say, or do—by what they eat and drink ;
Where and with whom, that question's to be tried
And statesmen are the judges to decide ;
No juries call'd, or, if call'd, kept in awe ;
They, facts confess'd, in themselves rest the law.
Each dish at Wildman's of sedition smacks ;
Blasphemy may be gospel at Almack's."
    Peace, good Discretion ! peace—thy fears are
            vain ;
Ne'er will I herd with Wildman's factious train ;
Never the vengeance of the great incur,   241

238 The first famous Almack's, a noted Tory club-house in
Pall Mall.
240 Wildman was a wine-merchant, and originally kept
a coffee-house in Bedford Street, Covent Garden, which was
frequented by the most vehement of Wilkes's supporters in
Westminster. In 1765, he obtained the situation of Cofferer
of the wine-cellar in the royal household.
    Wildman with Gay and Cotes acted subordinate parts in
the discreditable dispute between John Wilkes and John
Horne (afterwards Tooke), about some old clothes which the
latter alleged had been purchased for Wilkes when at Paris,
by Wildman, and sold or pawned by the former. Horne also
charged Wilkes with having given him a draft on his banker
for £1500, when he knew he had not fifteen pence in the
world.

Nor, without might, against the mighty stir.
If, from long proof, my temper you distrust,
Weigh my profession, to my gown be just;
Dost thou one parson know so void of grace
To pay his court to patrons out of place?

If still you doubt (though scarce a doubt remains)
Search through my alter'd heart, and try my reins;
There, searching, find, nor deem me now in sport,
A convert made by Sandwich to the court.　250
Let madmen follow error to the end,
I, of mistakes convinced, and proud to mend,
Strive to act better, being better taught,
Nor blush to own that change which reason wrought:
For such a change as this, must justice speak;
My heart was honest, but my head was weak.

Bigot to no one man, or set of men,
Without one selfish view, I drew my pen;
My country ask'd, or seem'd to ask, my aid,
Obedient to that call, I left off trade;　260
A side I chose, and on that side was strong,
Till time hath fairly proved me in the wrong:
Convinced, I change, (can any man do more?)
And have not greater patriots changed before?
Changed, I at once (can any man do less?)
Without a single blush, that change confess;
Confess it with a manly kind of pride,
And quit the losing for the winning side,
Granting, whilst virtuous Sandwich holds the rein,
What Bute for ages might have sought in vain. 270

250 John Montagu, fourth Earl of Sandwich, was in Sept. 1763, appointed one of the principal Secretaries of State. He acquired, at different periods, the soubriquets of Lothario, from the hero of the Fair Penitent, and of Jemmy Twitcher, one of Macheath's gang in the Beggar's Opera.

Hail, Sandwich—nor shall Wilkes resentment
    show,
Hearing the praises of so brave a foe!
Hail, Sandwich—nor, through pride, shalt thou
    refuse
The grateful tribute of so mean a Muse—
Sandwich, all hail—when Bute with foreign hand,
Grown wanton with ambition, scourged the land ;
When Scots, or slaves to Scotsmen, steer'd the helm;
When peace, inglorious peace, disgraced the realm,
Distrust, and general discontent prevail'd ;
But when, (he best knows why) his spirits fail'd ;
When, with a sudden panic struck, he fled,   281
Sneak'd out of power, and hid his miscreant head ;
When, like a Mars, (fear order'd to retreat)
We saw thee nimbly vault into his seat,
Into the seat of power, at one bold leap,
A perfect connoisseur in statesmanship ;
When, like another Machiavel, we saw
Thy fingers twisting, and untwisting law,
Straining, where godlike Reason bade, and where
She warranted thy mercy, pleased to spare ;   290
Saw thee resolved, and fix'd (come what come might)
To do thy God, thy king, thy country right ;
All things were changed ; suspense remain'd no
    more ;
Certainty reign'd where doubt had reign'd before :
All felt thy virtues, and all knew their use ;

281 Lord Bute, finding the whole English nation exas-
perated against him after the Excise Bill had received the
royal assent, resigned, having continued in power ten months
and ten days. He immediately retired to Harrowgate, glad
to escape from the threatening insults of the infuriated London populace.

What virtues such as thine must needs produce.
  Thy foes (for honour ever meets with foes)
Too mean to praise, too fearful to oppose,
In sullen silence sit; thy friends (some few,   299
Who, friends to thee, are friends to honour too)
Plaud thy brave bearing, and the Commonweal
Expects her safety from thy stubborn zeal.
A place amongst the rest the Muses claim,
And bring this free-will offering to thy fame;
To prove their virtue, make thy virtues known,
And, holding up thy fame, secure their own.
  From his youth upwards to the present day,
When vices, more than years, have mark'd him
        gray;
When riotous excess, with wasteful hand,   309
Shakes life's frail glass, and hastes each ebbing sand,
Unmindful from what stock he drew his birth,
Untainted with one deed of real worth,
Lothario, holding honour at no price,
Folly to folly added, vice to vice;
Wrought sin with greediness, and sought for shame
With greater zeal than good men seek for fame.
  Where (reason left without the least defence)
Laughter was mirth, obscenity was sense;
Where Impudence made Decency submit;   319
Where noise was humour, and where whim was wit;
Where rude, untemper'd license had the merit
Of liberty, and lunacy was spirit;
Where the best things were ever held the worst,
Lothario was, with justice, always first.
  To whip a top, to knuckle down at taw,
To swing upon a gate, to ride a straw,
To play at push-pin with dull brother peers,

To belch out catches in a porter's ears,
To reign the monarch of a midnight cell,
To be the gaping chairman's oracle,   330
Whilst, in most blessèd union, rogue and whore
Clap hands, huzza, and hiccup out Encore;
Whilst gray Authority, who slumbers there
In robes of watchman's fur, gives up his chair;
With midnight howl to bay the affrighted moon,
To walk with torches through the streets at noon;
To force plain nature from her usual way,
Each night a vigil, and a blank each day;
To match for speed one feather 'gainst another,
To make one leg run races with his brother;   340
'Gainst all the rest to take the northern wind,
Bute to ride first, and he to ride behind;
To coin newfangled wagers, and to lay 'em,
Laying to lose, and losing not to pay 'em,—
Lothario, on that stock which nature gives,
Without a rival stands, though March yet lives.

When Folly, (at that name in duty bound,
Let subject myriads kneel, and kiss the ground,
Whilst they who in the presence upright stand
Are held as rebels through the loyal land)   350
Queen every where, but most a queen in courts,
Sent forth her heralds, and proclaim'd her sports;
Bade fool with fool on her behalf engage,
And prove her right to reign from age to age,
Lothario, great above the common size,
With all engaged, and won from all the prize;
Her cap he wears, which from his youth he wore,
And every day deserves it more and more.

Nor in such limits rests his soul confined;
Folly may share, but can't engross his mind;   360

Vice, bold, substantial Vice puts in her claim,
And stamps him perfect in the books of shame.
Observe his follies well, and you would swear
Folly had been his first, his only care;
Observe his vices, you'll that oath disown,
And swear that he was born for vice alone.

Is the soft nature of some hapless maid,
Fond, easy, full of faith, to be betray'd;
Must she, to virtue lost, be lost to fame,   369
And he who wrought her guilt declare her shame;
Is some brave friend, who, men but little known,
Deems every heart as honest as his own,
And, free himself, in others fears no guile,
To be ensnared, and ruin'd with a smile;
Is law to be perverted from her course;
Is abject fraud to league with brutal force;
Is freedom to be crush'd, and every son
Who dares maintain her cause, to be undone;
Is base corruption, creeping through the land,
To plan, and work her ruin, underhand,   380
With regular approaches, sure, though slow;
Or must she perish by a single blow;
Are kings—who trust to servants, and depend
In servants (fond, vain thought!) to find a friend—
To be abused, and made to draw their breath
In darkness thicker than the shades of death;
Is God's most holy name to be profaned,
His word rejected, and his laws arraign'd,
His servants scorn'd, as men who idly dream'd,
His service laugh'd at, and his Son blasphemed;
Are debauchees in morals to preside;   391
Is faith to take an Atheist for her guide;

    367 The first ed. has "easy maid'

Is Science by a blockhead to be led ;
Are states to totter on a drunkard's head ;—
To answer all these purposes, and more,
More black than ever villain plann'd before,
Search earth, search hell, the devil cannot find
An agent, like Lothario, to his mind.

Is this nobility, which, sprung from kings,
Was meant to swell the power from whence it springs?
Is this the glorious produce, this the fruit,   401
Which Nature hoped for from so rich a root?
Were there but two, (search all the world around)
Were there but two such nobles to be found,
The very name would sink into a term
Of scorn, and man would rather be a worm
Than be a lord: but Nature, full of grace,
Nor meaning birth and titles to be base,
Made only one, and having made him, swore,
In mercy to mankind, to make no more :   410
Nor stopp'd she there, but, like a generous friend,
The ills which error caused, she strove to mend,
And having brought Lothario forth to view,
To save her credit, brought forth Sandwich too.

Gods ! with what joy, what honest joy of heart,
Blunt as I am, and void of every art,
Of every art which great ones in the state
Practise on knaves they fear, and fools they hate,
To titles with reluctance taught to bend,
Nor prone to think that virtues can descend,   420
Do I behold (a sight, alas ! more rare
Than honesty could wish) the noble wear
His father's honours, when his life makes known
They're his by virtue, not by birth alone ;
When he recals his father from the grave,

And pays with interest back that fame he gave:
Cured of her splenetic and sullen fits,
To such a peer my willing soul submits,
And to such virtue is more proud to yield
Than 'gainst ten titled rogues to keep the field.
Such, (for that truth e'en envy shall allow)   431
Such Wyndham was, and such is Sandwich now.

O gentle Montagu, in blessed hour
Didst thou start up, and climb the stairs of power;
England of all her fears at once was eased,
Nor, 'mongst her many foes was one displeased :
France heard the news, and told it cousin Spain ;
Spain heard, and told it cousin France again ;
The Hollander relinquish'd his design
Of adding spice to spice, and mine to mine;   440
Of Indian villanies he thought no more,
Content to rob us on our native shore :
Awed by thy fame, (which winds with open mouth
Shall blow from east to west, from north to south)
The western world shall yield us her increase,
And her wild sons be soften'd into peace ;
Rich eastern monarchs shall exhaust their stores,
And pour unbounded wealth on Albion's shores :
Unbounded wealth, which from those golden scenes,
And all acquired by honourable means,   450
Some honourable chief shall hither steer,
To pay our debts, and set the nation clear.

Nabobs themselves, allured by thy renown,

---

433 The affairs of the East India Company were at this
time in complete confusion. India was mismanaged by an
oligarchy perhaps more oppressive than any other government that has ever existed. The directors became the setters
up and pullers down of kings; Meer Jaffier and Meer Cossim
were the mere puppets of the council at Calcutta.

Shall pay due homage to the English crown ;
Shall freely as their king our king receive—
Provided the Directors give them leave.

Union at home shall mark each rising year,
Nor taxes be complain'd of, though severe ;
Envy her own destroyer shall become,   459
And Faction with her thousand mouths be dumb:
With the meek man thy meekness shall prevail,
Nor with the spirited thy spirit fail :
Some to thy force of reason shall submit,
And some be converts to thy princely wit :
Reverence for thee shall still a nation's cries,
A grand concurrence crown a grand excise :
And unbelievers of the first degree,
Who have no faith in God, have faith in thee.

When a strange jumble, whimsical and vain,
Possess'd the region of each heated brain ;   470
When some were fools to censure, some to praise,
And all were mad, but mad in different ways ;
When commonwealthsmen, starting at the shade
.Which in their own wild fancy had been made,
Of tyrants dream'd, who wore a thorny crown,
And with state bloodhounds hunted Freedom down:
When others, struck with fancies not less vain,
Saw mighty kings by their own subjects slain,
And, in each friend of liberty and law,
With horror big, a future Cromwell saw,   480
Thy manly zeal stept forth, bade discord cease,
And sung each jarring atom into peace ;
Liberty, cheer'd by thy all-cheering eye,
Shall, waking from her trance, live and not die ;
And, patronized by thee, Prerogative
Shall, striding forth at large, not die, but live ;

Whilst Privilege, hung betwixt earth and sky,
Shall not well know whether to live or die.
When on a rock which overhung the flood, 489
And seem'd to totter, Commerce shivering stood;
When Credit, building on a sandy shore,
Saw the sea swell, and heard the tempest roar,
Heard death in every blast, and in each wave
Or saw, or fancied that she saw her grave;
When property, transferr'd from hand to hand,
Weaken'd by change, crawl'd sickly through the
      land;
When mutual confidence was at an end,
And man no longer could on man depend;
Oppress'd with debts of more than common weight,
When all men fear'd a bankruptcy of state; 500
When, certain death to honour and to trade,
A sponge was talk'd of as our only aid;
That to be saved we must be more undone,
And pay off all our debts, by paying none;
Like England's better genius, born to bless,
And snatch his sinking country from distress,
Didst thou step forth, and, without sail or oar,
Pilot the shatter'd vessel safe to shore:
Nor shalt thou quit, till, anchor'd firm and fast,
She rides secure, and mocks the threatening blast!
Born in thy house, and in thy service bred, 511
Nursed in thy arms, and at thy table fed,
By thy sage councils to reflection brought,
Yet more by pattern than by precept taught,
Economy her needful aid shall join
To forward and complete thy grand design;

⁴⁹⁹ The national debt on the 5th of January, 1764,
amounted to about £130,000,000.

And, warm to save, but yet with spirit warm,
Shall her own conduct from thy conduct form.
Let friends of prodigals say what they will,
Spendthrifts at home, abroad are spendthrifts still.
In vain have sly and subtle sophists tried   521
Private from public justice to divide;
For credit on each other they rely;
They live together, and together die.
'Gainst all experience 'tis a rank offence,
High treason in the eye of common sense,
To think a statesman ever can be known
To pay our debts, who will not pay his own:
But now, though late, now may we hope to see
Our debts discharged, our credit fair and free, 530
Since rigid Honesty, (fair fall that hour!)
Sits at the helm, and Sandwich is in power.
With what delight I view thee, wondrous man!
With what delight survey thy sterling plan,
That plan which all with wonder must behold,
And stamp thy age the only age of Gold!
    Nor rest thy triumphs here—that Discord fled,
And sought with grief the hell where she was bred;
That Faction, 'gainst her nature forced to yield,
Saw her rude rabble scatter'd o'er the field,   540
Saw her best friends a standing jest become,
Her fools turn'd speakers, and her wits struck
       dumb;
That our most bitter foes (so much depends
On men of name) are turn'd to cordial friends;
That our offended friends (such terror flows
From men of name) dare not appear our foes;
That Credit, gasping in the jaws of death,
And ready to expire with every breath,

Grows stronger from disease ; that thou hast saved
Thy drooping country; that thy name, engraved
On plates of brass, defies the rage of time ;   551
Than plates of brass more firm that sacred rhyme
Embalms thy memory, bids thy glories live,
And gives thee what the muse alone can give—
These heights of virtue, these rewards of fame,
With thee in common other patriots claim.

But, that poor, sickly Science, who had laid
And droop'd for years beneath neglect's cold shade,
By those who knew her purposely forgot,   559
And made the jest of those who knew her not,
Whilst ignorance in power, and pamper'd pride,
" Clad like a priest, pass'd by on t'other side,"
Recover'd from her wretched state, at length
Puts on new health, and clothes herself with
          strength,
To thee we owe, and to thy friendly hand
Which raised, and gave her to possess the land :
This praise, though in a court, and near a throne,
This praise is thine, and thine, alas ! alone.

With what fond rapture did the goddess smile,
What blessings doth she promise to this isle,   570
What honour to herself, and length of reign,
Soon as she heard that thou didst not disdain
To be her steward ; but what grief, what shame,
What rage, what disappointment, shook her frame,
When her proud children dared her will dispute,
When youth was insolent, and age was mute !

That young men should be fools, and some wild few
To wisdom deaf, be deaf to interest too,

576 The younger members of the University were unani-
mous in favour of Lord Hardwicke.

Moved not her wonder ; but that men, grown gray
In search of wisdom ; men who own'd the sway
Of reason ; men who stubbornly kept down   581
Each rising passion ; men who wore the gown ;
That *they* should cross her will, that they should
     dare
Against the cause of Interest to declare ;
That they should be so abject and unwise,
Having no fear of loss before their eyes,
Nor hopes of gain ; scorning the ready means
Of being vicars, rectors, canons, deans,
With all those honours which on mitres wait,
And mark the virtuous favourites of state ;   590
That they should dare a Hardwicke to support,
And talk, within the hearing of a court,
Of that vile beggar Conscience, who, undone,
And starved herself, starves every wretched son ;—
This turn'd her blood to gall, this made her swear
No more to throw away her time and care
On wayward sons who scorn'd her love ; no more
To hold her courts on Cam's ungrateful shore.
Rather than bear such insults, which disgrace
Her royalty of nature, birth, and place,   600
Though Dulness there unrivall'd state doth keep,
Would she at Winchester with Burton sleep ;

602 Dr. John Burton, head master of Winchester school.
It was stated in the Auditor, that Wilkes, while stationed at
Winchester, in command of the Buckinghamshire militia,
had used the most insulting language towards the Earl of
Bute in the hearing of one of that nobleman's sons, who was
at school there. This story gaining ground, as it was un-
contradicted, if not circulated, by the young man, Wilkes
wrote a letter to Dr. Burton asking for an investigation ; but
he declined to concern himself in the affair.

Or, to exchange the mortifying scene
For something still more dull, and still more mean,
Rather than bear such insults, she would fly
Far, far beyond the search of English eye,
And reign amongst the Scots: to be a queen
Is worth ambition, though in Aberdeen.
O, stay thy flight, fair Science; what though some,
Some base-born children, rebels are become?   610
All are not rebels; some are duteous still,
Attend thy precepts, and obey thy will;
Thy interest is opposed by those alone
Who either know not, or oppose their own.

Of stubborn virtue, marching to thy aid,
Behold in black, the livery of their trade,
Marshall'd by Form, and by Discretion led,
A grave, grave troop, and Smith is at their head,
Black Smith of Trinity; on Christian ground
For faith in mysteries none more renown'd.   620

Next, (for the best of causes now and then
Must beg assistance from the worst of men)
Next (if old Story lies not) sprung from Greece,
Comes Pandarus, but comes without his niece:
Her, wretched maid! committed to his trust,
To a rank letcher's coarse and bloated lust
The arch, old, hoary hypocrite had sold,
And thought himself and her well damn'd for gold.
But (to wipe off such traces from the mind,

619 Dr. Smith, master of Trinity College, Cambridge, died
in 1768, in the 79th year of his age.   By his will he left the
interest of £2000 for the annual repairs of his college;
£2500 to the University.   He was master of mechanics to
the King, and had been preceptor to William, Duke of Cum-
berland.   He published in 1744, Harmonies, or the Philosophy of Musical Sounds, 8vo.

And make us in good humour with mankind)　630
Leading on men, who, in a college bred,
No woman knew, but those which made their bed ;
Who, planted virgins on Cam's virtuous shore,
Continued still male virgins at threescore,
Comes Sumner, wise, and chaste as chaste can be,
With Long, as wise, and not less chaste than he.
　　Are there not friends, too, enter'd in thy cause
Who, for thy sake, defying penal laws,
Were, to support thy honourable plan,
Smuggled from Jersey, and the Isle of Man ?　640
Are there not Philomaths of high degree
Who, always dumb before, shall speak for thee ?
Are there not Proctors, faithful to thy will,
One of full growth, others in embryo still,
Who may, perhaps, in some ten years, or more,
Be ascertain'd that two and two make four,
Or may a still more happy method find,
And, taking one from two, leave none behind ?
　　With such a mighty power on foot, to yield
Were death to manhood ; better in the field　650
To leave our carcasses, and die with fame,
Than fly, and purchase life on terms of shame.
Sackvilles alone anticipate defeat,
And ere they dare the battle, sound retreat.

[635] The Rev. Dr. Humphry Sumner, Vice-Chancellor of the University of Cambridge, and provost of King's College.
[636] Roger Long, D.D. F.R.S. master of Pembroke Hall, Cambridge, and professor of Astronomy in that University. He died in 1770, at the advanced age of 91.　He wrote a Treatise on Astronomy, 2 vols. 4to, and with a view to popularize that science, he caused to be constructed a hollow sphere, wherein thirty persons could sit conveniently, and on the inner surface of which was a representation of the heavens as they would appear in a north latitude.

But if persuasions ineffectual prove,
If arguments are vain, nor prayers can move,
Yet in thy bitterness of frantic woe
Why talk of Burton? why to Scotland go?
Is there not Oxford, she, with open arms,
Shall meet thy wish, and yield up all her charms;
Shall for thy love her former loves resign,   660
And jilt the banish'd Stuarts to be thine.

Bow'd to the yoke, and, soon as she could read,
Tutor'd to get, by heart, the despot's creed,
She, of subjection proud, shall knee thy throne,
And have no principles but thine alone;
She shall thy will implicitly receive,
Nor act, nor speak, nor think, without thy leave.
Where is the glory of imperial sway
If subjects none but just commands obey?   670
Then, and then only, is obedience seen,
When by command they dare do all that's mean:
Hither then wing thy flight, here fix thy stand,
Nor fail to bring thy Sandwich in thy hand.

Gods! with what joy, (for fancy now supplies,
And lays the future open to my eyes)
Gods! with what joy I see the worthies meet,
And Brother Lichfield Brother Sandwich greet!
Blest be your greetings, blest each dear embrace;
Blest to yourselves, and to the human race.   680
Sickening at virtues, which she cannot reach,
Which seem her baser nature to impeach,

---

678 George Henry Lee, third Earl of Lichfield, succeeded
the Earl of Westmoreland, as Chancellor of the University of
Oxford, in 1762, after a very severe contest between him
and Lords Foley and Suffolk; his success was principally
owing to the interference of Lord Bute in his favour.

Let Envy, in a whirlwind's bosom hurl'd,
Outrageous, search the corners of the world,
Ransack the present times, look back to past,
Rip up the future, and confess at last,
No times, past, present, or to come, could e'er
Produce, and bless the world with such a pair.

Phillips, the good old Phillips, out of breath, 689
Escaped from Monmouth, and escaped from death,
Shall hail his Sandwich with that virtuous zeal,
That glorious ardour for the commonweal,
Which warm'd his loyal heart and bless'd his tongue,
When on his lips the cause of rebels hung.

Whilst Womanhood, in habit of a nun,
At Mednam lies, by backward monks undone;

[689] Sir John Phillips, a barrister and an active member of
the House of Commons, who during the rebellion of 1745,
intrenching himself behind legal forms, had at a public
meeting threatened to present to the Court of King's Bench,
as an illegal levying of money upon the subject, the association formed for the defence of the family upon the throne.
In 1763 he was called to the privy council, and died the
following year.

[696] Medmenham, or, as it was commonly called, Mednam
Abbey, was a very large house on the banks of the Thames,
near Marlow, in Bucks. It was formerly a convent of Cis-
tertian Monks. The situation is remarkably fine. Sir Francis
Dashwood, Sir Thomas Stapleton, Paul Whitehead, Mr.
Wilkes, and other gentlemen, to the number of twelve,
rented the abbey, and often retired there in the summer.
Among other amusements they had sometimes a mock cele-
bration of the mysterious midnight orgies of Pagan worship,
and occasionally of the rites of the foreign religious orders
among the Roman Catholics.

" Over the grand entrance was the famous inscription on
Rabelais' abbey of Theleme, *Fay ce que voudras*.   At the end
of the passage over the door was *Aude, hospes, contemnere opes.*
At one end of the refectory was Harpocrates, the god of
silence; at the other the goddess Angerona, that the same
duty might be enjoined on both sexes."

A nation's reckoning, like an alehouse score,
Whilst Paul, the aged, chalks behind a door,
Compell'd to hire a foe to cast it up,
Dashwood shall pour, from a communion cup,   700
Libations to the goddess without eyes,
And hob or nob in cyder and excise.

   From those deep shades, where Vanity, unknown.
Doth penance for her pride, and pines alone,
Cursed in herself, by her own thoughts undone,
Where she sees all, but can be seen by none;
Where she no longer, mistress of the schools,
Hears praise loud pealing from the mouths of fools,
Or hears it at a distance; in despair
To join the crowd, and put in for a share,   710
Twisting each thought a thousand different ways,
For his new friends new-modelling old praise;
Where frugal sense so very fine is spun,
It serves twelve hours, though not enough for one,
King shall arise, and, bursting from the dead,
Shall hurl his piebald Latin at thy head.

   Burton (whilst awkward affectation's hung
In quaint and labour'd accents on his tongue;
Who 'gainst their will makes junior blockheads
     speak,
Ignorant of both, new Latin and new Greek,   720

---

   698 Paul Whitehead. See The Ghost, Book iii. l. 95, note.
   715 Dr. William King, LL.D. principal of St. Mary's
Hall, died at an advanced age in 1764, at which time he was
the oldest head of any house in the University of Oxford,
having been appointed to that situation in 1719. The composition of his celebrated Radcliffe harangue and the Tory
principles it advocated afforded an ample field of controversy
to critics, but it earned for him an elegant compliment from
Warton in his Triumph of Isis.

Not such as was in Greece and Latium known,
But of a modern cut, and all his own;
Who threads, like beads, loose thoughts on such a
     string,
They're praise and censure; nothing, every thing;
Pantomime thoughts, and style so full of trick,
They even make a Merry Andrew sick;
Thoughts all so dull, so pliant in their growth,
They're verse, they're prose, they're neither, and
     they're both)
Shall (though by nature ever loath to praise)
Thy curious worth set forth in curious phrase; 730
Obscurely stiff, shall press poor sense to death,
Or in long periods run her out of breath;
Shall make a babe, for which, with all his fame.
Adam could not have found a proper name,
Whilst, beating out his features to a smile,
He hugs the bastard brat, and calls it Style.

    Hush'd be all nature as the land of death;
Let each stream sleep, and each wind hold his breath;
Be the bells muffled, nor one sound of care,
Pressing for audience, wake the slumbering air; 740
Browne comes—behold how cautiously he creeps—
How slow he walks, and yet how fast he sleeps—
But to thy praise in sleep he shall agree;
He cannot wake, but he shall dream of thee.

    Physic, her head with opiate poppies crown'd,
Her loins by the chaste matron Camphire bound;
Physic, obtaining succour from the pen

---

741 Dr. William Browne, Lord Lichfield's Vice-Chancellor
of the University of Oxford from 1759 to 1769; he was also
provost of Queen's College.

Of her soft son, her gentle Heberden,
If there are men who can thy virtue know,
Yet spite of virtue treat thee as a foe,   750
Shall, like a scholar, stop their rebel breath,
And in each recipe send classic death.

So deep in knowledge, that few lines can sound
And plumb the bottom of the vast profound,
Few grave ones with such gravity can think,
Or follow half so fast as he can sink;
With nice distinctions glossing o'er the text,
Obscure with meaning, and in words perplexed;
With subtleties on subtleties refined,
Meant to divide and subdivide the mind,   760
Keeping the forwardness of youth in awe,
The scowling Blackstone bears the train of law.

Divinity, enrobed in college fur,
In her right hand a New Court Kalendar
Bound like a book of prayer, thy coming waits

[749] Dr. William Heberden, the celebrated physician; he
died in 1801, in the 91st year of his age.

[762] Dr. Blackstone, principal of New Inn Hall in the
University of Oxford, and Vinerian Professor of Law; afterwards Sir William Blackstone, Solicitor-General, and a
Judge of the Court of Common Pleas. His reputation as a
sound lawyer and accomplished writer is too well established
to be affected by this random hit of the satirist. Blackstone's
great work, his Commentaries on the Laws of England,
being the improved and enlarged substance of his Vinerian
Lectures, superseded the dry abridgments of Hale, Hawkins,
and Wood, and still retain their popularity and position,
notwithstanding the great legal changes since their publication.

He was, no doubt, attacked by Churchill on account of
the part he took, in the House of Commons, against Wilkes,
on the subject of privilege, for which he was also severely
censured by Junius and Sir William Meredith. He died in
1780, at the age of 56.

With all her pack, to hymn thee in the gates.
　Loyalty, fix'd on Isis' alter'd shore,
A stranger long, but stranger now no more,
Shall pitch her tabernacle, and with eyes
Brim-full of rapture, view her new allies;　　770
Shall, with much pleasure and more wonder, view
Men great at court, and great at Oxford too.
　O sacred Loyalty! accursed be those
Who, seeming friends, turn out thy deadliest foes,
Who prostitute to kings thy honour'd name,
And sooth their passions to betray their fame;
Nor praised be those, to whose proud nature clings
Contempt of government, and hate of kings;
Who, willing to be free, not knowing how,
A strange intemperance of zeal avow,　　780
And start at Loyalty, as at a word
Which without danger Freedom never heard.
　Vain errors of vain men—wild both extremes,
And to the state not wholesome, like the dreams,
Children of night, of indigestion bred,
Which, reason clouded, seize and turn the head;
Loyalty without Freedom, is a chain
Which men of liberal notice can't sustain,
And Freedom without Loyalty, a name
Which nothing means, or means licentious shame.
　Thine be the art, my Sandwich, thine the toil, 791
In Oxford's stubborn and untoward soil
To rear this plant of union, till at length,
Rooted by time, and foster'd into strength,
Shooting aloft, all danger it defies,
And proudly lifts its branches to the skies;
Whilst, Wisdom's happy son, but not her slave,
Gay with the gay, and with the grave ones grave,

Free from the dull impertinence of thought,
Beneath that shade, which thy own labours wrought,
And fashion'd into strength, shalt thou repose 801
Secure of liberal praise, since Isis flows
True to her Tame, as duty hath decreed,
Nor longer, like a harlot, lusts for Tweed,
And those old wreaths, which Oxford once dared
        twine
To grace a Stuart brow, she plants on thine.

THE FAREWELL.

IN this poem the author combats the cold philsosophy which was formerly in so much favour with some theorists, and vindicates the reasonableness and the usefulness of patriotic feelings. The Farewell contains less satire and more argument than any of Churchill's other poems; and though it is not one of his most powerful productions, it is one of the soundest and most unobjectionable pieces he ever wrote.

Cosmopolitanism has now, happily, but few disciples. The profession of "that nobler love which comprehends the whole world," is generally a veil for cynicism; and loving all men and all countries equally, invariably means loving none much.

Poet.

FAREWELL to Europe, and at once, farewell
To all the follies which in Europe dwell;
To Eastern India now, a richer clime,
Richer, alas! in everything, but rhyme,
The Muses steer their course; and, fond of change,
At large, in other worlds, desire to range,
Resolved, at least, since they the fool must play,
To do it in a different place, and way.

Friend. What whim is this, what error of the brain,
What madness worse than in the dog-star's reign?
Why into foreign countries would you roam,   11
Are there not knaves and fools enough at home?
If satire be thy object, and thy lays

As yet have shown no talents fit for praise ;
If satire be thy object, search all round,
Nor to thy purpose can one spot be found
Like England, where, to rampant vigour grown,
Vice chokes up every virtue ; where, self-sown,
The seeds of folly shoot forth rank and bold,
And every seed brings forth a hundred-fold.   20
  Poet. No more of this—though Truth (the more
    our shame ;
The more our guilt) though Truth perhaps may claim,
And justify her part in this, yet here,
For the first time, e'en Truth offends my ear.
Declaim from morn to night, from night to morn,
Take up the theme anew, when day's new-born,
I hear, and hate—be England what she will,
With all her faults she is my country still.
  Friend. Thy country ? and what then ? Is that
    mere word
Against the voice of Reason to be heard ?   30
Are prejudices, deep imbibed in youth,
To counteract, and make thee hate the truth ?
'Tis the sure symptom of a narrow soul
To draw its grand attachment from the whole,
And take up with a part ; men, not confined
Within such paltry limits, men design'd
Their nature to exalt, where'er they go,
Wherever waves can roll, and winds can blow,
Where'er the blessed sun, placed in the sky
To watch this subject world, can dart his eye,   40
Are still the same, and prejudice outgrown,
Consider every country as their own ;
At one grand view they take in Nature's plan,
Not more at home in England than Japan.
  Poet. My good, grave Sir of Theory, whose wit,

Grasping at shadows, ne'er caught substance yet,
'Tis mighty easy o'er a glass of wine
On vain refinements vainly to refine,
To laugh at poverty in plenty's reign,
To boast of apathy when out of pain,   50
And in each sentence, worthy of the schools,
Varnish'd with sophistry, to deal out rules
Most fit for practice, but for one poor fault,
That into practice they can ne'er be brought.

  At home, and sitting in your elbow-chair,
You praise Japan, though you was never there :
But was the ship this moment under sail,
Would not your mind be changed, your spirits fail?
Would you not cast one longing eye to shore,
And vow to deal in such wild schemes no more?
Howe'er our pride may tempt us to conceal   61
Those passions which we cannot choose but feel,
There's a strange something, which, without a brain,
Fools feel, and which e'en wise men can't explain,
Planted in man to bind him to that earth,
In dearest ties, from whence he drew his birth.

  If honour calls, where'er she points the way
The sons of honour follow, and obey ;
If need compels, wherever we are sent
'Tis want of courage not to be content ;   70
But, if we have the liberty of choice,
And all depends on our own single voice,
To deem of every country as the same
Is rank rebellion, 'gainst the lawful claim
Of Nature, and such dull indifference
May be philosophy, but can't be sense.
    Friend. Weak and unjust distinction, strange
       design,
Most peevish, most perverse, to undermine

Philosophy, and throw her empire down
By means of sense, from whom she holds her crown!
Divine Philosophy, to thee we owe   81
All that is worth possessing here below;
Virtue and wisdom consecrate thy reign,
Doubled each joy, and pain no longer pain.

    When, like a garden, where, for want of toil
And wholesome discipline, the rich, rank soil
Teems with incumbrances; where all around,
Herbs noxious in their nature make the ground,
Like the good mother of a thankless son,
Curse her own womb, by fruitfulness undone;   90
Like such a garden, when the human soul,
Uncultured, wild, impatient of control,
Brings forth those passions of luxuriant race,
Which spread, and stifle every herb of grace;
Whilst Virtue, check'd by the cold hand of scorn,
Seems withering on the bed where she was born,
Philosophy steps in, with steady hand
She brings her aid, she clears the encumber'd land;
Too virtuous to spare Vice one stroke, too wise
One moment to attend to Pity's cries,   100
See with what godlike, what relentless power
She roots up every weed!

    Poet.   And every flower.
Philosophy, a name of meek degree,
Embraced, in token of humility,
By the proud sage, who, whilst he strove to hide,
In that vain artifice, reveal'd his pride;

[107] Diogenes of Synope affected complete indifference not
only to the luxuries, but to the comforts and decencies of
life. Treading upon Plato's robe, he exclaimed, "Thus I
trample under foot the pride of Plato;" "With greater pride
on your part," was Plato's just retort.

Philosophy, whom Nature had design'd
To purge all errors from the human mind,
Herself misled by the philosopher, 110
At once her priest and master made us err :
Pride, pride, like leaven in a mass of flour,
Tainted her laws, and made e'en virtue sour.
Had she, content within her proper sphere,
Taught lessons suited to the human ear,
Which might fair Virtue's genuine fruits produce,
Made not for ornament but real use,
The heart of man, unrivall'd, she had sway'd,
Praised by the good, and by the bad obey'd ;
But when she, overturning Reason's throne, 120
Strove proudly in its place to plant her own ;
When she with apathy the breast would steel,
And teach us, deeply feeling, not to feel ;
When she would wildly all her force employ,
Not to correct our passions, but destroy ;
When, not content our nature to restore,
As made by God, she made it new all o'er ;
When, with a strange and criminal excess,
To make us more than men she made us less ;
The good her dwindled power with pity saw, 130
The bad with joy, and none but fools with awe.
Truth with a simple and unvarnish'd tale,
E'en from the mouth of Norton might prevail,
Could she get there ; but Falsehood's sugar'd strain
Should pour her fatal blandishments in vain,
Nor make one convert, though the Siren hung,
Where she too often hangs, on Mansfield's tongue.
Should all the Sophs, whom in his course the sun
Hath seen, or past, or present, rise in one ;
Should *he*, whilst pleasure in each sentence flows,

Like Plato, give us poetry in prose;   141
Should he, full orator, at once impart
The Athenian's genius with the Roman's art;
Genius and art should in this instance fail,
Nor Rome, though join'd with Athens, here prevail.
'Tis not in man, 'tis not in more than man,
To make me find one fault in Nature's plan.
Placed low ourselves, we censure those above,
And, wanting judgment, think that she wants love,
Blame, where we ought in reason to commend, 150
And think her most a foe, when most a friend.
Such be philosophers—their specious art,
Though Friendship pleads, shall never warp my
      heart;
Ne'er make me from this breast one passion tear,
Which Nature, my best friend, hath planted there.
   Friend. Forgiving as a friend, what, whilst I live,
As a philosopher I can't forgive,
In this one point at last I join with you,
To Nature pay all that is Nature's due;
But let not clouded Reason sink so low,   160
To fancy debts she does not, cannot owe:
Bear, to full manhood grown, those shackles bear
Which Nature meant us for a time to wear,
As we wear leading-strings, which, useless grown,
Are laid aside, when we can walk alone;
But on thyself by peevish humour sway'd
With thou lay burdens Nature never laid?
Wilt thou make faults, whilst Judgment weakly errs,
And then defend, mistaking them for hers?
Darest thou to say, in our enlighten'd age,   170
That this grand master passion, this brave rage
Which flames out for thy country, was imprest

And fix'd by Nature in the human breast?
   If you prefer the place where you was born,
And hold all others in contempt and scorn
On fair comparison ; if on that land
With lib'ral, and a more than equal hand,
Her gifts, as in profusion, Plenty sends ;
If Virtue meets with more and better friends ;
If Science finds a patron 'mongst the great ;   180
If Honesty is minister of state ;
If Power, the guardian of our rights design'd,
Is to that great, that only end confined ;
If riches are employ'd to bless the poor ;
If law is sacred, liberty secure ;
Let but these facts depend on proofs of weight,
Reason declares thy love can't be too great,
And, in this light could he our country view,
A very Hottentot must love it too.
   But if by Fate's decrees, you owe your birth 190
To some most barren and penurious earth,
Where, every comfort of this life denied,
Her real wants are scantily supplied ;
Where power is reason, liberty a joke,
Laws never made, or made but to be broke ;
To fix thy love on such a wretched spot,
Because in lust's wild fever there begot ;
Because, thy weight no longer fit to bear,
By chance, not choice, thy mother dropt thee there,
Is folly, which admits not of defence ;   200
It can't be nature, for it is not sense.
By the same argument which here you hold,
(When Falsehood's insolent, let Truth be bold)
If propagation can in torments dwell,
A devil must, if born there, love his hell.

Poet. Had Fate, to whose decrees I lowly bend,
And e'en in punishment confess a friend,
Ordain'd my birth in some place yet untried,
On purpose made to mortify my pride;
Where the sun never gave one glimpse of day, 210
Where science never yet could dart one ray;
Had I been born on some bleak, blasted plain
Of barren Scotland, in a Stuart's reign,
Or in some kingdom, where men, weak, or worse,
Turn'd Nature's every blessing to a curse;
Where crowns of freedom, by the fathers won,
Dropp'd leaf by leaf from each degenerate son,
In spite of all the wisdom you display,
All you have said, and yet may have to say,
My weakness here, if weakness, I confess,   220
I as my country had not loved her less.

Whether strict reason bears me out in this,
Let those who, always seeking, always miss
The ways of reason, doubt with precious zeal;
Theirs be the praise to argue, mine to feel.
Wish we to trace this passion to the root,
We, like a tree, may know it by its fruit;
From its rich stem ten thousand virtues spring,
Ten thousand blessings on its branches cling;
Yet in the circle of revolving years   230
Not one misfortune, not one vice, appears.
Hence, then, and what you reason call adore;
This, if not reason, must be something more.

But (for I wish not others to confine;
Be their opinions unrestrain'd as mine)
Whether this love's of good, or evil growth,
A vice, a virtue, or a spice of both,
Let men of nicer argument decide;

If it is virtuous, soothe an honest pride
With liberal praise; if vicious, be content,   240
It is a vice I never can repent;
A vice, which, weigh'd in heaven, shall more avail
Than ten cold virtues in the other scale.

  Friend. This wild, untemper'd zeal (which, after all,
We, candour unimpeach'd, might madness call)
Is it a virtue? that you scarce pretend;
Or can it be a vice, like virtue's friend,
Which draws us off from and dissolves the force
Of private ties, nay, stops us in our course
To that grand object of the human soul,   250
That nobler love which comprehends the whole?
Coop'd in the limits of this petty isle,
This nook, which scarce deserves a frown or smile
Weigh'd with Creation, you, by whim undone,
Give all your thoughts to what is scarce worth one.
The generous soul, by Nature taught to soar,
Her strength confirm'd in philosophic lore,
At one grand view takes in a world with ease,
And, seeing all mankind, loves all she sees.   259

  Poet. Was it most sure, which yet a doubt endures,
Not found in Reason's creed, though found in yours,
That these two services, like what we're told
And know of God's and Mammon's, cannot hold
And draw together; that, however loth,
We neither serve, attempting to serve both,
I could not doubt a moment which to choose,
And which in common reason to refuse.
  Invented oft for purposes of art,
Born of the head, though father'd on the heart,
This grand love of the world must be confest   270

A barren speculation at the best.
Not one man in a thousand, should he live
Beyond the usual term of life, could give,
So rare occasion comes, and to so few,
Proof whether his regards are feign'd, or true.

   The love we bear our country, is a root
Which never fails to bring forth golden fruit;
'Tis in the mind an everlasting spring
Of glorious actions, which become a king,
Nor less become a subject; 'tis a debt   280
Which bad men, though they pay not, can't forget;
A duty which the good delight to pay,
And every man can practise every day.

   Nor, for my life (so very dim my eye,
Or dull your argument) can I descry
What you with faith assert, how that dear love
Which binds me to my country, can remove,
And make me of necessity forego,
That general love which to the world I owe.
Those ties of private nature, small extent,   29
In which the mind of narrow cast is pent,
Are only steps on which the generous soul
Mounts, by degrees, till she includes the whole.
That spring of love, which, in the human mind,
Founded on self, flows narrow and confined,
Enlarges as it rolls, and comprehends
The social charities of blood and friends,
Till smaller streams included, not o'erpast,
It rises to our country's love at last;
And he, with liberal and enlargèd mind,   300
Who loves his country, cannot hate mankind.

   Friend. Friend as you would appear to common
     sense,

Tell me, or think no more of a defence,
Is it a proof of love by choice to run
A vagrant from your country?

    Poet.   Can the son
(Shame, shame on all such sons) with ruthless eye,
And heart more patient than the flint, stand by,
And by some ruffian, from all shame divorced,
All virtue, see his honour'd mother forced!   310
Then—no, by Him that made me, not e'en then,
Could I with patience, by the worst of men,
Behold my country plunder'd, beggar'd, lost
Beyond redemption, all her glories cross'd,
E'en when occasion made them ripe, her fame
Fled like a dream, while she awakes to shame.

    Friend. Is it not more the office of a friend,
The office of a patron, to defend
Her sinking state, than basely to decline
So great a cause, and in despair resign?   320

    Poet. Beyond my reach, alas! the grievance lies,
And, whilst more able patriots doubt, she dies. .
From a foul source, more deep than we suppose,
Fatally deep and dark, this grievance flows.
'Tis not that peace our glorious hopes defeats;
'Tis not the voice of faction in the streets;
'Tis not a gross attack on freedom made;
'Tis not the arm of privilege display'd
Against the subject, whilst she wears no sting
To disappoint the purpose of a king;   .   330
These are no ills, or trifles, if compared
With those which are contrived though not declared.
    Tell me, Philosopher, is it a crime
To pry into the secret womb of Time,
Or, born in ignorance, must we despair

To reach events, and read the future there?
Why, be it so—still 'tis the right of man,
Imparted by his Maker, where he can,
To former times and men his eye to cast,
And judge of what's to come, by what is past. 340
    Should there be found, in some not distant year,
(O how I wish to be no prophet here)
Amongst our British Lords should there be found
Some great in power, in principles unsound,
Who look on freedom with an evil eye,
In whom the springs of loyalty are dry;
Who wish to soar on wild Ambition's wings,
Who hate the Commons, and who love not Kings;
Who would divide the people and the throne,
To set up separate interests of their own;   350
Who hate whatever aids their wholesome growth,
And only join with, to destroy them both;
Should there be found such men in after-times,
May Heaven, in mercy to our grievous crimes,
Allot some milder vengeance, nor to them,
And to their rage, this wretched land condemn.
    Thou God above, on whom all states depend,
Who knowest from the first their rise, and end,
If there's a day mark'd in the book of Fate,
When ruin must involve our equal state;   360
When law, alas! must be no more, and we,
To freedom born, must be no longer free,
Let not a mob of tyrants seize the helm,
Nor titled upstarts league to rob the realm;
Let not, whatever other ills assail,
A damnèd aristocracy prevail:
If, all too short, our course of freedom run,
'Tis Thy good pleasure, we should be undone,

Let us, some comfort in our griefs to bring,
Be slaves to one, and be that one a king.   370
    Friend. Poets, accustom'd by their trade to feign,
Oft substitute creations of the brain
For real substance, and, themselves deceived,
Would have the fiction by mankind believed.
Such is your case—but grant, to soothe your pride,
That you know more than all the world beside,
Why deal in hints, why make a moment's doubt?
Resolved, and like a man, at once speak out;
Shew us our danger, tell us where it lies,
And, to ensure our safety, make us wise.   380
    Poet. Rather than bear the pain of thought, fools
       stray;
The proud will rather lose than ask their way:
To men of sense what needs it to unfold,
And tell a tale which they must know untold?
In the bad, interest warps the canker'd heart,
The good are hoodwink'd by the tricks of art;
And, whilst arch, subtle hypocrites contrive
To keep the flames of discontent alive;
Whilst they, with arts to honest men unknown,
Breed doubts between the people and the throne,
Making us fear, where reason never yet   391
Allow'd one fear, or could one doubt admit,
Themselves pass unsuspected in disguise,
And 'gainst our real danger seal our eyes.
    Friend. Mark them, and let their names recorded
       stand
On Shame's black roll, and stink through all the
       land.
    Poet. That might some courage, but no prudence
       be;

No hurt to them, and jeopardy to me.

   Friend. Leave out their names.

   Poet.   For that kind caution, thanks;

But may not judges sometimes fill up blanks?   401

   Friend. Your country's laws in doubt then you
      reject.

Poet. The laws I love, the lawyers I suspect.

Amongst Twelve Judges may not one be found

(On bare, bare possibility I ground

This wholesome doubt) who may enlarge, retrench,

Create, and uncreate, and from the bench,

With winks, smiles, nods, and such like paltry arts,

May work and worm into a jury's hearts?

Or, baffled there, may, turbulent of soul,   410

Cramp their high office, and their rights control;

Who may, though judge, turn advocate at large,

And deal replies out by the way of charge,

Making interpretation all the way,

In spite of facts, his wicked will obey;

And, leaving law without the least defence,

May damn his conscience to approve his sense?

   Friend. Whilst, the true guardians of this char-
      ter'd land,

In full and perfect vigour, juries stand,

A judge in vain shall awe, cajole, perplex.   420

   Poet. Suppose I should be tried in Middlesex?

   Friend. To pack a jury they will never dare.

   Poet. There's no occasion to pack juries there.

---

[423] Most probably alluding to the then recent acquittal by
the petty jury, of Mr. Philip Carteret Webb, solicitor to the
Treasury, against whom an indictment had been found by the
grand jury for Middlesex, for perjury, alleged to have been
committed by him, in the evidence he had given upon the
trial of the action brought by Wilkes against Mr. Wood, the

Friend. 'Gainst prejudice all arguments are weak;
Reason herself without affect must speak.
Fly then thy country, like a coward fly;
Renounce her interest, and her laws defy.
But why, bewitch'd, to India turn thine eyes?
Cannot our Europe thy vast wrath suffice?
Cannot thy misbegotten Muse lay bare   430
Her brawny arm, and play the butcher there?
  Poet. Thy counsel taken, what should Satire do?
Where could she find an object that is new?
Those travell'd youths, whom tender mothers wean,
And send abroad to see, and to be seen;
With whom, lest they should fornicate, or worse,
A tutor's sent by way of a dry nurse;
Each of whom just enough of spirit bears
To shew our follies, and to bring home theirs,
Have made all Europe's vices so well known,   440
They seem almost as natural as our own.
  Friend. Will India for thy purpose better do?
  Poet. In one respect at least—there's something
        new.
  Friend. A harmless people, in whom Nature speaks
Free and untainted, 'mongst whom Satire seeks,
But vainly seeks, so simply plain their hearts,
One bosom where to lodge her poison'd darts.
  Poet. From knowledge speak you this, or doubt
        on doubt
Weigh'd and resolved, hath Reason found it out?
Neither from knowledge, nor by reason taught,   450

Earl of Egremont's secretary. Lord Mansfield, in his charge
to the jury, on this occasion, too pointedly delivered his
sentiments in favour of the defendant. The verdict was
however generally approved, as a righteous termination of a
frivolous and vexatious proceeding.

You have faith every where, but where you ought.
India or Europe—what's there in a name?
Propensity to vice in both the same,
Nature alike in both works for man's good,
Alike in both by man himself withstood.
Nabobs, as well as those who hunt them down,
Deserve a cord much better than a crown,
And a Mogul can thrones as much debase
As any polish'd prince of Christian race.

 Friend. Could you, a task more hard than you
   suppose,   460
Could you, in ridicule whilst Satire glows,
Make all their follies to the life appear,
'Tis ten to one you gain no credit here;
Howe'er well drawn, the picture, after all,
Because we know not the original,
Would not find favour in the public eye.

 Poet. That, having your good leave, I mean to try:
And if your observations sterling hold,
If the piece should be heavy, tame, and cold,
To make it to the side of Nature lean,   470
And meaning nothing, something seem to mean:
To make the whole in lively colours glow,
To bring before us something that we know,
And from all honest men applause to win,
I'll group the Company and put them in.

 Friend. Be that ungenerous thought by shame
   suppress'd
Add not distress to those too much distress'd.
Have they not, by blind zeal misled, laid bare,
Those sores which never might endure the air?

---

[475] The conduct of the Directors and the debates in the
East India House at this time excited much attention.

Have they not brought their mysteries so low, 480
That what the wise suspected not, fools know?
From their first rise e'en to the present hour,
Have they not proved their own abuse of power,
Made it impossible, if fairly view'd,
Ever to have that dangerous power renew'd,
Whilst unseduced by ministers, the throne
Regards our interest, and knows its own?

Poet. Should every other subject chance to fail,
Those who have sail'd, and those who wish'd to sail
In the last fleet, afford an ample field, 490
Which must beyond my hopes a harvest yield.

Friend. On such vile food Satire can never thrive.

Poet. She cannot starve, if there was only Clive.

[489] In 1764, Lord Clive, with a select committee of his own nomination, sailed for India, invested by the Directors with full powers for settling the differences with the native princes, and for regulating the abuses which the rapacity of the company's servants there had introduced into every department of government. In the former object he was eminently successful, and an addition of nearly two millions sterling of annual revenue was the result. The latter he failed to accomplish, for standing alone in a sincere wish to effect a reform, his plans were counteracted from every quarter; but he palliated evils which he could not remove.

Lord Clive returned to England in 1767, and in 1773 a motion being made in the House of Commons, of which he was a member, purporting "that he had abused the powers with which he was intrusted," he delivered an eloquent and spirited vindication of his conduct. The House of Commons rejected the motion, and resolved "that Lord Clive had rendered great and meritorious services to his country."

Lord Clive's charities were extensive; the present he made of £70,000 as a provision for the invalids in the company's service was one of the noblest donations ever made by a private individual. He stood high in the esteem of the great Earl of Chatham, who used to say, that he looked upon him as a heaven-born general.

THE TIMES.

If the Times were really as depraved when the poet wrote as he represents them to have been, we should have cause to rejoice in the ameliorated condition of our countrymen at this period. But we are persuaded that Englishmen never merited the general execration, so nervously bestowed upon them in this poem. A depraved few have occasionally imported from abroad crimes at the mention of which every good man must shudder; but neither rank nor fortune have been able to shield them from the indignation and abhorrence of all ranks of people.

In this poem we have abstained from elucidating the obscurities that occur; we should deem ourselves inexcusable were we, in an attempt to gratify the curiosity of our readers, to fix a stain upon the memory of persons, who have either been the victims of the most injurious calumny, or if guilty, have appeared before that tribunal, the judgments of which neither wealth nor influence can evade.

HE time hath been, a boyish, blushing
    time,
  When modesty was scarcely held a crime;
  When the most wicked had some touch
    of grace,
And trembled to meet Virtue face to face;
When those, who, in the cause of Sin grown gray,
Had served her without grudging, day by day,

Were yet so weak an awkward shame to feel,
And strove that glorious service to conceal :
We, better bred, and than our sires more wise,
Such paltry narrowness of soul despise :　　　10
To virtue every mean pretence disclaim,
Lay bare our crimes, and glory in our shame.

Time was, ere Temperance had fled the realm,
Ere Luxury sat guttling at the helm
From meal to meal, without one moment's space
Reserved for business, or allow'd for grace ;
Ere Vanity had so far conquer'd sense
To make us all wild rivals in expense,
To make one fool strive to outvie another,
And every coxcomb dress against his brother ;　20
Ere banish'd Industry had left our shores,
And Labour was by Pride kick'd out of doors ;
Ere idleness prevail'd sole queen in courts,
Or only yielded to a rage for sports ;
Ere each weak mind was with externals caught,
And dissipation held the place of thought ;
Ere gambling lords in vice so far were gone
To cog the die, and bid the sun look on ;
Ere a great nation, not less just than free,
Was made a beggar by Economy ;　　　　30
Ere rugged honesty was out of vogue ;
Ere fashion stamp'd her sanction on the rogue ;
Time was that men had conscience, that they made
Scruples to owe what never could be paid.

Was one then found, however high his name,
So far above his fellows damn'd to shame,
Who dared abuse, and falsify his trust,

---

30 The party-cry of Lord Bute's administration was
" Economy."

Who, being great, yet dared to be unjust—
Shunn'd like a plague, or but at distance view'd,
He walk'd the crowded streets in solitude ;   40
Nor could his rank, and station in the land
Bribe one mean knave to take him by the hand.
Such rigid maxims (O, might such revive
To keep expiring honesty alive !)
Made rogues, all other hopes of fame denied,
Not just through principle, be just through pride.
    Our times, more polish'd, wear a different face ;
Debts are an honour, payment a disgrace.
Men of weak minds, high-placed on folly's list,
May gravely tell us trade cannot subsist,   50
Nor all those thousands who're in trade employ'd,
If faith 'twixt man and man is once destroy'd.
Why—be it so—we in that point accord ;
But what are trade, and tradesmen to a lord?
    Faber, from day to day, from year to year,
Hath had the cries of tradesmen in his ear,
Of tradesmen by his villany betray'd,
And, vainly seeking justice, bankrupts made.
What is't to Faber?   Lordly, as before,
He sits at ease, and lives to ruin more :   60
Fix'd at his door, as motionless as stone,
Begging, but only begging for their own,
Unheard they stand, or only heard by those,
Those slaves in livery who mock their woes.
What is't to Faber? he continues great,
Lives on in grandeur, and runs out in state.
The helpless widow, wrung with deep despair,
In bitterness of soul pours forth her prayer,
Hugging her starving babes with streaming eyes,
And calls down vengeance, vengeance from the skies.

What is't to Faber? he stands safe and clear, 71
Heaven can commence no legal action here;
And on his breast a mighty plate he wears,
A plate more firm than triple brass, which bears
The name of privilege, 'gainst vulgar awe;
He feels no conscience, and he fears no law.

Nor think, acquainted with small knaves alone,
Who have not shame outlived, and grace outgrown,
The great world hidden from thy reptile view,
That on such men, to whom contempt is due, 80
Contempt shall fall, and their vile author's name
Recorded stand through all the land of shame.
No—to his porch, like Persians to the sun,
Behold contending crowds of courtiers run;
See, to his aid what noble troops advance,
All sworn to keep his crimes in countenance:
Nor wonder at it—they partake the charge,
As small their conscience, and their debts as large.

Propp'd by such clients, and without control
From all that's honest in the human soul; 90
In grandeur mean, with insolence unjust,
Whilst none but knaves can praise, and fools will
    trust,
Caress'd and courted, Faber seems to stand
A mighty pillar in a guilty land.
And (a sad truth, to which succeeding times
Will scarce give credit, when 'tis told in rhymes)
Did not strict honour with a jealous eye
Watch round the throne, did not true piety
(Who, link'd with honour for the noblest ends,
Ranks none but honest men amongst her friends) 100
Forbid us to be crush'd with such a weight,
He might in time be minister of state.

But why enlarge I on such petty crimes?
They might have shock'd the faith of former times,
But now are held as nothing—we begin
Where our sires ended, and improve in sin ;
Rack our invention, and leave nothing new
In vice and folly for our sons to do.

Nor deem this censure hard ; there's not a place
Most consecrate to purposes of grace,　　　110
Which vice hath not polluted ; none so high,
But with bold pinion she hath dared to fly,
And build there for her pleasure ; none so low
But she hath crept into it, made it know
And feel her power; in courts, in camps she reigns,
O'er sober citizens, and simple swains ;
E'en in our temples she hath fix'd her throne,
And 'bove God's holy altars placed her own.

More to increase the horror of our state,
To make her empire lasting as 'tis great ;　　120
To make us, in full grown perfection feel
Curses which neither art nor time can heal ;
All shame discarded, all remains of pride,
Meanness sits crown'd, and triumphs by her side ;
Meanness, who gleans out of the human mind
Those few good seeds which vice had left behind,
Those seeds which might in time to virtue tend,
And leaves the soul without a power to mend ;
Meanness, at sight of whom, with brave disdain,
The breast of manhood swells, but swells in vain ; 130
Before whom Honour makes a forced retreat,
And Freedom is compell'd to quit her seat ;
Meanness, which, like that mark by bloody Cain
Borne in his forehead for a brother slain,
God, in his great and all-subduing rage,

Ordains the standing mark of this vile age.
    The venal hero trucks his fame for gold,
The patriot's virtue for a place is sold,
The statesman bargains for his country's shame,
And for preferment priests their God disclaim ; 140
Worn out with lust, her day of lech'ry o'er,
The mother trains the daughter which she bore
In her own paths ; the father aids the plan,
And, when the innocent is ripe for man,
Sells her to some old lecher for a wife,
And makes her an adulteress for life,
'Or in the papers bids his name appear,
And advertises for a L———— :
Husband and wife, (whom avarice must applaud)
Agree to save the charge of pimp and bawd ; 150
These parts they play themselves, a frugal pair,
And share the infamy, the gain to share ;
Well pleased to find, when they the profits tell,
That they have play'd the whore and rogue so well.
    Nor are these things (which might imply a spark
Of shame still left) transacted in the dark :
No—to the public they are open laid,
And carried on like any other trade ;
Scorning to mince damnation, and too proud
To work the works of darkness in a cloud, 160
In fullest vigour Vice maintains her sway ;
Free are her marts, and open at noon-day.
Meanness, now wed to Impudence, no more
In darkness skulks, and trembles, as of yore,
When the light breaks upon her coward eye ;
Boldly she stalks on earth, and to the sky
Lifts her proud head, nor fears lest time abate,
And turn her husband's love to canker'd hate,

Since fate, to make them more sincerely one,
Hath crown'd their loves with Montagu their son; 170
A son so like his dam, so like his sire,
With all the mother's craft, the father's fire,
An image so express in every part,
So like in all bad qualities of heart,
That, had they fifty children, he alone
Would stand as heir apparent to the throne.

    With our own island vices not content,
We rob our neighbours on the Continent;
Dance Europe round, and visit every court,
To ape their follies and their crimes import: 180
To different lands for different sins we roam,
And, richly freighted, bring our cargo home,
Nobly industrious to make vice appear
In her full state, and perfect only here.

    To Holland, where politeness ever reigns,
Where primitive sincerity remains,
And makes a stand; where Freedom in her course
Hath left her name, though she hath lost her force
In that as other lands; where simple Trade
Was never in the garb of Fraud array'd; 190
Where Avarice never dared to shew his head ·
Where, like a smiling cherub, Mercy, led
By Reason, blesses the sweet-blooded race;
And cruelty could never find a place;
To Holland for that charity we roam,
Which happily begins and ends at home.

    France, in return for peace and power restored,
For all those countries, which the hero's sword
Unprofitably purchased, idly thrown
Into her lap, and made once more her own; 200
France hath afforded large and rich supplies

Of vanities full-trimm'd ; of polish'd lies,
Of soothing flatteries, which through the ears
Steal to, and melt the heart ; of slavish fears
Which break the spirit, and of abject fraud—
For which, alas ! we need not send abroad.
    Spain gives us pride—which Spain to all the
        Earth
May largely give, nor fear herself a dearth—
Gives us that jealousy, which, born of fear
And mean distrust, grows not by nature here ; 210
Gives us that superstition, which pretends
By the worst means to serve the best of ends ;
That cruelty, which, stranger to the brave,
Dwells only with the coward and the slave ;
That cruelty, which led her Christian bands
With more than savage rage o'er savage lands,
Bade them, without remorse, whole countries thin,
And hold of nought, but mercy, as a sin.
    Italia, nurse of every softer art,
Who, feigning to refine, unmans the heart ; 220
Who lays the realms of Sense and Virtue waste ;
Who mars while she pretends to mend our taste ;
Italia, to complete and crown our shame,
Sends us a fiend, and Legion is his name.
The farce of greatness without being great,
Pride without power, titles without estate,
Souls without vigour, bodies without force,
Hate without cause, revenge without remorse,
Dark, mean revenge, murder without defence,
Jealousy without love, sound without sense, 230
Mirth without humour, without wit grimace,
Faith without reason, Gospel without grace,
Zeal without knowledge, without nature art,

Men without manhood, women without heart;
Half-men, who, dry and pithless, are debarr'd
From man's best joys—no sooner made than
      marr'd—
Half-men, whom many a rich and noble dame,
To serve her lust, and yet secure her fame,
Keeps on high diet, as we capons feed,
To glut our appetites at last decreed;   240
Women, who dance in postures so obscene,
They might awaken shame in Aretine;
Who, when, retired from the day's piercing light,
They celebrate the mysteries of Night,
Might make the Muses, in a corner placed
To view their monstrous lusts, deem Sappho chaste:
These, and a thousand follies rank as these,
A thousand faults, ten thousand fools, who please
Our pall'd and sickly taste, ten thousand knaves,
Who serve our foes as spies, and us as slaves, 250
Who, by degrees, and unperceived, prepare
Our necks for chains which they already wear,
Madly we entertain, at the expense
Of fame, of virtue, taste, and common sense.
   Nor stop we here: the soft luxurious East,
Where man, his soul degraded, from the beast
In nothing different but in shape we view—
They walk on four legs, and he walks on two—
Attracts our eye; and flowing from that source
Sins of the blackest character, sins worse   260
Than all her plagues, which truly to unfold,
Would make the best blood in my veins run cold,
And strike all manhood dead; which but to name,
Would call up in my cheeks the marks of shame;
Sins, if such sins can be, which shut out grace;

Which for the guilty leave no hope, no place,
E'en in God's mercy; sins 'gainst Nature's plan
Possess the land at large; and man for man
Burns in those fires which hell alone could raise
To make him more than damn'd; which, in the days
Of punishment, when guilt becomes her prey, 271
With all her tortures she can scarce repay.

Be grace shut out, be mercy deaf, let God
With tenfold terrors arm that dreadful nod
Which speaks them lost, and sentenced to despair;
Distending wide her jaws, let hell prepare
For those who thus offend amongst mankind,
A fire more fierce, and tortures more refined:
On earth, which groans beneath their monstrous
        weight,
On earth, alas! they meet a different fate, 280
And whilst the laws, false grace, false mercy, shown,
Are taught to wear a softness not their own,
Men, whom the beasts would spurn, should they
        appear
Amongst the honest herd, find refuge here.

No longer by vain fear, or shame controll'd,
From long, too long security grown bold,
Mocking rebuke, they brave it in our streets:
And Lumley e'en at noon his mistress meets:
So public in their crimes, so daring grown,
They almost take a pride to have them known, 290
And each unnatural villain scarce endures
To make a secret of his vile amours.
Go where we will, at every time and place,
Sodom confronts, and stares us in the face;
They ply in public at our very doors,
And take the bread from much more honest whores.

Those who are mean high paramours secure,
And the rich guilty screen the guilty poor ;
The sin too proud to feel from reason awe,
And those who practise it too great for law.   300
    Woman, the pride and happiness of man,
Without whose soft endearments Nature's plan
Had been a blank, and life not worth a thought ;
Woman, by all the Loves and Graces taught
With softest arts, and sure, though hidden skill,
To humanize, and mould us to her will ;
Woman, with more than common grace form'd here,
With the persuasive language of a tear
To melt the rugged temper of our isle,
Or win us to her purpose with a smile ;   310
Woman, by fate the quickest spur decreed,
The fairest, best reward of every deed
Which bears the stamp of honour ; at whose name
Our ancient heroes caught a quicker flame,
And dared beyond belief, whilst o'er the plain,
Spurning the carcases of princes slain,
Confusion proudly strode, whilst Horror blew
The fatal trump, and Death stalk'd full in view ;
Woman is out of date, a thing thrown by
As having lost its use : no more the eye,   320
With female beauty caught, in wild amaze,
Gazes entranced, and could for ever gaze ;
No more the heart, that seat where Love resides,
Each breath drawn quick and short, in fuller tides
Life posting through the veins, each pulse on fire,
And the whole body tingling with desire,
Pants for those charms, which Virtue might engage,
To break his vow, and thaw the frost of Age,
Bidding each trembling nerve, each muscle strain,

And giving pleasure which is almost pain.   330
Women are kept for nothing but the breed;
For pleasure we must have a Ganymede,
A fine, fresh Hylas, a delicious boy,
To serve our purposes of beastly joy.
    Fairest of nymphs, where every nymph is fair,
Whom Nature form'd with more than common care,
With more than common care whom Art improved,
And both declared most worthy to be loved,
———— neglected wanders, whilst a crowd
Pursue and consecrate the steps of ————.   340
She, hapless maid, born in a wretched hour,
Wastes life's gay prime in vain, like some fair flower,
Sweet in its scent, and lively in its hue,
Which withers on the stalk from whence it grew,
And dies uncropp'd; whilst he admired, caress'd,
Beloved, and every where a welcome guest,
With brutes of rank and fortune plays the whofe,
For this unnatural lust a common sewer.
    Dine with Apicius; at his sumptuous board
Find all the world of dainties can afford;   350
And yet (so much distemper'd spirits pall ·
The sickly appetite) amidst them all
Apicius finds no joy, but whilst he carves
For every guest, the landlord sits and starves.
    The forest haunch, fine, fat, in flavour high,
Kept to a moment, smokes before his eye,
But smokes in vain; his heedless eye runs o'er
And loathes what he had deified before:
The turtle, of a great and glorious size,
Worth its own weight in gold, a mighty prize,   360
For which a man of taste all risks would run,
Itself a feast, and every dish in one;

The turtle in luxurious pomp comes in,
Kept, kill'd, cut up, prepared, and dress'd by Quin ;
In vain it comes, in vain lays full in view ;
As Quin hath dress'd it, he may eat it too ;
Apicius cannot.   When the glass goes round,
Quick-circling, and the roofs with mirth resound,
Sober he sits, and silent ; all alone   369
Though in a crowd, and to himself scarce known :
On grief he feeds : nor friends can cure, nor wine
Suspend his cares, and make him cease to pine.

    Why mourns Apicius thus ? why runs his eye,
Heedless, o'er delicates, which from the sky
Might call down Jove ?   Where now his generous
       wish
That, to invent a new and better dish,
The world might burn, and all mankind expire,
So he might roast a phœnix at the fire ?
Why swims that eye in tears, which, through a race
Of sixty years, ne'er shew'd one sign of grace ? 380
Why feels that heart, which never felt before ?
Why doth that pamper'd glutton eat no more,
Who only lived to eat, his stomach pall'd,
And drown'd in floods of sorrow ? hath Fate call'd
His father from the grave to second life ?
Hath Clodius on his hands return'd his wife ?
Or hath the law, by strictest justice taught,
Compell'd him to restore the dower she brought ?
Hath some bold creditor, against his will,   389
Brought in, and forced him to discharge, a bill,
Where eating had no share ? hath some vain wench
Run out his wealth, and forced him to retrench ?

    [366] Quin, the actor, was celebrated for providing scarce
and choice dishes for dinner, and high-flavoured wines.

Hath any rival glutton got the start,
And beat him in his own luxurious art?
Bought cates for which Apicius could not pay,
Or dress'd old dainties in a newer way?
Hath his cook, worthy to be slain with rods,
Spoil'd a dish fit to entertain the gods?
Or hath some varlet, cross'd by cruel fate,
Thrown down the price of empires in a plate? 400
　　None, none of these—his servants all are tried:
So sure, they walk on ice and never slide;
His cook, an acquisition made in France,
Might put a Chloe out of countenance;
Nor, though old Holles still maintains his stand,
Hath he one rival glutton in the land.
Women are all the objects of his hate;
His debts are all unpaid, and yet his state
In full security and triumph held,
Unless for once a knave should be expell'd;　　410
His wife is still a whore, and in his power,
The woman gone, he still retains the dower;
Sound in the grave (thanks to his filial care
Which mix'd the draught, and kindly sent him
　　　　there)
His father sleeps, and till the last trump shake
The corners of the earth, shall not awake.
　　Whence flows this sorrow, then? Behind his
　　　　chair,
Didst thou not see, deck'd with a solitaire
Which on his bare breast glittering play'd, and
　　　　graced
With nicest ornaments, a stripling placed,　　420

---

[404] M. St. Clouet, or Chloe, as he was more familiarly
called, was *chef de cuisine* to Holles, Duke of Newcastle.

A smooth, smug stripling, in life's fairest prime?
Didst thou not mind, too, how from time to time,
The monstrous lecher, tempted to despise
All other daintics, thither turn'd his eyos?
How he seem'd inly to reproach us all,
Who strove his fix'd attention to recal,
And how he wish'd, e'en at the time of grace,
Like Janus, to have had a double face?
His cause of grief behold in that fair boy.
Apicius dotes, and Corydon is coy.   430
    Vain and unthinking stripling! when the glass
Meets thy too curious eye, and, as you pass,
Flattering, presents in smiles thy image there,
Why dost thou bless the gods, who made thee fair?
Blame their large bounties, and with reason blame;
Curse, curse thy beauty, for it leads to shame;
When thy hot lord, to work thee to his end,
Bids showers of gold into thy breast descend,
Suspect his gifts, nor the vile giver trust;
They're baits for virtue, and smell strong of lust.
On those gay, gaudy trappings, which adorn   441
The temple of thy body, look with scorn;
View them with horror; they pollution mean,
And deepest ruin: thou hast often seen
From 'mongst the herd, the fairest and the best
Carefully singled out, and richly drest,
With grandeur mock'd, for sacrifice decreed,
Only in greater pomp at last to bleed.
Be warn'd in time, the threaten'd danger shun,
To stay a moment is to be undone.   450
What though, temptation proof, thy virtue shine,
Nor bribes can move, nor arts can undermine?
All other methods failing, one resource

Is still behind, and thou must yield to force.
Paint to thyself the horrors of a rape,
Most strongly paint, and, while thou canst, escape:
Mind not his promises—they're made in sport—
Made to be broke—was he not bred at court?
Trust not his honour; he's a man of birth:
Attend not to his oaths—they're made on earth,
Not register'd in heaven—he mocks at grace,   461
And in his creed God never found a place;
Look not for Conscience—for he knows her not,
So long a stranger, she is quite forgot;
Nor think thyself in law secure and firm;
Thy master is a lord, and thou a worm,
A poor, mean reptile, never meant to think,
Who, being well supplied with meat and drink,
And suffer'd just to crawl from place to place,
Must serve his lusts, and think he does thee grace.

Fly, then, whilst yet 'tis in thy power to fly;   471
But whither canst thou go? on whom rely
For wish'd protection?   Virtue's sure to meet
An armed host of foes in every street.
What boots it, of Apicius fearful grown,
Headlong to fly into the arms of Stone?
Or why take refuge in the house of prayer
If sure to meet with an Apicius there?
Trust not old age, which will thy faith betray;
Saint Socrates is still a goat, though grey: 480
Trust not green youth; Florio will scarce go down,
And, at eighteen, hath surfeited the town:
Trust not to rakes—alas! 'tis all pretence—
They take up raking only as a fence
'Gainst common fame—place H—— in thy view;
He keeps one whore as Barrowby kept two:

Trust not to marriage—T—— took a wife,
Who chaste as Dian might have pass'd her life,
Had she not, far more prudent in her aim,
(To propagate the honours of his name,   490
And save expiring titles) taken care,
Without his knowledge, to provide an heir:
Trust not to marriage, in mankind unread;
S——'s a married man, and S—— new wed.

   Wouldst thou be safe? society forswear,
Fly to the desert, and seek shelter there;
Herd with the brutes—they follow Nature's plan
There's not one brute so dangerous as man.
In Afric's wilds—'mongst them that refuge find
Which lust denies thee here among mankind: 500
Renounce thy name, thy nature, and no more
Pique thy vain pride on manhood: on all four
Walk, as you see those honest creatures do,
And quite forget that once you walk'd on two.

   But, if the thought of solitude alarm,
And social life hath one remaining charm;
If still thou art to jeopardy decreed
Amongst the monsters of Augusta's breed,
Lay by thy sex, thy safety to procure,
Put off the man, from men to live secure;   510
Go forth a woman to the public view,
And with their garb assume their manners too.
Had the light-footed Greek of Chiron's school
Been wise enough to keep this single rule,

---

[487] This initial applies to the nobleman so severely stig-
matised under the name of Apicius. His excesses of all
kinds rendering it inconvenient, if not unsafe, to continue to
reside in this country, he exchanged the neighbourhood of
Epping for the more congenial air of Italy.

The maudlin hero, like a puling boy
Robb'd of his plaything, on the plains of Troy
Had never blubber'd at Patroclus' tomb,
And placed his minion in his mistress' room;
Be not in this than catamites more nice,
Do that for virtue, which they do for vice;   520
Thus shalt thou pass untainted life's gay bloom,
Thus stand uncourted in the drawing-room;
At midnight, thus, untempted, walk the street,
And run no danger but of being beat.

   Where is the mother, whose officious zeal,
Discreetly judging what her daughters feel
By what she felt herself in days of yore,
Against that lecher man makes fast the door
Who not permits, e'en for the sake of prayer,
A priest, uncastrated, to enter there,   530
Nor (could her wishes, and her care prevail)
Would suffer in the house a fly that's male?
Let her discharge her cares, throw wide her doors,
Her daughters cannot, if they would, be whores;
Nor can a man be found, as times now go,
Who thinks it worth his while to make them so.

   Though they more fresh, more lively than the
       morn,
And brighter than the noon-day sun, adorn
The works of Nature; though the mother's grace
Revives improved, in every daughter's face;   540
Undisciplined in dull Discretion's rules,
Untaught and undebauch'd by boarding-schools,
Free and unguarded, let them range the town,
Go forth at random, and run pleasure down,
Start where she will; discard all taint of fear,
Nor think of danger, when no danger's near.

Watch not their steps—they're safe without thy
    care,
Unless, like Jennets, they conceive by air,
And every one of them may die a nun,
Unless they breed, like carrion, in the sun.   550
Men, dead to pleasure, as they're dead to grace,
Against the law of Nature set their face,
The grand primeval law, and seem combined
To stop the propagation of mankind;
Vile pathics read the Marriage Act with pride,
And fancy that the law is on their side.
    Broke down, and strength a stranger to his bed,
Old Ligonier, though yet alive, is dead;
T—— lives no more, or lives not to our isle;
No longer bless'd with a Czarina's smile;   560
T—— is at Petersburg disgraced,
And M—— grown gray, perforce grows chaste;
Nor to the credit of our modest race,
Rises one stallion to supply their place.
A maidenhead, which, twenty years ago,
In mid December, the rank fly would blow
Though closely kept, now, when the Dog-star's heat
Inflames the marrow, in the very street
May lie untouch'd, left for the worms, by those
Who daintily pass by, and hold their nose.   570
Poor, plain Concupiscence is in disgrace,
And simple Lechery dares not shew her face,
Lest she be sent to Bridewell; bankrupts made,

---

555 The marriage act was passed in 1753, which prescribes
the forms now in use; it immediately put an end to the cele-
bration of clandestine and irregular marriages by the chaplain of the Fleet prison, and by a class of trading parsons
throughout England.

To save their fortunes, bawds leave off their trade,
Which first had left off them ; to Wellclose square
Fine, fresh young strumpets (for Dodd preaches
     there)
Throng for subsistence : pimps no longer thrive,
And pensions only keep L—— alive.
  Where is the mother, who thinks all her pain,
And all her jeopardy of travail, gain   580
When a man-child is born ; thinks every prayer
Paid to the full, and answer'd in an heir ?
Short-sighted Woman ! little doth she know
What streams of sorrow from that source may flow ;
Little suspect, while she surveys her boy,
Her young Narcissus, with an eye of joy
Too full for continence, that Fate could give
Her darling as a curse ; that she may live,
Ere sixteen winters their short course have run,

<hr>

[576] The Rev. Dr. William Dodd was the eldest son of the
Rev. William Dodd, many years vicar of Bourne, in Lincoln-
shire; he was born in 1729, educated at Cambridge as a
sizar of Clare Hall, where he took his degree of B.A., and on
leaving the university, married very imprudently in 1751;
took orders, and became a popular preacher. His first preferment was the lectureship of West Ham. He was then
chosen lecturer of St. Olave, Hart Street, after which Bishop
Squire gave him a prebendal stall in Brecon, and he was
appointed one of the chaplains in ordinary to the King; and
became tutor to Mr. Stanhope, afterwards Earl of Chesterfield. Dr. Dodd was one of the founders of the Magdalen
Hospital, and its first chaplain on its original establishment
in Wellclose Square, to the chapel of which he attracted
overflowing congregations by his florid and declamatory
eloquence. He became embarrassed in consequence of his
extravagant and dissipated habits, in which he was encouraged by his wife; in 1777 he forged and negociated a bond
from the Earl of Chesterfield to himself for £4,200, for which
crime he was hanged.

In agonies of soul, to curse that son.   590
    Pray then for daughters, ye wise Mothers, pray ;
They shall reward your love, not make ye gray
Before your time with sorrow ; they shall give
Ages of peace, and comfort ; whilst ye live
Make life most truly worth your care, and save,
In spite of death, your memories from the grave.
    That sense with more than manly vigour fraught,
That fortitude of soul, that stretch of thought,
That genius, great beyond the narrow bound
Of earth's low walk, that judgment perfect found
When wanted most, that purity of taste   601
Which critics mention by the name of chaste ;
Adorn'd with elegance, that easy flow
Of ready wit, which never made a foe ;
That face, that form, that dignity, that ease,
Those powers of pleasing, with that will to please,
By which Lepel, when in her youthful days,
E'en from the currish Pope extorted praise,
We see, transmitted, in her daughter shine,
And view a new Lepel in Caroline.   610
    Is a son born into this world of woe ?
In never-ceasing streams let sorrow flow ;

---

[607] Mary, daughter of Brigadier-General Lepel, famous in
song as " Molly " Lepel, was married, in 1720, to John Lord
Hervey (eldest son of the Earl of Bristol) who was called
up to the House of Lords during his father's life-time. Lord
John Hervey died in 1743, and his eldest son succeeded to
the earldom in 1751 ; at which time his Majesty by warrant
granted to his Lordship's sisters the same precedency as
daughters of an Earl of Great Britain, as if their father had
lived to enjoy that dignity. Lady Hervey died in 1768,
leaving issue surviving her, the late Earl of Bristol and
Bishop of Derry, Colonel Hervey, and three daughters, of
whom Lady Caroline, mentioned by our author, was one.

Be from that hour the house with sables hung,
Let lamentations dwell upon thy tongue,
E'en from the moment that he first began
To wail and whine, let him not see a man:
Lock, lock him up, far from the public eye:
Give him no opportunity to buy,
Or to be bought; B——, though rich, was sold,
And gave his body up to shame for gold. 620
 Let it be bruited all about the town,
That he is coarse, indelicate, and brown,
An antidote to lust; his face deep scarr'd
With the small-pox, his body maim'd and marr'd;
Ate up with the king's evil, and his blood
Tainted throughout, a thick and putrid flood,
Where dwells corruption, making him all o'er,
From head to foot, a rank and running sore.
Shouldst thou report him, as by nature made,
He is undone, and by thy praise betray'd: 630
Give him out fair, lechers, in number more,
More brutal, and more fierce, than throng'd the door
Of Lot in Sodom, shall to thine repair,
And force a passage, though a god is there.
 Let him not have one servant that is male;
Where lords are baffled, servants oft prevail.
Some vices they propose, to all agree;
H—— was guilty, but was M—— free?
 Give him no tutor—throw him to a punk,
Rather than trust his morals to a monk; 640
Monks we all know—we, who have lived at home,
From fair report, and travellers who roam,
More feelingly; nor trust him to the gown;
'Tis oft a covering in this vile town
For base designs: ourselves have lived to see

More than one parson in the pillory.
Should he have brothers, (image to thy view
A scene, which, though not public made, is true)
Let not one brother be to t'other known,
Nor let his father sit with him alone.   650
Be all his servants female, young and fair,
And if the pride of Nature spur thy heir
To deeds of venery; if, hot and wild,
He chance to get some score of maids with child,
Chide, but forgive him; whoredom is a crime
Which, more at this than any other time,
Calls for indulgence, and, 'mongst such a race,
To have a bastard is some sign of grace.
    Born in such times, should I sit tamely down,
Suppress my rage, and saunter through the town
As one who knew not, or who shared these crimes?
Should I at lesser evils point my rhymes,   662
And let this giant sin, in the full eye
Of observation, pass unwounded by?
Though our meek wives, passive obedience taught,
Patiently bear those wrongs, for which they ought,
With the brave spirit of their dams possess'd,
To plant a dagger in each husband's breast,
To cut off male increase from this fair isle,
And turn our Thames into another Nile;   70
Though, on his Sunday, the smug pulpiteer,
Loud 'gainst all other crimes, is silent here,
And thinks himself absolved, in the pretence
Of decency, which, meant for the defence
Of real virtue, and to raise her price,
Becomes an agent for the cause of vice;
Though the law sleeps, and through the care they take
To drug her well, may never more awake,

Born in such times, nor with that patience curst
Which saints may boast of, I must speak or burst.
   But if, too eager in my bold career,   681
Haply I wound the nice, and chaster ear ;
If, all unguarded, all too rude, I speak,
And call up blushes in the maiden's cheek,
Forgive, ye fair—my real motives view,
And to forgiveness add your praises too.
For you I write—nor wish a better plan,
The cause of woman is most worthy man ;
For you I still will write, nor hold my hand
Whilst there's one slave of Sodom in the land. 690
   Let them fly far, and skulk from place to place,
Not daring to meet manhood face to face ;
Their steps I'll track, nor yield them one retreat
Where they may hide their heads, or rest their feet,
Till God, in wrath, shall let his vengeance fall,
And make a great example of them all,
Bidding in one grand pile, this town expire,
Her towers in dust, her Thames a lake of fire ;
Or they (most worth our wish) convinced though late
Of their past crimes and dangerous estate,   700
Pardon of women with repentance buy,
And learn to honour them as much as I.

INDEPENDENCE.

This poem was published in the last week of September, 1764, and is the latest of Churchill's productions that appeared in his life-time. He soon afterwards went to France, where he was attacked by the disorder which prematurely swept him to the grave.

Adverting to the title, we may observe, that at this time Churchill had so far acquired the Independence which he loved, as to be altogether out of debt, and had he lived, he might, with the profits arising from the sale of his former still popular poems, and of his future productions, have realized a sufficient competence for life.

 APPY the bard (though few such bards we find)
    Who, 'bove controlment, dares to speak his mind;
Dares, unabash'd, in every place appear,
And nothing fears, but what he ought to fear:
Him fashion cannot tempt, him abject need
Cannot compel, him pride cannot mislead
To be the slave of greatness, to strike sail
When, sweeping onward with her peacock's tail,
Quality in full plumage passes by;

He views her with a fix'd, contemptuous eye,   10
And mocks the puppet, keeps his own due state,
And is above conversing with the great.

Perish those slaves, those minions of the quill,
Who have conspired to seize that sacred hill
Where the nine sisters pour a genuine strain,
And sunk the mountain level with the plain;
Who, with mean, private views and servile art,
No spark of virtue living in their heart,
Have basely turn'd apostates; have debased
Their dignity of office: have disgraced,   20
Like Eli's sons, the altars where they stand,
And caused their name to stink through all the
    land;
Have stoop'd to prostitute their venal pen
For the support of great, but guilty men;
Have made the bard, of their own vile accord,
Inferior to that thing we call a lord.

What is a lord? Doth that plain simple word
Contain some magic spell? As soon as heard,
Like an alarum bell on Night's dull ear,
Doth it strike louder, and more strong appear   30
Than other words? Whether we will or no,
Through reason's court doth it unquestion'd go
E'en on the mention, and of course transmit
Notions of something excellent; of wit
Pleasing, though keen; of humour free, though
    chaste;
Of sterling genius, with sound judgment graced ·
Of virtue far above temptation's reach,
And honour, which not malice can impeach?
Believe it not—'twas nature's first intent,
Before their rank became their punishment,   40

They should have pass'd for men, nor blush'd to
    prize
The blessings she bestow'd—she gave them eyes,
And they could see; she gave them ears—they
    heard;
The instruments of stirring, and they stirr'd;
Like us, they were design'd to eat, to drink,
To talk, and every now and then, to think;
Till they, by pride corrupted, for the sake
Of singularity, disclaim'd that make:
Till they, disdaining nature's vulgar mode,
Flew off, and struck into another road,   50
More fitting Quality, and to our view
Came forth a species altogether new,
Something we had not known, and could not know,
Like nothing of God's making here below;
Nature exclaim'd with wonder: "Lords are things
Which, never made by me, were made by kings."

A lord, (nor let the honest and the brave,
The true old noble, with the fool and knave
Here mix his fame; cursed be that thought of mine,
Which with a Bute and Fox should Grafton join)

[60] The third Duke of Grafton was then just at the ontset
of his political career, which was commenced under the ban-
ners of the Earl of Chatham. On the dismissal of the Duke
of Bedford's ministry in 1765, the Duke of Grafton took the
office of secretary of state, with an engagement to support
the Marquess of Rockingham's administration. He resigned
however in a short time, under the pretence that he could
not act without Lord Chatham, nor bear to see his friend
Mr. Wilkes abandoned. This was the signal for Lord
Rockingham's dismissal. When Lord Chatham came in, the
duke got possession of the treasury; soon afterwards Lord
Chatham complained of a gradual deviation on his part from
every thing that had been previously agreed to between
them, and resigned in 1767. The Duke of Grafton then be-

A lord, (nor here let Censure rashly call   61
My just contempt of some, abuse of all,
And, as of late, when Sodom was my theme,
Slander my purpose, and my muse blaspheme,
Because she stops not, rapid in her song,
To make exceptions as she goes along—
Though well she hopes to find, another year,
A whole minority exceptions here)
A mere, mere lord, with nothing but the name,
Wealth all his worth, and title all his fame,   70
Lives on another man, himself a blank,
Thankless he lives, or must some grandsire thank
For smuggled honours, and ill-gotten pelf;
A bard owes all to nature, and himself.

Gods, how my soul is burnt up with disdain,
When I see men, whom Phœbus in his train
Might view with pride, lackey the heels of those
Whom genius ranks among her greatest foes!
And what's the cause? why, these same sons of
          scorn,
No thanks to them, were to a title born,   80
And could not help it; by chance hither sent,
And only deities by accident.
Had fortune on our getting chanced to shine,
Their birthright honours had been yours or mine.
'Twas a mere random stroke, and should the throne

came the only efficient minister and the chief promoter of the
measures against Wilkes. In 1770 he took the privy seal,
and Lord North the treasury. His grace continued in office
till 1777, and died in 1811.

  64 Churchill's preceding poem, the Times, had been severely and justly censured for the imputation it conveyed, of
the prevalence in this country of a crime, the very allusion
to which was condemned as offensive to delicacy.

Eye thee with favour, proud and lordly grown,
Thou, though a bard, might'st be their fellow yet:
But Felix never can be made a wit.
No, in good faith—that's one of those few things
Which fate hath placed beyond the reach of kings:
Bards may be lords, but 'tis not in the cards,   91
Play how we will, to turn lords into bards.

A bard—a lord—why, let them, hand in hand,
Go forth as friends, and travel through the land,
Observe which word the people can digest
Most readily, which goes to market best,
Which gets most credit, whether men will trust
A bard, because they think he may be just,
Or on a lord will choose to risk their gains,
Though privilege in that point still remains.   ·100

A bard—a lord—Let Reason take her scales,
And fairly weigh those words, see which prevails,
Which in the balance lightly kicks the beam,
And which, by sinking, we the victor deem.

'Tis done, and Hermes, by command of Jove,
Summons a synod in the sacred grove;
Gods throng with gods to take their chairs on high,
And sit in state, the senate of the sky,
Whilst, in a kind of parliament below,
Men stare at those above, and want to know   110
What they're transacting: Reason takes her stand
Just in the midst, a balance in her hand,
Which o'er and o'er she tries, and finds it true:
From either side, conducted full in view,
A man comes forth, of figure strange and queer;

92 It is curious to reflect that a "lord" who was also a
"bard," should have written, in 1816, a poem on "Churchill's grave," which has largely helped to keep our author's
fame alive.

We now and then see something like them here.
   The first was meagre, flimsy, void of strength,
But nature kindly had made up in length
What she in breadth denied : erect and proud,
A head and shoulders taller than the crowd,   120
He deem'd them pigmies all : loose hung his skin
O'er his bare bones : his face so very thin,
So very narrow, and so much beat out,
That physiognomists have made a doubt,
Proportion lost, expression quite forgot,
Whether it could be call'd a face or not :
At end of it, howe'er, unbless'd with beard,
Some twenty fathom length of chin appear'd :
With legs, which we might well conceive that Fate
Meant only to support a spider's weight,   130
Firmly he strove to tread, and with a stride,
Which shew'd at once his weakness and his pride,
Shaking himself to pieces, seem'd to cry,
" Observe, good people, how I shake the sky."
   In his right hand a paper did he hold,
On which, at large, in characters of gold,
Distinct and plain for those who run to see,
Saint Archibald had wrote L,O,R,D.

[138] This allusion to Archibald Bower fixes the portrait of the lord upon the amiable historian of Henry the Second, who was through life his firm friend and patron. The descriptions of his person, though highly caricatured, conveys some points of resemblance; his slender, uncompact frame and meagre face, had also been ludicrously described in a political print levelled against Sir Robert Walpole:

   " But who be dat so lank, so lean, so bony?
   O dat be de great orator, Lytteltony."

Nothing could be more injudicious in other respects, than the selection of Lord Lyttelton as a depreciating representative

This, with an air of scorn, he from afar
Twirl'd into Reason's scales, and on that bar,   140
Which from his soul he hated, yet admired,
Quick turn'd his back, and, as he came, retired.
The judge to all around his name declared ;
Each goddess titter'd, each god laugh'd, Jove stared,
And the whole people cried, with one accord,
" Good Heaven bless us all ! is that a lord ?"

Such was the first—the second was a man
Whom nature built on quite a diff'rent plan ;
A bear, whom, from the moment he was born,
His dam despised, and left unlick'd in scorn ;   150
A Babel, which, the power of art outdone,
She could not finish when she had begun ;
An utter Chaos, out of which no might
But that of God, could strike one spark of light.

Broad were his shoulders, and from blade to
    blade,
A H—— might at full length have laid :
Vast were his bones, his muscles twisted strong ;
His face was short, but broader than 'twas long ;
His features, though by nature they were large,
Contentment had contrived to overcharge,   160
And bury meaning, save that we might spy
Sense lowering on the penthouse of his eye ;
His arms were two twin oaks ; his legs so stout
That they might bear a Mansion-house about ;

of the peerage ; his character as a statesman was marked with
the strictest integrity and patriotism ; and his productions as
a poet, historian, and miscellaneous writer, though not in the
first style of composition, are still read.

155-176 In these lines the author gives a ludicrous description of his own person ; and of his mode of dressing, after
he had laid aside the clerical profession.

Nor were they, look but at his body there,
Design'd by fate a much less weight to bear.
  O'er a brown cassock, which had once been black,
Which hung in tatters on his brawny back,
A sight most strange, and awkward to behold,
He threw a covering of blue and gold.   170
Just at that time of life, when man by rule,
The fop laid down, takes up the graver fool,
He started up a fop, and, fond of show,
Look'd like another Hercules turn'd beau ;
A subject met with only now and then,
Much fitter for the pencil than the pen ;
Hogarth would draw him (Envy must allow)
E'en to the life, was Hogarth living now.
  With such accoutrements, with such a form,
Much like a porpoise just before a storm,   180
Onward he roll'd : a laugh prevail'd around ;
E'en Jove was seen to simper ; at the sound
(Nor was the cause unknown, for from his youth
Himself he studied by the glass of truth)
He join'd their mirth ; nor shall the gods condemn
If, whilst they laugh'd at him, he laugh'd at them.
Judge Reason view'd him with an eye of grace,
Look'd through his soul, and quite forgot his face,
And, from his hand received, with fair regard
Placed in her other scale, the name of Bard.   190
  Then, (for she did as judges ought to do ;
She nothing of the case beforehand knew,

---

[178] How little did Churchill imagine, while he affected to
consider his antagonist as already dead, that the power of
pleasing was so soon to cease in both ! Hogarth died within
four weeks after the publication of Independence, and
Churchill survived him but nine days.

Nor wish'd to know ; she never stretch'd the laws,
Nor, basely to anticipate a cause,
Compell'd solicitors, no longer free,
To show those briefs she had no right to see)
Then she with equal hand her scales held out,
Nor did the cause one moment hang in doubt ;
She held her scales out fair to public view,
The Lord, as sparks fly upwards, upwards flew, 200
More light than air, deceitful in the weight ;
The Bard, preponderating, kept his state ;
Reason approved, and with a voice, whose sound
Shook earth, shook heaven, on the clearest ground
Pronouncing for the Bards a full decree,
Cried—"Those must honour them, who honour me;
They from this present day, where'er I reign,
In their own right, precedence shall obtain ;
Merit rules here ; be it enough that birth
Intoxicates, and sways the fools of earth."   210

Nor think that here, in hatred to a lord,
I've forged a tale, or alter'd a record ;
Search when you will, (I am not now in sport)
You'll find it register'd in Reason's court.

Nor think that envy here hath strung my lyre,
That I depreciate what I most admire,
And look on titles with an eye of scorn,
Because I was not to a title born.
By Him that made me, I am much more proud,
More inly satisfied, to have a crowd   220
Point at me as I pass, and cry—"That's he—
A poor but honest bard, who dares be free

212 In allusion to the substitution of the word "tenor" for
"purport," in the record against Mr. Wilkes, which was
sanctioned by Lord Mansfield.

Amidst corruption," than to have a train
Of flickering levee slaves, to make me vain
Of things I ought to blush for; to run, fly,
And live but in the motion of my eye;
When I am less than man, my faults t'adore,
And make me think that I am something more.
Recal past times, bring back the days of old,
When the great noble bore his honours bold,　230
And in the face of peril, when he dared
Things which his legal bastard, if declared,
Might well discredit; faithful to his trust,
In the extremest points of justice, just;
Well knowing all, and loved by all he knew;
True to his king, and to his country true;
Honest at court, above the baits of gain;
Plain in his dress, and in his manners plain;
Moderate in wealth, generous, but not profuse,
Well worthy riches, for he knew their use;　240
Possessing much, and yet deserving more;
Deserving those high honours which he wore
With ease to all, and in return gain'd fame
Which all men paid, because he did not claim;
When the grim war was placed in dread array,
Fierce as the lion roaring for his prey,
Or lioness of royal whelps foredone;
In peace, as mild as the departing sun;
A general blessing wheresoe'er he turn'd,
Patron of learning, nor himself unlearn'd;　250
Ever awake at Pity's tender call,
A father of the poor, a friend to all—
Recal such times, and from the grave bring back
A worth like this, my heart shall bend, or crack,
My stubborn pride give way, my tongue proclaim,

And every Muse conspire to swell his fame,
Till Envy shall to him that praise allow
Which she cannot deny to Temple now.

This justice claims, nor shall the bard forget,
Delighted with the task, to pay that debt,   260
To pay it like a man, and in his lays,
Sounding such worth, prove his own right to praise,
But let not pride and prejudice misdeem,
And think that empty titles are my theme;
Titles, with me, are vain, and nothing worth;
I reverence virtue, but I laugh at birth.
Give me a lord that's honest, frank, and brave,
I am his friend, but cannot be his slave;
Though none, indeed, but blockheads would pretend
To make a slave, where they may make a friend.
I love his virtues, and will make them known, 271
Confess his rank, but can't forget my own.
Give me a lord, who, to a title born,
Boasts nothing else, I'll pay him scorn with scorn.
What! shall my pride (and pride is virtue here)
Tamely make way, if such a wretch appear?
Shall I uncover'd stand, and bend my knee
To such a shadow of nobility,
A shred, a remnant? he might rot unknown
For any real merit of his own,   280
And never had come forth to public note
Had he not worn, by chance, his father's coat.
To think a Melcombe worth my least regards
Is treason to the majesty of bards.

By nature form'd (when, for her honour's sake
She something more than common strove to make,

[283] Bubb Doddington—who, by the way, was the *first*
Lord Melcombe.

When, overlooking each minute defect,
And all too eager to be quite correct,
In her full heat and vigour she imprest
Her stamp most strongly on the favour'd breast)
The bard, (nor think too lightly that I mean   291
Those little, piddling witlings, who o'erween
Of their small parts, the Murphys of the stage,
The Masons and the Whiteheads of the age,
Who all in raptures their own works rehearse,
And drawl out measured prose, which they call
          verse)
The real bard, whom native genius fires,
Whom every maid of Castaly inspires,
Let him consider wherefore he was meant,
Let him but answer nature's great intent,   300
And fairly weigh himself with other men,
Would ne'er debase the glories of his pen,
Would in full state, like a true monarch, live,
Nor bate one inch of his prerogative.
    Methinks I see old Wingate frowning here,
(Wingate may in the season be a peer,
Though now, against his will, of figures sick,
He's forced to diet on arithmetic,
E'en whilst he envies every Jew he meets,   309
Who cries old clothes to sell about the streets)
Methinks (his mind with future honours big,
His Tyburn bob turn'd to a dress'd bag wig)
I hear him cry—" What doth this jargon mean ?
Was ever such a damn'd dull blockhead seen ?
Majesty—Bard—Prerogative ;—disdain
Hath got into, and turn'd the fellow's brain :
To Bethlem with him—give him whips and straw—
I'm very sensible he's mad in law.

A saucy groom, who trades in reason, thus
To set himself upon a par with us ;   320
If this here's suffer'd, and if that there fool
May when he pleases send us all to school,
Why, then our only business is outright
To take our caps, and bid the world good night.
I've kept a bard myself this twenty years,
But nothing of this kind in him appears ;
He, like a thorough, true-bred spaniel, licks
The hand which cuffs him, and the foot which kicks ;
He fetches and he carries, blacks my shoes,
Nor thinks it a discredit to his muse ;   330
A creature of the right chameleon hue,
He wears my colours, yellow or true blue,
Just as I wear them : 'tis all one to him
Whether I change through conscience, or through
          whim.
Now this is something like ; on such a plan
A bard may find a friend in a great man ;
But this proud coxcomb—Zounds, I thought that all
Of this queer tribe had been like my old Paul."
    Injurious thought ! accursed be the tongue
On which the vile insinuation hung,   340
The heart where 'twas engender'd ! curst be those,
Those bards, who not themselves alone expose,
But me, but all, and make the very name
By which they're call'd a standing mark of shame.
    Talk not of custom—'tis the coward's plea,
Current with fools, but passes not with me ;
An old, stale trick, which guilt hath often tried
By numbers to o'erpower the better side.
Why tell me then that from the birth of rhyme,
        [338] Paul Whitehead.

No matter when, down to the present time,   350
As by the original decree of fate,
Bards have protection sought amongst the great;
Conscious of weakness, have applied to them
As vines to elms, and twining round their stem,
Flourish'd on high ; to gain this wish'd support
E'en Virgil to Mecænas paid his court.
As to the custom, 'tis a point agreed,
But 'twas a foolish diffidence, not need,
From which it rose ; had bards but truly known
That strength which is most properly their own,
Without a lord, unpropp'd they might have stood,
And overtopp'd those giants of the wood.

But why, when present times my care engage,
Must I go back to the Augustan age?
Why, anxious for the living, am I led
Into the mansions of the ancient dead?
Can they find patrons no where but at Rome,
And must I seek Mecænas in the tomb?
Name but a Wingate, twenty fools of note
Start up, and from report Mecænas quote ;   370
Under his colours lords are proud to fight,
Forgetting that Mecænas was a knight:
They mention him, as if to use his name
Was, in some measure, to partake his fame,
Though Virgil, was he living, in the street,
Might rot for them, or perish in the Fleet.
See how they redden, and the charge disclaim—
" Virgil, and in the Fleet—forbid it, Shame ! "
Hence, ye vain boasters, to the Fleet repair,
And ask, with blushes ask if Lloyd is there.   380

<hr>

[380] The imprudent conduct of this unfortunate man, and
the steady attachment our author on all occasions evinced

Patrons in days of yore were men of sense,
Were men of taste, and had a fair pretence
To rule in letters—some of them were heard
To read off-hand, and never spell a word;
Some of them, too, to such a monstrous height
Was learning risen, for themselves could write,
And kept their secretaries, as the great
Do many other foolish things, for state.
   Our patrons are of quite a different strain,
With neither sense nor taste; against the grain 390
They patronize for fashion's sake—no more—

towards him, have been noticed before. Lloyd entertained
golden hopes of the success of the St. James's Magazine, a
publication almost entirely of his own composition, which
he commenced on his quitting Westminster school; it however proceeded no farther than two volumes, and never having
had a sale adequate to his expectations and consequent mode
of living, poor Lloyd was immured by his creditors in the
Fleet prison.

An effort was made to raise a sufficient sum for his support
by a subscription among his friends, but it was so coldly
entertained that the expedient was not resorted to, and he
was principally supported by the bounty of Churchill. He
also received some trifling sums from the booksellers, for a
translation of Marmontel's Tales, and some other hasty
translations and original pieces, which did not contribute to
increase his reputation.

The news of Churchill's death being announced somewhat
abruptly to him while sitting at dinner, he was seized with
a sudden sickness, the forerunner of a bilious fever, and
saying, " I shall follow poor Charles," took to his bed, from
which he never rose again, and literally did within a month
" follow poor Charles."

In his sickness he was attended by Miss Patty Churchill,
the sister of his deceased friend, who possessed a considerable
portion of the sense, spirit, and genius of her brother. It is
said that she was betrothed to Lloyd, and that the melancholy deaths of her lover and brother preyed upon her spirits,
and did not permit her long to survive them.

And keep a bard, just as they keep a whore.
Melcombe (on such occasions I am loath
To name the dead) was a rare proof of both.
Some of them would be puzzled e'en to read,
Nor could deserve their clergy by their creed;
Others can write, but such a Pagan hand,
A Willes should always at our elbow stand:
Many, if begg'd, a chancellor, of right,
Would order into keeping at first sight.   400
Those who stand fairest to the public view
Take to themselves the praise to others due;
They rob the very 'Spital, and make free
With those, alas, who've least to spare—we see
———— hath not had a word to say,
Since winds and waves bore Singlespeech away.
    Patrons in days of yore, like patrons now,
Expected that the bard should make his bow

---

[398] Dr. Edward Willes, Bishop of Bath and Wells, and joint decypherer, with his son Edward Willes, afterwards chief justice of the common pleas, to the king. Dr. Willes was first employed in that capacity upon the proceedings against Atterbury, Bishop of Rochester, for a treasonable correspondence; a considerable pension was settled on him for his services. He died in 1773. Churchill was ordained a deacon by Bishop Willes to the curacy of Cadbury, Somerset.

[406] The gentleman distinguished by this name, was the Right Honourable William Gerrard Hamilton, who was so called from the circumstance of his having, as his maiden speech, delivered a very forcible and eloquent harangue, and having never again gratified the house with any farther specimens of his oratory. In 1761, he went to Ireland as principal secretary of state to the Lord-Lieutenant, the Earl of Halifax; and in 1763, we find him Chancellor of the Exchequer for that kingdom. Having secured a pension of £2000 a-year on the Irish establishment, he returned to England, and died in 1796, in the 69th year of his age.

At coming in, and every now and then
Hint to the world that they were more than men;
But, like the patrons of the present day,   410
They never bilk'd the poet of his pay.
Virgil loved rural ease, and, far from harm,
Mecænas fix'd him in a neat, snug farm,
Where he might free from trouble pass his days
In his own way, and pay his rent in praise.
Horace loved wine, and, through his friend at court,
Could buy it off the quay in every port:
Horace loved mirth, Mecænas loved it too;
They met, they laugh'd, as Goy and I may do,   420
Nor in those moments paid the least regard
To which was minister, and which was bard.

    Not so our patrons—grave as grave can be,
They know themselves, they keep up dignity;
Bards are a forward race, nor is it fit
That men of fortune rank with men of wit:
Wit, if familiar made, will find her strength—
'Tis best to keep her weak, and at arm's length.
'Tis well enough for bards, if patrons give,
From hand to mouth, the scanty means to live.   430
Such is their language, and their practice such;
They promise little, and they give not much.
Let the weak bard, with prostituted strain,
Praise that proud Scot whom all good men disdain;
What's his reward? why, his own fame undone,
He may obtain a patent for the run

    [429] M. Pierre Goy, a French gentleman of brilliant accom-
plishments, but dissipated habits, was introduced by Wilkes
to Churchill, who, in his last letter to his friend, thus ex-
presses his gratitude to him for the introduction—"I am
now to thank you for the acquaintance of Goy, which I deem
one of the greatest obligations you have conferred on me'

Of his lord's kitchen, and have ample time,
With offal fed, to court the cook in rhyme;
Or (if he strives true patriots to disgrace)
May at the second table get a place,   440
With somewhat greater slaves allow'd to dine,
And play at crambo o'er his gill of wine.

And are there bards, who, on creation's file,
Stand rank'd as men, who breathe in this fair isle
The air of freedom, with so little gall,
So low a spirit, prostrate thus to fall
Before these idols, and without a groan
Bear wrongs might call forth murmurs from a stone?
Better, and much more noble, to abjure
The sight of men, and in some cave, secure   450
From all the outrages of pride, to feast
On Nature's salads, and be free at least.
Better (though that, to say the truth, is worse
Than almost any other modern curse)
Discard all sense, divorce the thankless Muse,
Critics commence, and write in the Reviews,
Write without tremor—Griffiths cannot read;
No fool can fail, where Langhorne can succeed.

But (not to make a brave and honest pride,
Try those means first she must disdain when tried)
There are a thousand ways, a thousand arts,   461

---

[412] *Crambo* or *Crambe*, formerly a very favourite amusement. " I saw in a corner . . . a cluster of men and women
diverting themselves with a game of crambo. I heard several
double rhymes . . . which raised a great deal of mirth."—
ADDISON. Crabbe says, "Crambo is a play in rhyming in
which he that repeats a word that was said before forfeits
something."

[458] Dr. Langhorne succeeded Smollett as editor of the
Critical Review, which was ably conducted, and was for
many years the only competitor of the Monthly Review.

By which, and fairly, men of real parts
May gain a living, gain what Nature craves;
Let those, who pine for more, live, and be slaves.
Our real wants in a small compass lie;
But lawless appetite, with eager eye,
Kept in a constant fever, more requires,
And we are burnt up with our own desires.
Hence our dependence, hence our slavery springs;
Bards, if contented, are as great as kings.   470
Ourselves are to ourselves the cause of ill;
We may be independent, if we will.
The man who suits his spirit to his state
Stands on an equal footing with the great;
Moguls themselves are not more rich, and he
Who rules the English nation, not more free.
Chains were not forged more durable and strong
For bards than others, but they've worn them long,
And therefore wear them still; they've quite forgot
What freedom is, and therefore prize her not.   480
Could they, though in their sleep, could they but
        know
The blessings which from Independence flow;
Could they but have a short and transient gleam
Of liberty, though 'twas but in a dream,
They would no more in bondage bend their knee,
But, once made freemen, would be always free.
The Muse, if she one moment freedom gains,
Can never more submit to sing in chains.
Bred in a cage, far from the feather'd throng,
The bird repays his keeper with his song;   490
But, if some playful child sets wide the door,
Abroad he flies, and thinks of home no more;
With love of liberty begins to burn,

And rather starves than to his cage return.

Hail, Independence—by true reason taught,
How few have known, and prized thee as they ought!
Some give thee up for riot ; some, like boys,
Resign thee, in their childish moods, for toys ;
Ambition some, some avarice misleads,
And in both cases Independence bleeds.   500
Abroad, in quest of thee, how many roam,
Nor know they had thee in their reach at home !
Some, though about their paths, their beds about,
Have never had the sense to find thee out :
Others, who know of what they are possess'd,
Like fearful misers, lock thee in a chest,
Nor have the resolution to produce,
In these bad times, and bring thee forth for use.
Hail, Independence—though thy name's scarce
          known,
Though thou, alas ! art out of fashion grown,   510
Though all despise thee, I will not despise,
Nor live one moment longer than I prize
Thy presence, and enjoy : by angry fate
Bow'd down, and almost crush'd, thou cam'st,
          though late,
Thou cam'st upon me, like a second birth,
And made me know what life was truly worth.
Hail, Independence—never may my cot,
Till I forget thee, be by thee forgot :
Thither, O thither, oftentimes repair ;
Cotes, whom thou lovest too, shall meet the there :

---

[520] Humphry Cotes, a wine merchant in St. Martin's
Lane, and a strenuous advocate for Wilkes in all his political
struggles. He was an honest, well-meaning tool of Wilkes,
whose business he transacted, to the injury of his own ; he

All thoughts but what arise from joy give o'er, 521
Peace dwells within, and Law shall guard the door.
   O'erweening Bard! Law guard thy door! what
     law?
The law of England.—To control and awe
Those saucy hopes, to strike that spirit dumb,
Behold, in state, Administration come.
   Why, let her come, in all her terrors too;
I dare to suffer all she dares to do.
I know her malice well, and know her pride,
I know her strength, but will not change my side.
This melting mass of flesh she may control   531
With iron ribs, she cannot chain my soul.
No—to the last resolved her worst to bear,
I'm still at large, and independent there.
   Where is this minister? where is the band
Of ready slaves, who at his elbow stand
To hear, and to perform his wicked will?
Why, for the first time, are they slow to ill?
When some grand act 'gainst law is to be done,
Doth — — sleep; doth blood-hound — — run 540
To L— — —, and worry those small deer,
When he might do more precious mischief here?
Doth Webb turn tail? doth he refuse to draw
Illegal warrants, and to call them Law?
Doth —, at Guilford kick'd, from Guilford run,
With that cold lump of unbaked dough, his son,

became bankrupt in 1767, and was treated in his difficulties
with the most mortifying indifference and neglect by Mr.
Wilkes. They were, however, reconciled, and poor Cotes
again became the drudge of the great patriot, the renewal
of whose pretended friendship he thought a sufficient recom-
pense for the slights he had endured from him in his mis-
fortunes.

And, his more honest rival Ketch to cheat,
Purchase a burial-place where three ways meet?
Believe it not; —— is —— still,
And never sleeps, when he should wake to ill: 550
—— doth lesser mischiefs by the bye,
The great ones till the term in petto lie:
—— lives, and, to the strictest justice true,
Scorns to defraud the hangman of his due.

O my poor Country—weak, and overpower'd
By thine own sons—ate to the bone—devour'd
By vipers, which, in thine own entrails bred,
Prey on thy life, and with thy blood are fed—
With unavailing grief thy wrongs I see,
And, for myself not feeling, feel for thee.   560
I grieve, but can't despair—for, lo, at hand
Freedom presents a choice, but faithful band
Of loyal patriots; men who greatly dare
In such a noble cause; men fit to bear
The weight of empires; Fortune, Rank, and Sense,
Virtue and Knowledge, leagued with Eloquence,
March in their ranks; Freedom from file to file
Darts her delighted eye, and with a smile
Approves her honest sons, whilst down her cheek,
As 'twere by stealth, (her heart too full to speak)
One tear in silence creeps, one honest tear,   571
And seems to say, Why is not Granby here?

[572] The Marquess of Granby, in 1763, accepted the office of
Master-General of the Ordnance, and was, in 1766, appointed
Commander-in-chief of all his Majesty's land forces in Great
Britain. Junius accuses him of an improper partiality to
his own family and connections in the exercise of his patronage; but admits that "in private life he was unquestionably
that good man, who, for the interest of his country, ought to
have been a great one. *Bonum virum facile dixeris:—mag-*

O ye brave few, in whom we still may find
A love of virtue, freedom, and mankind,
Go forth—in majesty of woe array'd,
See at your feet your country kneels for aid,
And, (many of her children traitors grown)
Kneels to those sons she still can call her own ;
Seeming to breathe her last in every breath,
She kneels for freedom, or she begs for death. 580
Fly, then, each duteous son, each English chief,
And to your drooping parent bring relief.
Go forth—nor let the Siren voice of ease
Tempt ye to sleep, whilst tempests swell the seas;
Go forth—nor let Hypocrisy, whose tongue
With many a fair, false, fatal art is hung,
Like Bethel's fawning prophet, cross your way,
When your great errand brooks not of delay ;
Nor let vain Fear, who cries to all she meets,
Trembling and pale, " A lion in the streets ! " 590
Damp your free spirits ; let not threats affright,
Nor bribes corrupt, nor flatteries delight :
Be as one man—concord success ensures—
There's not an English heart but what is yours.
Go forth—and Virtue, ever in your sight,
Shall be your guide by day, your guard by night.
Go forth—the champions of your native land,
And may the battle prosper in your hand.
It may, it must : ye cannot be withstood.
Be your hearts honest, as your cause is good. 600

num libenter. I speak of him now without partiality :—
I never spoke of him with resentment. His mistakes in public conduct did not arise either from want of sentiment or
want of judgment, but, in general, from the difficulty of
saying NO to the bad people who surrounded him."

THE JOURNEY.*

SOME of my friends, (for friends I must suppose
All, who, not daring to appear my foes,
Feign great good will, and, not more full of spite
Than full of craft, under false colours fight)
Some of my friends, (so lavishly I print)
As more in sorrow than in anger, hint
(Though that indeed will scarce admit a doubt)
That I shall run my stock of genius out,
My no great stock, and, publishing so fast,
Must needs become a bankrupt at the last.   10
  "The husbandman, to spare a thankful soil,
Which, rich in disposition, pays his toil
More than a hundredfold, which swells his store
E'en to his wish, and makes his barns run o'er,
By long experience taught, who teaches best,
Foregoes his hopes a while, and gives it rest:
The land, allow'd its losses to repair,

* This short piece was published soon after the author's
death, and was the only complete poem, if such it may be
considered, which he left behind him in manuscript.

Refresh'd, and full in strength, delights to wear
A second youth, and to the farmer's eyes
Bids richer crops, and double harvests rise.   20
    " Nor think this practice to the earth confined,
It reaches to the culture of the mind.
The mind of man craves rest, and cannot bear
Though next in power to God's, continual care.
Genius himself (nor here let Genius frown)
Must, to ensure his vigour, be laid down,
And fallow'd well: had Churchill known but this,
Which the most slight observer scarce could miss,
He might have flourish'd twenty years, or more,
Though now, alas! poor man! worn out in four."
    Recover'd from the vanity of youth,   31
I feel, alas! this melancholy truth,
Thanks to each cordial, each advising friend,
And am, if not too late, resolved to mend ·
Resolved to give some respite to my pen,
Apply myself once more to books and men,
View what is present, what is past review,
And, my old stock exhausted, lay in new.
For twice six moons, (let winds, turn'd porters, bear
This oath to heaven) for twice six moons, I swear,
No Muse shall tempt me with her Siren lay,   41
Nor draw me from improvement's thorny way.
Verse I abjure, nor will forgive that friend,
Who, in my hearing, shall a rhyme commend.
    It cannot be—whether I will, or no,
Such as they are, my thoughts in measure flow.
Convinced, determined, I in prose begin,

---

[30] Our author did not live to complete even his fourth
poetic year; the Rosciad having been published in March,
1761, and Independence in September, 1764.

But ere I write one sentence, verse creeps in,
And taints me through and through; by this good
    light
In verse I talk by day, I dream by night!   50
If now and then I curse, my curses chime,
Nor can I pray, unless I pray in rhyme.
E'en now I err, in spite of common sense,
And my confession doubles my offence.
    Rest then, my friends;—spare, spare your pre-
    cious breath,
And be your slumbers not less sound than death;
Perturbëd spirits, rest, nor thus appear
To waste your counsels in a spendthrift's ear;
On your grave lessons I cannot subsist,
Nor e'en in verse become economist.   60
Rest then, my friends, nor hateful to my eyes,
Let Envy, in the shape of Pity, rise
To blast me ere my time; with patience wait,
('Tis no long interval) propitious Fate
Shall glut your pride, and every son of phlegm
Find ample room to censure and condemn.
Read some three hundred lines, (no easy task,
But probably the last that I shall ask)
And give me up for ever; wait one hour—
Nay, not so much—revenge is in your power,   70
And ye may cry, ere Time hath turn'd his glass,
" Lo ! what we prophesied is come to pass."
    Let those who poetry in poems claim,
Or not read this, or only read to blame;
Let those who are by fiction's charms enslaved,
Return me thanks for half-a-crown well saved;
Let those who love a little gall in rhyme
Postpone their purchase now, and call next time;

Let those who, void of nature, look for art,
Take up their money, and in peace depart;   8ʔ
Let those who energy of diction prize,
For Billingsgate quit Flexney, and be wise:
Here is no lie, no gall, no art, no force,
Mean are the words, and such as come of course;
The subject not less simple than the lay;
A plain, unlabour'd Journey of a Day.

    Far from me now be every tuneful maid;
I neither ask, nor can receive their aid.
Pegasus turn'd into a common hack,
Alone I jog, and keep the beaten track,   90
Nor would I have the Sisters of the hill
Behold their bard in such a dishabille.
Absent, but only absent for a time,
Let them caress some dearer son of rhyme;
Let them, as far as decency permits,
Without suspicion, play the fool with wits,
'Gainst fools be guarded; 'tis a certain rule,
Wits are safe things; there's danger in a fool.

    Let them, though modest, Gray, more modest,
      woo;

---

⁸² The publisher of his poems. Mr. Flexney died Jan.
7, 1808, aged 77, having handed over to Mr. W. Tooke, who
first edited the Aldine edition of Churchill's poems, in
1803, the very few manuscripts he had preserved of, or
relating to, the poet, from which but little information
could be collected; he was at the same time confident that
none others existed, which the lapse of time has confirmed.
Few instances occur in the literary world of a man who has
filled so eminent a position as Churchill leaving so few me-
morials of himself behind; the fact is, he destroyed most
of his manuscripts, and his dissipated associates were too
much occupied with their own irregular pursuits to care to
collect the *disjecta membra* of their friend.

Let them with Mason bleat, and bray, and coo; 100
Let them with Francklin, proud of some small Greek,
Make Sophocles, disguised, in English speak;
Let them with Glover o'er Medea doze;
Let them with Dodsley wail Cleone's woes,
Whilst he, fine-feeling creature, all in tears,
Melts as they melt, and weeps with weeping peers;
Let them with simple Whitehead taught to creep
Silent and soft, lay Fontenelle asleep;
Let them with Brown contrive, no vulgar trick,
To cure the dead, and make the living sick; 110
Let them, in charity to Murphy, give
Some old French piece, that he may steal and live;
Let them with antic Foote subscriptions get,
And advertise a summer-house of wit.

Thus, or in any better way they please,
With these great men, or with great men like these,
Let them their appetite for laughter feed;
I on my Journey all alone proceed.

If fashionable grown, and fond of power, 119
With humorous Scots let them disport their hour;

103 Mr. Glover, in his tragedy of Medea, attempted to improve upon Euripides and Seneca; the unities are preserved throughout, and the diction is, in general, harmonious and picturesque. Mrs. Yates usually selected this play for her benefit.

104 Cleone, a tragedy by Robert Dodsley, the bookseller, having been rejected by Garrick, was first acted at Covent Garden in 1758: it is founded upon the old legend of St. Genevieve, written originally in French, and translated into English by Sir William Lower about two hundred years ago. The play was acted a few seasons with some success, but has now been neglected for many years.

107 Whitehead's "School for Lovers" was dedicated to the memory of Fontenelle.

109 The cure of Saul, a sacred ode by Dr. Brown.

Let them dance, fairy-like, round Ossian's tomb ;
Let them forge lies and histories for Hume ;
Let them with Home, the very prince of verse,
Make something like a tragedy in Erse ;
Under dark allegory's flimsy veil
Let them with Ogilvie spin out a tale
Of rueful length ; let them plain things obscure,
Debase what's truly rich, and what is poor
Make poorer still by jargon most uncouth ;
With every pert, prim prettiness of youth,   130
Born of false taste ; with Fancy (like a child
Not knowing what it cries for) running wild ;
With bloated style, by affectation taught,
With much false colouring, and little thought,
With phrases strange, and dialect decreed
By reason never to have pass'd the Tweed ;
With words, which nature meant each other's foe,
Forced to compound whether they will or no ;
With such materials, let them, if they will,
To prove at once their pleasantry and skill,   140
Build up a bard to war 'gainst common sense,
By way of compliment to Providence ;
Let them with Armstrong, taking leave of sense,

[122] David Hume's strong bias in favour of the Stuarts rendered him extremely obnoxious to the Whigs.   .

[126] John Ogilvie, A.M. was the author of Providence, a poem, published in 1764, in which the most cogent arguments in favour of a divine providence are adorned with pleasing allegorical imagery and harmonious numbers.

[143] Dr. John Armstrong, author of the poems "Benevolence, an Epistle to Eumenes," and "The Art of Preserving Health," was, until the publication of the North Briton, on the most intimate footing of friendship with Wilkes and Churchill. He could not however but feel hurt at the constant attacks made upon his countrymen the Scotch ; and in politics he by

Read musty lectures on Benevolence,
Or con the pages of his gaping Day,
Where all his former fame was thrown away,
Where all but barren labour was forgot,
And the vain stiffness of a letter'd Scot;
Let them with Armstrong pass the term of light,
But not one hour of darkness: when the night 150
Suspends this mortal coil, when memory wakes,
When for our past misdoings conscience takes
A deep revenge, when, by reflection led,
She draws his curtains, and looks comfort dead,
Let every muse be gone; in vain he turns,
And tries to pray for sleep; an Ætna burns,
A more than Ætna, in his coward breast,
And guilt, with vengeance arm'd, forbids him rest:
Though soft as plumage from young Zephyr's wing,
His couch seems hard, and no relief can bring;
Ingratitude hath planted daggers there 161
No good man can deserve, no brave man bear.

Thus, or in any better way they please,
With these great men, or with great men like these,
Let them their appetite for laughter feed;
I on my journey all alone proceed.

no means approved of the system adopted by his friends. In
1761, while physician to the English army in Germany, he
wrote a careless epistle to Wilkes, called Day, which was
published (as the prefatory advertisement confesses) "without the knowledge or consent of the author, or of the gentleman to whom it was addressed." In this poem he hazarded
some reflections, which drew on him the unrelenting vengeance of our satirist.

DEDICATION TO DR. W. WARBURTON,

BISHOP OF GLOUCESTER.

THE manuscript of this unfinished poem was found among the few papers Churchill left behind him at his death, and appears to have been intended by him as the dedication of a volume of sermons to the learned prelate, against whom he on all occasions aimed the most malignant shafts of satire.

EALTH to great Glo'ster—from a man unknown,
 Who holds thy health as dearly as his own,
Accept this greeting—nor let modest fear
Call up one maiden blush—I mean not here
To wound with flattery; 'tis a villain's art,
And suits not with the frankness of my heart.
Truth best becomes an orthodox divine,
And, spite of hell, that character is mine :
To speak e'en bitter truths I cannot fear ;
But truth, my Lord, is panegyric here. 10
 Health to great Glo'ster—nor, through love of ease,
Which all priests love, let this address displease.
I ask no favour ; not one *note* I crave ;
And when this busy brain rests in the grave,

(For till that time it never can have rest)
I will not trouble you with one bequest.
Some humbler friend, my mortal journey done,
More near in blood, a nephew or a son,
In that dread hour executor I'll leave,
For I, alas! have many to receive— 20
To give, but little.—To great Glo'ster health;
Nor let thy true and proper love of wealth
Here take a false alarm—in purse though poor,
In spirit I'm right proud, nor can endure
The mention of a bribe—thy pocket's free:
I, though a dedicator, scorn a fee.
Let thy own offspring all thy fortunes share;
I would not Allen rob, nor Allen's heir.

Think not—a thought unworthy thy great soul,
Which pomps of this world never could control; 30
Which never offer'd up at Power's vain shrine—
Think not that pomp and power can work on mine.
'Tis not thy name, though that indeed is great,
'Tis not the tinsel trumpery of state,
'Tis not thy title, Doctor though thou art,
'Tis not thy mitre which hath won my heart.
State is a farce; names are but empty things;

[20] The active benevolence of Mr. Allen is celebrated by
Pope in these lines:

> "Let humble Allen, with an awkward shame,
> Do good by stealth, and blush to find it fame."

Warburton, in his notes upon nearly every word of the
above quotation, takes the opportunity of exalting the character of his patron, representing Pope as considering him
"all and much more than he had feigned in the imaginary
virtues of the Man of Ross. One, who, whether he be considered in his civil, social, domestic, or religious capacity, is
an ornament to human nature."

Degrees are bought; and, by mistaken kings,
Titles are oft' misplaced; mitres, which shine
So bright in other eyes, are dull in mine,   40
Unless set off by virtue; who deceives
Under the sacred sanction of lawn sleeves
Enhances guilt, commits a double sin,
So fair without, and yet so foul within.
'Tis not thy outward form, thy easy mien,
Thy sweet complacency, thy brow serene,
Thy open front, thy love-commanding eye,
Where fifty Cupids, as in ambush, lie,
Which can from sixty to sixteen impart
The force of Love, and point his blunted dart;   50
'Tis not thy face, though that by nature's made
An index to thy soul; though there display'd
We see thy mind at large, and through thy skin
Peeps out that courtesy which dwells within;
'Tis not thy birth, for that is low as mine;
Around our heads no lineal glories shine;
But what is birth, when, to delight mankind,
Heralds can make those arms they cannot find;
When thou art to thyself, thy sire unknown,
A whole Welsh genealogy alone?   60
No; 'tis thy inward man, thy proper worth,
Thy right just estimation here on earth,
Thy life and doctrine uniformly join'd,
And flowing from that wholesome source, thy mind;
Thy known contempt of persecution's rod,
Thy charity for man, thy love of God,
Thy faith in Christ, so well approved 'mongst men,
Which now give life and utterance to my pen.
Thy virtue, not thy rank, demands my lays;
'Tis not the Bishop, but the Saint, I praise: 70

Raised by that theme, I soar on wings more strong,
And burst forth into praise withheld too long.

Much did I wish, e'en whilst I kept those sheep
Which, for my curse, I was ordain'd to keep,
Ordain'd, alas! to keep through need, not choice,
Those sheep which never heard their shepherd's
 voice;
Which did not know, yet would not learn their way;
Which stray'd themselves, yet grieved that I should
 stray;
Those sheep which my good father (on his bier
Let filial duty drop the pious tear)   80
Kept well, yet starved himself; e'en at that time
Whilst I was pure and innocent of rhyme;
Whilst, sacred dulness ever in my view,
Sleep at my bidding crept from pew to pew,
Much did I wish, though little could I hope,
A friend in him who was the friend of Pope.

His hand, said I, my youthful steps shall guide,
And lead me safe where thousands fall beside;
His temper, his experience shall control,
And hush to peace the tempest of my soul;   90
His judgment teach me, from the critic school

75 Churchill succeeded his father in the curacy and lecture-ship of St. John the Evangelist, Westminster; his conduct there was for some time exemplary, but latterly, the complete dereliction of his duty justly incurred the displeasure of his parishioners, who complained to his diocesan of his excesses; upon which Churchill, in January 1763, resigned his situation, and with it the dress, the last remaining badge of his clerical function.

77-78 In the author's first manuscript these lines stood thus:

"Which, accents of rebuke could never bear,
Nor would have heeded Christ, had Christ been there."

How not to err, and how to err by rule;
Instruct me, mingle profit with delight,
Where Pope was wrong, where Shakspeare was
        not right;
Where they are justly praised, and where through
        whim
How little's due to them, how much to him.
Raised 'bove the slavery of common rules,
Of common-sense, of modern, ancient schools;
Those feelings banish'd which mislead us all,
Fools as we are, and which we Nature call,   100
He by his great example might impart
A better something, and baptize it Art;
He, all the feelings of my youth forgot,
Might shew me what is taste by what is not;
By him supported with a proper pride,
I might hold all mankind as fools beside;
He (should a world, perverse and peevish grown,
Explode his maxims and assert their own)
Might teach me, like himself to be content,
And let their folly be their punishment;   110
Might, like himself, teach his adopted son,
'Gainst all the world, to quote a Warburton.

[112] The literary tyranny assumed and exercised by Warburton and his disciples could not be exceeded, and has never
been equalled since the days of the Scaligers. Hume, whose
liberality and amenity of disposition, rendered him a perfect
contrast to these sturdy dogmatists, thus characterizes their
style of criticism. " In this interval I published, at London,
my Natural History of Religion, along with some other small
pieces: its public entry was rather obscure, except only that
Dr. Hurd wrote a pamphlet against it, with all the illiberal
petulance, arrogance, and scurrility, which distinguish the
Warburtonian school. This pamphlet gave me some conso-
lation for the otherwise indifferent reception of my performance."—*Hume's Memoirs of his own Life.*

Fool that I was! could I so much deceive
My soul with lying hopes? could I believe
That he, the servant of his Maker sworn,
The servant of his Saviour, would be torn
From their embrace, and leave that dear employ,
The cure of souls, his duty and his joy,
For toys like mine, and waste his precious time,
On which so much depended, for a rhyme?   120
Should he forsake the task he undertook,
Desert his flock, and break his pastoral crook?
Should he (forbid it, Heaven!) so high in place,
So rich in knowledge, quit the work of grace,
And, idly wandering o'er the Muses' hill,
Let the salvation of mankind stand still?

Far, far be that from thee—yes, far from thee
Be such revolt from grace, and far from me
The will to think it—guilt is in the thought.
Not so, not so hath Warburton been taught,   130
Not so learn'd Christ—recal that day, well known,
When (to maintain God's honour—and his own)
He call'd blasphemers forth: methinks I now
· See stern rebuke enthronëd on his brow,
And arm'd with tenfold terrors: from his tongue,
Where fiery zeal and Christian fury hung,

---

¹³¹ On the 15th of November, 1763, the Bishop of Glou-
cester made a complaint, in the House of Lords, against
Mr. Wilkes for breach of privilege in putting the name of
Warburton to a variety of notes upon the Essay on Woman.
The Bishop, with great warmth, laying his hand upon his
heart, declared that he did not write any one of them, and
called his God to witness the truth of his assertion; in his
opinion, he said, no one except the devil could be the author
of this atrocious publication, but, added he, after a pause,
"I beg the devil's pardon, for I do not think even him
capable of so infamous a production."

Methinks I hear the deep-toned thunders roll,
And chill with horror every sinner's soul;
In vain they strive to fly—flight cannot save;
And Potter trembles even in his grave;   140
With all the conscious pride of innocence
Methinks I hear him, in his own defence,
Bear witness to himself, whilst all men knew,
By gospel rules his witness to be true.

   O glorious man! thy zeal I must commend,
Though it deprived me of my dearest friend;
The real motives of thy anger known,
Wilkes must the justice of that anger own;
And, could thy bosom have been bared to view,
Pitied himself, in turn had pitied you.   150
Bred to the law, you wisely took the gown,
Which I, like Demas, foolishly laid down;
Hence double strength our Holy Mother drew,
Me she got rid of, and made prize of you.
I, like an idle truant fond of play,
Doting on toys, and throwing gems away,
Grasping at shadows, let the substance slip;
But you, my lord, renounced attorneyship
With better purpose, and more noble aim,
And wisely play'd a more substantial game: 160
Nor did Law mourn, bless'd in her younger son,
For Mansfield does what Glo'ster would have done.

   Doctor! Dean! Bishop! Glo'ster! and my Lord,
If haply these high titles may accord
With thy meek spirit; if the barren sound
Of pride delights thee, to the topmost round

---

[140] Thomas Potter, author of the notes to the Essay on
Woman. He was the son of the Archbishop of Canterbury,
and an intimate friend of Wilkes.

Of Fortune's ladder got, despise not one
For want of smooth hypocrisy undone,
Who, far below, turns up his wondering eye,
And, without envy, sees thee placed so high: 170
Let not thy brain (as brains less potent might)
Dizzy, confounded, giddy with the height,
Turn round, and lose distinction, lose her skill
And wonted powers of knowing good from ill,
Of sifting truth from falsehood, friends from foes;
Let Glo'ster well remember how he rose,
Nor turn his back on men who made him great;
Let him not, gorged with power, and drunk with
      state,
Forget what once he was, though now so high;
How low, how mean, and full as poor as I. 180

*   *   *   *   *   *
*   *   *   *   *

Cætera desunt.

INDEX.*

* In constructing this Index an attempt has been made to facilitate reference not only to the persons and events mentioned in the notes, but also to the more striking passages that occur in the poems.

www.ingramcontent.com/pod-product-compliance
Lightning Source LLC
Chambersburg PA
CBHW060529030726
47498CB00004B/1126